CHRISTMAS AT CORNER COTTAGE

SARAH HOPE

B
Boldwood

First published in 2019. This edition first published in Great Britain in 2023 by Boldwood Books Ltd.

Cover Design by Head Design Ltd

Cover Illustration: Shutterstock

A CIP catalogue record for this book is available from the British Library.

Paperback ISBN 978-1-80549-111-8

Large Print ISBN 978-1-80549-110-1

Hardback ISBN 978-1-80549-109-5

Ebook ISBN 978-1-80549-112-5

Kindle ISBN 978-1-80549-113-2

Audio CD ISBN 978-1-80426-104-0

MP3 CD ISBN 978-1-80549-105-7

Digital audio download ISBN 978-1-80549-108-8

Boldwood Books Ltd
23 Bowerdean Street
London SW6 3TN
www.boldwoodbooks.com

For my children,
Let's change our stars
xXx

1

Biting down on her bottom lip, the sharp metallic taste of blood filled her mouth, momentarily focusing Chrissy Marsden's attention. Shifting the hamster cage onto her hip, she politely shook Evan Shaw's hand.

'Pleasure doing business with you. Well, under different circumstances...' Evan looked down at his feet before heading back inside the house and firmly shutting the front door.

'Do you want me to take Star?' Andrew indicated to the rusty heap on the driveway, the soppy face of a collie cross pressed against the passenger window.

'Now you ask! You know how difficult it was for me to find a place to rent that allowed dogs! If you'd said you'd have taken her before I'd signed, I would have said "yes, sure, make my life a little easier". But no, you watched me go through the ordeal of actually thinking I'd have to make the choice between taking her to a rescue centre or making the kids homeless.' Shaking her head, she looked back at her car, Star pawing the window, desperate to escape the injustice of being cooped up while they'd dragged the last of their possessions out of the house. 'Plus, the kids are expecting her to come now.'

'OK, I only asked.' Holding his hands up, he shook his head. 'Evan did offer to rent this place to you.'

'Yes, well, I don't think that would have been such a good idea, do you? For the kids, I mean.' She knew a lot of women stayed in the marital home when their marriage ended, but with it being sold to a landlord? Nope, it wouldn't be the same. She couldn't picture living in their old home that wasn't theirs any more. No.

'I'm just saying this was your choice.' Again, Andrew waved his right arm, taking in her car with the trailer attached piled high with their belongings.

'Right, my choice. Of course.'

'No need to be like that.' He looked back at the house. 'I'm going to get off now.'

'Bye then.' Chrissy looked down at the hamster as

he squirmed out of his little plastic house, eyeing her nervously. 'It's OK, Patch, I'm not going to drop you. I know how that feels.' Twisting around, she watched Andrew stroll up to her car as Evie and Sophia tumbled out and ran towards their father.

'Dad, why don't you come with us? You and Mum can change your minds. This doesn't even have to happen.' Looking up at him, Evie hugged her dad.

'Don't be stupid, Evie. It's done. Look, our old home is sold now. They've made their decision.'

'I don't care, Sophia. It doesn't mean Dad can't come with us. Does it, Mum?' Evie's eyes flickered from her dad to Chrissy.

Looking down, Chrissy stared at Patch. She'd been through this so many times with the girls. Both her and Andrew had spoken to them numerous times in the long eight months since he'd told her he didn't love her any more. Sophia had understood, but Evie, well, she was forever the optimist and Chrissy didn't have the heart to tell her the real reason Andrew was leaving.

'Dad, please?'

'Evie, I'm sorry, I've got to get back to work now.' Andrew kissed them both on their heads and straightened his tie before walking to his car.

Chrissy shrugged, she obviously wasn't even

worthy of a second more of his time. A minute later and he was gone, his company car pulling away, not even a second glance back at her.

'Come on, girls. In the car. Let's begin our new adventure.' Chrissy nudged them both with the hamster cage. 'Who's having this one on their laps?'

'She can. It was Evie who wanted a hamster.' Scowling, Sophia pointed at Evie.

'OK. Here you go, Evie.' Chrissy plonked the cage on Evie's lap before sliding into the driver's seat, pushing Star back onto her side of the car. 'Sit still, you daft dog.'

'Don't call her daft, Mum! You're not daft, are you, Star? You just don't like the car, do you?'

In the rear-view mirror Chrissy watched as Sophia rolled her eyes and punched her sister on the arm. 'Sophia Marsden! How many times do I have to tell you not to hurt your sister?'

'Well, she's being stupid. Again. I don't know why you don't just tell her the truth that daft dogs can't answer back or understand what humans say?'

'She can too!'

'What? Talk? Right, OK, Evie. Whatever.'

'No, she can understand. Can't you, Star? You're a clever girl, aren't you? Yes, you are.'

'Girls, please stop. Star, get down.' She pulled Star

down, her front paws finally unclinging from the back of the chair as she tried to get to Evie. Chrissy shook her head, the girls had begun to get their signature teenage moods already. They were only ten. She shrugged, she supposed it was inevitable that things would be worse with twins.

She remembered when they'd found out she was expecting twins, her and Andrew had spoken endlessly about how lovely it would be that their girls would have a best friend for life. Unfortunately, the reality was somewhat different, instead, they just bounced off each other. And the older they got, the more they seemed to revel in annoying one another. At least, Sophia did. Poor Evie, the meeker of the two, just seemed to wind her sister up unintentionally.

'Are we there yet?' Evie looked up from cooing over Patch.

'We've only just left our old town. We've got at least another hour and a half, possibly longer, because I can't go very fast with the trailer.'

'Yes, well, if we'd been allowed to be like a normal family and stay in the same town, we'd be at our crummy new house by now.' Sophia crossed her arms.

Chrissy gritted her teeth, she could hardly tell them that as an unemployed single mum with two kids, a dog and a hamster the only way she'd been able to secure a tenancy had been to find a private landlord who had agreed to take a hefty deposit and six months' rent upfront. Of course, if their father had told her he would have taken Star before today then things may have been different, but as it stood, he hadn't, and so here they were, moving to a remote village an hour and a half away from all their friends. It was all very well Andrew saying the landlord who had brought their small but much loved marital home had offered it to her, but she couldn't have afforded the six months' rent, not at the rate they charged in their old town. No, she'd had no choice.

'I know you're upset to be leaving, Sophia, but it'll be an adventure. A new start.'

'A lonely start away from all my friends, you mean.'

'You'll make new friends.'

'No, I won't and I won't even try because you've forced me into this, Mum. You've taken me away from my home and I'll never forgive you.' Sophia jutted out her chin, closed her eyes and pulled her headphones on.

Chrissy could hear the beat of the angry bass even from the front of the car, but also knew it would make things worse if she said anything. Having her iPod up that loud once wasn't going to harm her hearing, was it?

'Mum, I can hear Sophia's music. Can you tell her to turn it down? It's giving me a headache.'

'Evie, sweetheart, just leave her be for a bit. You can see she's upset.'

'I'm upset too. I really thought you wouldn't make Dad go. I thought you'd get back together.'

Staring at the road ahead, she switched the headlights on. 'I didn't make Dad go. You know that, don't you? It's just one of those things, adults break up sometimes. I'm sorry.'

'I just miss him.'

'You've only just said bye to him. Plus, you'll see him every other weekend.' Watching Evie's cheeks glisten with tears broke Chrissy's heart. It wasn't her fault, she had to remember that. Chrissy hadn't asked for any of this.

'I still miss him. I don't want us to live away from him. I want us to be a family again.' Balancing Patch's cage on her knees, she quickly swiped the tears away with the sleeves of her hoodie.

'We'll still be a family. We just won't live with Daddy. Lots of families are the same. Didn't Mattie's parents from your old class split up last year?'

'Yes, and his dad moved abroad.' Evie burst into fresh sobs.

Of course he did, why hadn't Chrissy remembered that? What a stupid example. 'Hey, don't cry. Daddy's not going to move abroad.'

'He might do. Anything can happen now.'

'He won't, I promise. Now, why don't you open that pack of sweets I got you for the journey?' Reaching behind, Chrissy patted Evie's leg before fixing her attention back to the road. The sky was darkening still, rain was all she needed with only a tarp (and a good few gaps around the outside) protecting their things in the trailer.

'Sorry, Mum.'

'Sorry about what, Evie?' Chrissy strained to hear Evie's soft whisper.

'Sorry for saying it was your fault. I know it's not. I'm just sad.'

'Oh darling, that's OK.' Chrissy pulled a few strands of hair from her messy bun and twisted them around her finger.

'Mum?'

'Yes, Evie?'

'When are we going to get there?'

'It shouldn't be much further.' Chrissy tapped the satnav. They should have been there at least twenty minutes ago. Maybe there were roadworks or some reason the satnav was taking her a longer route. 'Another fifteen minutes, perhaps.'

'I'm hungry. Can we stop and get something, please?'

The windscreen wipers sped backwards and forward as they cruised along the sheen covered road. Looking in the rear-view mirror, Chrissy could see a line of cars trailing behind them. She shrugged, there wasn't much she could do, she realised she was barely doing half the speed limit but even at that speed the trailer was bouncing behind them. Trying to avoid the potholes seemed to make it worse, the trailer just weaved across the road. But she was doing it. She was pulling the trailer, despite the fact that Andrew had told her that her little car wouldn't cope with the weight. 'I don't think so. We'll be there soon.'

2

'Here we go, Moorfield. Our new home!' As they drove into the village, Chrissy twisted around to smile at Evie and Sophia. Evie still clung to Patch's cage whilst Sophia had nodded off, her head leaning against the window, headphones pushed down to her neck. 'Evie, love, can you wake Sophia for me, please?'

'Sophia. Sophia!'

Chrissy watched in the rear-view mirror as Evie poked her sister. Sophia stirred, moving slightly before closing her eyes again.

'Sophia! You need to wake up now. We're here!' Chrissy jiggled Sophia's leg with one hand before returning to the ten to two position on the steering wheel that her driving instructor had ingrained in her.

'OK, OK, I'm awake!' Rubbing her eyes, Sophia peered out of the window.

'There's a good girl. Now, look out of Evie's window, we're just about to go past your new school.' Chrissy pointed towards the left. An old Victorian building peeked above a camouflage of trees, the recent cold weather having stolen a number of leaves, leaving the school building more exposed to the roadside than it had been when they had visited three weeks ago.

'Yuck! It still looks as old and creepy as it did last time.'

'Sophia! It doesn't look creepy in the slightest. Yes, it looks different from your old school but that's only because it was built over a hundred years ago. It's full of character. It's beautiful.' It was true, the ornate archway leading into the building from the playground stood proud, pale bricks fanning the entrance way.

'I don't like it. I liked our old school. You know the one I mean, Mum? The one where I actually *had* friends. I'm going to be miserable here. I hate it.' Crossing her arms, Sophia pursed her lips.

'You'll make friends here, Sophia. I promise.'

Chrissy tapped her fingers against the steering wheel, she was certain they would settle and make friends easily. Especially Sophia, she had always been the more outgoing one, the one who took the lead and went off to search for people she deemed to be friend-worthy when they started a new club. She nodded, Sophia would make friends anywhere. They both would. She'd always done her best to socialise them both. The amount of money she had spent on various clubs for them over the years had always been a sore point between her and Andrew.

'There's no point me trying to make friends here anyway. I'll get settled here and then we'll just move again.'

'No we won't. We'll make a new life here. A really good life. You'll see.'

'How can anything be good around here? Look at it.'

'It's lovely here. There's a lovely park and lots of places to take Star for walks. Plus, Stratford-Upon-Avon is just a few minutes away and there's always something going on there.'

'A park? You do know that we're ten now, right? And who wants to go on a stupid walk with Star? I bet it always rains here too.'

'Now you're just being silly, Sophia. You're excited

about starting school tomorrow, aren't you, Evie?' Looking back at Evie, she silently pleaded for backup.

'Umm, not really, Mum.' Evie looked down at Patch who was poking his head out of his little plastic house again, probably wondering what all the commotion was about. 'I'm feeling a tiny bit nervous really.'

'Evie, it'll be OK. You'll soon make friends, both of you will. Plus, you've got each other, most people would have to start on their own, so you're ahead of the game already.' Smiling, she blinked against the sting in her eyes. When they had looked around primary schools before the girls had started, both her and Andrew had fallen in love with the newly built, busy, dynamic school they had ended up sending them to. And it had been the right decision. They had both been happy there, but now, moving an hour and a half away, it just wasn't possible to keep them there.

When she had taken the girls to look around Moorfield Primary it had seemed nice. Not as bright and airy as their old school, but small and friendly. Like a little family really, the Headteacher had known every child he had come across by name. Plus, the class sizes were smaller, which could only be a good thing.

'I hope so.'

'It will, you'll see.' Taking a deep breath in, Chrissy reminded herself again that she hadn't had a choice. It wasn't as though she had wanted them to have to swap schools, it had just worked out that way. When they had accepted the offer on the marital home she'd had to find somewhere for them to live, and this place in Moorfield had seemed perfect. The private land-lord had agreed to allow Star and to sign a tenancy over to her if she paid six months' rent upfront, unlike all of the estate agents she'd contacted who seemed to have a 'computer says no' generic fit for single mums with no income and a dog. No, the best thing had been to take this house in this village.

'Where's the stupid cottage then?' Sophia looked up.

'Umm, the next turning on the left I believe. Are you excited to finally see inside? I know we saw the photos the landlord sent us, but it's not the same, is it?'

'Not excited, no. But I bagsy the bigger bedroom.' Sophia glanced sideways at Evie, a slow grin spreading across her face.

'That's fine, she can have the bigger bedroom. I liked the small pink room anyway. It looked so cosy in the photo.'

'OK, that was easy then. Bedrooms chosen! I wonder what the front garden looks like now.'

'Hopefully better than it did before.'

'Yes, it should do. The landlord, Mr Lowen, was going to get a gardener in, so it should be lovely now.' When they had driven by after visiting the school, the cottage garden had looked so overgrown, ivy had been swamping the short fence around the garden and it had looked as though the couple of hedges flanking the gateway had been left to their own devices for years. When Chrissy emailed her concerns, Mr Lowen had promised to get a gardener round before they moved in.

'Almost there now.' As she took the sharp left turn, Chrissy smiled, she was looking forward to village life, to a new start. Even with the rain pelting against the windscreen, their little lane looked beautiful. Brick cottages tucked away on one side with a large green opposite which would be perfect for the twins to run off some energy. At the end of the lane, a wood arched around the back of the cottages and the park and local shop were a short walk away at the end of the High Street.

'Look, Sophia, we could play tag on the green!'

'Tag is for babies.' Sophia looked over at Star who

had begun to whimper and paw at the door. 'What's wrong with the stupid dog?'

'Don't call her stupid. Mum! Sophia called Star stupid again.' Holding on to Patch's cage with one hand, Evie leant forward and patted Star.

'She's just eager to get out and explore our new home, that's all.' Pulling up against the narrow pathway in front of the cottage, the trailer bounced to a stop behind them. 'Umm, that's strange.' Leaning across Star, Chrissy wiped the condensation from the passenger window and peered out. The garden was untouched. Leaves, soggy from the rain covered the small cracked slabbed pathway towards the front door and the hedges still competed with each to see which could cover the small gap between them the most.

'He didn't send a gardener then?' Sophia crossed her arms, her eyes narrowing.

'Maybe he couldn't get someone to come and sort it out in time. I'll send him an email when we're all settled in. Right, I'm going to go and get the key and open up. You two may as well stay here in the dry.'

'You'll be quick, won't you, Mum?' Evie looked nervously up and down the lane.

'Of course I will.' Pulling her hood up, Chrissy slipped into the rain, making her way to the gate. The landlord had said the key would be under a rock with their door number written on somewhere near the front door.

Pushing the gate gently open, she squeezed between the hedges and made her way down the path, careful to avoid the puddles filling the gaping holes between the slabs.

Now, where was that rock? There it was, marked with a number 3. Squatting down, she lifted it up, feeling around in the moss underneath for a key. There it was. It was a bit rusty, but that was to be expected, it being left out here in weather like this.

Standing up, Chrissy listened, she could hear voices from the back garden, she was sure of it. Maybe Mr Lowen had sent a gardener after all. Would she be able to ask him to fill in a few of the cracks in the path? Chrissy smiled, there was no harm in asking, right?

Making her way around the side of the cottage she saw two men, one in a suit holding a large black umbrella and a clipboard, the other in torn jeans and a hoodie with the hood pulled up against the rain.

Chrissy tucked a stray hair behind her ear. The landlord must have come to oversee the gardening. She hadn't expected to meet him. She was sure he'd said he was now living in Spain. Unless he hadn't liked the sound of her through the emails and had wanted to meet her in person. What if he decided he didn't like her? That he didn't want her living in his house? He couldn't go back on their agreed tenancy now, could he? She was pretty sure that a tenancy agreement was legally binding once signed.

Taking a deep breath, she walked up behind them. 'Hello, I'm Chrissy.'

Twisting around quickly, the gardener looked at her and smiled, taking her hand. 'Hello, Chrissy. I'm Luke.'

'Nice to finally meet you.' Chrissy smiled and turned to look at the man in the suit, Mr Lowen, holding her hand out to him.

Glancing up from his clipboard, the man nodded before returning his gaze and scribbling something on the paper.

Lowering her hand, Chrissy tugged her hood further down. He had seemed so friendly through the emails. She shrugged, she guessed it wasn't as though you can really find out what someone is like through stilted online conversation. Maybe he was just quite a shy person in real life, maybe that's why he had dealt with everything online. Unless something *had* happened and he didn't want them to move in any more. Biting the bottom of her lip, Chrissy tried to push away the thought of having to rock up on her parents' doorstep, kids, dog and hamster in tow. They hadn't spoken to her since Andrew had said he wanted out of the marriage. Maybe they were right, maybe marriage had become a throwaway commodity in this day and age and she should have tried harder to please Andrew. She shook her head, they had some funny views, always had.

'So...' What was she supposed to do now, just move her stuff in with him out here, or should she wait until he invited her to go in? She shuffled her feet and turned to the gardener, if she struck up a conversation with him then maybe Mr Lowen would join in and make her feel a little more at ease. 'Are you OK starting with the hedges, please? It's just I've got a lot to get through that small gap.'

'The hedges? I think they're the least of our worries.' Luke grinned, the skin around his blue eyes creasing.

'Oh, really?' Pulling her eyes away from him, she looked around, taking in the knee length grass and the mound of grey rocks poking up in the centre of the lawn, a nod to a long forgotten rock garden feature maybe. She nodded, it was worse around the back she supposed, but it still made more sense to start at the front, surely? 'It's just it would make my life easier, or else I've got to lift everything up and over them.'

'Everything?' Luke tilted his head, shallow lines forming across his forehead.

'Well, yes, it's not furnished. It's not, is it, Mr Lowen?' She looked across to Mr Lowen, pen still in hand, head still dipped across his paper.

'Me?' Looking up, he tapped his pen against his chest. 'I'm afraid I'm not Mr Lowen.' He looked towards Luke. 'I'll leave you to it, Mr Cravish. I've got an appointment at half past anyway. I'll get these plans drawn up and emailed across as soon as I can.'

Luke shook the man's hand and they both watched him pick his way carefully across the lawn around to the front of the house.

'I believe we may have crossed wires here.' Luke crossed his arms and grinned at Chrissy.

'Sorry, I assumed...' She pointed towards the front garden.

'That he was Mr Lowen? The Mr Lowen that currently owns this cottage?'

'Well, yes.' Chrissy rubbed her hands together, it felt colder here than it had done when they had left their old house. 'You are the gardener, right? Sorry, I should never have suggested you started with the hedges, it's your job, you know what you're doing.'

Dipping his head, a strange sound, halfway between a laugh and a cough escaped his lips. Was he laughing at her? Subconsciously touching her cheek with the back of her hand, she felt a blush flushing across her face.

'I'm not a gardener. Why would Mr Lowen have employed a gardener to sort this place out anyway? And what are you here for, Chrissy?'

'I'm here to move my stuff in, of course. It's the day my tenancy starts.'

Luke shoved his hands in his pockets and took a few steps away from her, turning his back and dipping his head.

'Who are you, then?' She shook her head, if she didn't hurry up, the twins would no doubt start another argument cooped up in the car.

'Are you sure you've got the right place?' Turning back towards Chrissy Luke looked up, his lips straightened and his brow furrowed.

'Of course! I can show you my tenancy if I need to. Are you working on behalf of Mr Lowen?'

'I'm buying this place.' Taking his arms out of his pockets he swung them at his side.

'Are you? When? Are you going to keep renting it out? Mr Lowen didn't say anything about it being sold.'

'No, I'm knocking it down.'

'What? Mr Lowen promised me it would be a long

term let. I wouldn't have even considered the place if I had known we'd have to move again after the six months was up.' Why would he have not been straight with her? Now, what was she supposed to do? It had been hard enough finding this place when no estate agents would even look at her. And the girls? What about their school? There couldn't be many places up for rent in a village as small as this one. She'd promised them they wouldn't have to move schools again.

'Six months? You've got to be kidding me.' Luke kicked a loose stone, watching as it sprang and landed at the foot of a tree to the side of the garden.

'Hold on. Let me get this straight.' Chrissy held her hands up in front of her. None of this made any sense whatsoever. 'Mr Lowen has sold you this place, but didn't tell you I was moving in today?'

'Not exactly.'

'What do you mean? He either told you about us or not.'

'I mean, it's not exactly sold. He promised to sell it to me if he didn't get a tenant.'

'So, you haven't brought it then? You're not knocking it down?' Chrissy folded her arms.

'Yes, no. No, I haven't brought it yet, but we had a gentleman's agreement that he would sell it to me if he couldn't get a tenant by the end of the year and, well,' Luke swept his arm around the garden. 'I took it for a given that he wouldn't be able to.'

'Why not? Yes, the garden may be a little over-grown, to say the least, but he's promised to get a gardener in to sort that out so...'

'Have you been inside?' Luke interrupted her.

'I've seen photos of the inside. Mr Lowen is in Spain and as it's a private rental he couldn't get anyone to show me around, but the photos look lovely so...' Why was he looking at her like that? With his head tilted, he looked as if he was trying to decide if she was lying or just a little crazy.

'You do know he's not been able to rent it out for over three years, don't you?'

'Three years? No, I didn't. I guess with it being in a village the location might put people off.' She knew some people liked the hustle and bustle of town living and having everything on your doorstep, but if she was honest, she was looking forward to embracing a slower pace of life.

'Those photos you were talking about. They didn't happen to have a blue Citroen out the front, did they?'

'Umm, there may have been, I didn't take much notice of what car the previous tenants had.' Chrissy scrunched her nose and looked at him from under her hood. What was he playing at?

'The photos are from when this place was sold, seven years ago. My old mate used to live here, he drove a blue Citroen.'

'Oh, right.'

'Evie! Stop following me!'

Chrissy turned around, Sophia was stomping up the path, stepping over puddles and ducking under branches. Evie and Star close behind. Patch must have been left in the car.

'Star hasn't got her lead on!' Walking quickly towards them she pulled Star's lead out from the bag slung across her shoulder.

'She's OK. She listens to me. Look, sit, paw.' Evie smiled as she took hold of Star's uplifted paw.

'That may be so, but she's never been here before, if she runs off she won't be able to find her way back to us.' Clipping the lead onto Star's red collar, Chrissy looked back at Luke. 'If you've not got anything in writing, then I guess I'm going to move our stuff in.'

'Go ahead.' Luke held his hand out towards the cottage.

'Who's he?' Sophia asked.

'I'm not entirely sure. A friend of the landlord, I presume. Are you ready to have a look inside?'

'No, I'd much rather stand here in this rubbish dump of a garden and get a little bit wetter.' Sophia crossed her arms and stared at Chrissy.

'Sophia, please. I know this is difficult for you, but please don't talk to me like that.' She patted Sophia on the shoulder, she knew it was tough for the girls. She was finding it difficult, and she was an adult, she couldn't imagine what the twins were feeling.

'Get off me.' Jerking her shoulder away from her, Sophia stomped to the front door standing to the side, waiting for Chrissy.

'OK, here we go. Home sweet home.' Smiling, Chrissy twisted the key in the lock and pushed open the door.

'Urgh. It stinks!' Sophia and Evie both staggered back, covering their noses with their sleeves.

'I'm sorry, Mum, but we can't live in a place that stinks like that.'

'It's OK, girls. It's not been lived in for a few years so probably just needs the windows opening and some air let in.' Chrissy took a deep breath and stepped inside. The tiled hallway, though caked in mud, looked OK.

Opening the door on the left to the living room, Chrissy paused, gagging. Looking around the bare room, the dark wooden floorboards were covered in thick dust and the windows barely let any light in. In the far corner, Chrissy spotted what looked like a splash of black paint thrown against the wall. Stamping the rain off of her trainers, she walked across to the wall. It wasn't paint. It was mould growing across the wall. A windowpane was smashed in the corner of the window next to it. That must be why it was so mouldy.

The smell was worse near the fireplace. Coughing into her sleeve, Chrissy backed away.

'Yuck! What's that on the wall? It's all black!' Sophia came to stand next to her, her scarf pulled up over her mouth and nose.

'It's mould. The rain must have been getting in through the broken window.'

'Is that what smells?'

'No, I think there might be a dead bird or something stuck up the chimney.'

'Oh no! The poor little thing. Can we save it?'

'Mum said it was dead. Nothing can be saved when it's dead.' Sophia turned her back on her sister and rolled her eyes.

'Anyway. Let's go and have a look at the other rooms, shall we?' Chrissy shepherded them both towards the kitchen and gingerly opened the door.

'And we're supposed to actually cook in here?'

Sophia pointed to the oven. 'I'm not going to be eating anything that comes out of that.'

The glass panel was missing from the oven door and judging by the amount of ingrained food around the rings, the previous tenants had been worse cooks than Chrissy herself.

'Oh, Mum, look at the tap.' Evie shook her head at the dripping tap, a ring of limescale circling the plughole. 'What a waste of water.'

'Yes, what a shame.' With her hands on her hips, Chrissy swivelled around, taking in the small galley kitchen. The only drawer lay on its side propped against the back of the work surface and one, no two, cupboard doors were hanging off.

'A little different to the photos Mr Lowen sent you, isn't it?'

'Luke! How did you get in?' Chrissy spun around.

'The front door.' Lowering his hood, Luke ruffled his ash blond hair with his fingers.

'A little different, yes.'

'Mr Lowen couldn't be bothered to fix anything after he got the bailiffs to kick the last tenants out. Hence, why it's in such a state and he hasn't been able to get a tenant.'

'Oh, OK.'

'Never mind, I'm sure you can find some other

place to rent. Somewhere that has a working oven, maybe?'

'It's not as easy as that.' Curling a loose piece of hair around her finger, Chrissy blinked back the tears.

'Sure it is. Just pop along to an estate agent and, voila, you'll soon be the proud tenant of a habitable house.'

'Girls, why don't you go and check on Patch for me?' Chrissy watched as Evie and Sophia ran back through the living room and out to the car.

'Let me find out where the nearest estate agent is for you. We used to have one down on the High Street, but that shut down years ago.' Bending his head, he scrolled through his phone.

Looking out into the garden, Chrissy tried to slow her breathing. She was being daft, panicking. All she needed to do was to send an email to Mr Lowen and he'd send some contractors round to make the repairs and clean the cottage up.

'I don't suppose you have Mr Lowen's number, do you?'

'No,' Luke laughed. 'I'm sorry, I shouldn't laugh, but he doesn't give out his number to us villagers. He had too many complaints about his last tenants so he changed his phone number.'

'But you said you had an agreement with him about buying this place? You must have his number.'

'Nope, afraid not. We had an agreement in place from when I saw him last. He lost a poker game, the prize being that he'd sell up if he couldn't get a tenant.'

'Well, he has. Sorry, you lost.'

'Nah, you don't want to stay here, not with two kids in tow. It's a health hazard.'

'It's less of a health hazard than living on the streets.'

'Now that's just being melodramatic.'

'Is it?' With the pads of her thumbs, Chrissy wiped her eyes before turning around and facing Luke. 'All my money is wrapped up in this tenancy. I've paid six months in advance.'

Luke whistled through his teeth. 'Without seeing it?'

'Yep, without seeing it. The estate agents wouldn't even consider a single, unemployed mum with a dog. This place seemed perfect, our only choice.'

Tapping his fingers on the grimy work surface, Luke looked at her, a half smile on his face. 'No chance you're walking away from this place then?'

'Not for six months anyway.' Chrissy slapped her forehead. 'How could I be so stupid?'

'You're not stupid, just trusting, that's all.'

'I think that's been the problem my whole life.' Why was she even talking to a complete stranger like this? Especially one who wanted to make her and the twins homeless.

'In that case, I guess my grand plans of knocking this dump down to build a four-bedroom money-maker will have to wait.'

'Thank you. Right, I need to get on, it's getting late and my girls start their new school in the morning.'

'Are you seriously going to sleep here with it in this state? You've no idea what it's like upstairs.'

'Nope, I'm going to see if they have room in a little B&B for tonight and then I'll clean it tomorrow once Mr Lowen has replied to the strongly worded email I'm going to send him.'

'OK, good plan. You never know, Mr Lowen might give you your money back.'

'Umm, I doubt that very much from what you've told me about him.'

'Stranger things have happened. I think they let dogs stay at the B&B in the centre of the village, so your luck might be changing.'

'You think they'll let us take a hamster in too?' Now that she had a proper plan in place, she felt calmer. Things would be OK. The worst-case scenario would be that Mr Lowen would refuse to make good the repairs. She just wouldn't let herself think about what might happen to them if he decided it was too much bother and terminated the tenancy. But he couldn't do that legally, could he? Chrissy was sure he couldn't. It would be fine.

3

'Hey, hey. Chrissy, stop!'

Lifting her knee up, Chrissy rested her foot on the trailer's tyre, bearing the brunt of the chest of drawers on her hip. She twisted her body to see who was in such a hurry to speak to her. 'Luke. What's the matter?'

'That's the matter.' As he jogged towards her, he pointed to the chest of drawers. 'Here, let me help. You'll give yourself an injury.'

'I'm fine. Honest.' Or she would be if she could just get on with it. The wood was digging into her hip.

'Let me help.' Gripping hold of the chest of drawers, he lifted it away from Chrissy's hip bone. 'You grab the other end.'

'Yes, sir!' As Luke slowly backed away, pulling the chest of drawers towards him, Chrissy grabbed the other end and pulled it out of the trailer.

'No need to be sarcastic, I'm only helping you.'

'Umm.' Shaking her head, she reminded herself that this was Luke, a virtual stranger, trying to be nice. It wasn't Andrew who had always insisted on 'helping' her and doing things for her, rendering her incapable or at least believing she, herself, was incapable. 'Sorry, thank you.'

'Have you heard back from Mr Lowen?'

'Yes, I got a curt email back basically saying I could either sort it all out myself or find somewhere else but he would keep my money regardless. I signed the contract, didn't I? It was my fault for not insisting on viewing the place. Plus, nowhere else would take me on anyway, so it's all immaterial. Sorry, your plans are well and truly scuppered.'

'No worries. I'm sure I can talk him into selling it to me at a later date.'

Backing into the cottage, Chrissy noticed Luke's muscles flexing under his jumper.

'I need to go to the gym more.' Luke laughed and lifted his end of the chest of drawers up and down impersonating a weightlifter.

'You look fine as you are.' She averted her eyes

quickly, she hadn't meant for it to come out like that. Feeling the heat of a blush rapidly racing across her cheeks, she jerked her head trying to flick her hair across her face to cover it. 'I didn't mean it like that. I meant...'

'It's OK, I'm happy to take a compliment.' Luke laughed, seemingly revelling in her discomfort. 'Is this going upstairs?'

'Yes, I can manage myself though, if you need to get off?'

'What are you going to do? Pull it up the stairs?'

'I could do.'

'You could. Or you could just let me help. I figure I probably owe you a couple of hours' hard graft after the way I tried to make you homeless yesterday.'

'Thank you.' Chrissy allowed him to shepherd her up the stairs first, him taking the majority of the weight at the bottom.

* * *

'Right, is that the last of it? I think I've racked up more than a few days off from the gym with all the lifting.' Flexing his arms, his muscles strained at the thin maroon wool of his jumper.

'Yes, that's it and thank you again. I owe you big time.' Looking sideways at him she added, 'But that doesn't mean I'm going to move out so you can make your fortune.'

'Good, I don't want you to move out for a very long time, not if I have to help you carry everything back out again anyway. Now, surely I've at least earned a coffee.'

'Of course.' Leading the way into the small kitchen, Chrissy switched the kettle on as Luke leant against the work surface.

'I'd forgotten how good this place can look. It looks like a home again now you've got all your things in.'

'I like it. Here you go, one coffee and you can help yourself to a biscuit too, if you like?'

'I am spoilt.' Luke took the packet of digestives from Chrissy's hand, his skin brushing hers.

'Take a seat.' In the living room, Chrissy indicated a furry pink beanbag.

'I'm too old for this.' Lowering himself down, Luke held his coffee away from him, taking care not to spill it. 'It's comfy at least. Haven't you got a sofa?'

'Yep, our sofa and beds are currently in a van sat in my ex's work car park. They wouldn't fit in the trailer, so he managed to borrow a van from his work. He's bringing them on Saturday when he picks the twins up. So it's not long we've got to cope on beanbags and airbeds.' Squatting down, she sank in Sophia's fluffy beanbag.

'You stink!' Luke scrunched his nose up and laughed.

'Sorry, I probably do. Sweat mixed with bleach, by any chance?' Chrissy shuffled to the edge of the beanbag, her coffee sloshing precariously close to the rim of her mug, she was glad she hadn't filled it to the brim.

'The bleach is quite overpowering, I must say.'

'Yes, well, have you noticed the wall over there?' She pointed to where the mould used to smother the whitewashed wall.

'Wow! You have been busy! You'd never know it was covered in mould yesterday.'

'It took me a good hour to clean though, and my arms feel like they're going to drop off.' Chrissy rubbed her upper arms. She'd done it though, despite the fact that getting the cottage clean and liveable had seemed like an impossible task, she'd won. She'd scrubbed every wall with a bleach solution, mouldy or not, and washed the floorboards, twice. And with the amount of bleach she'd used on the kitchen work surfaces, she'd feel happy eating dinner off of them.

'I bet they do.' Placing his coffee mug on the floor, Luke shimmied to the edge of the beanbag, leant forward and began to massage Chrissy's shoulders. 'How's that?'

'Absolutely divine.' Chrissy closed her eyes and smiled. Luke's fingers working into her taut muscles were strong and confident. Andrew would never even have thought to give her a massage.

'What's happening about that broken window? It's cold enough in here already and it's only going to get colder.'

'Just having the wood across it has made a heck of a difference.' Chrissy glanced across at the thin piece of plywood she'd found in the shed outside. She wouldn't mention it was stuck to the window frame with some ancient wood glue she'd also unearthed in the shed. 'I'll email Mr Lowen again later and see if I can get him to agree to fix it. I need to badger him to fix the oven door too.'

'Have you got any wood for the wood burner?' Luke nodded towards the fireplace. 'It's surprising how much heat they can pump out.'

'Not yet. I'll have to pop somewhere tomorrow.'

She twisted around to face him. 'As lovely as this is, I need to jump in the shower before I pick the girls up.'

* * *

Jogging the last few metres to the school gates, Chrissy bundled her wet hair up into a messy bun before slowing down and rounding the corner into the playground.

'Hello, I haven't seen you here before. You must be mum to the twin girls, is that right?'

'Hi, yes I am. We just moved here yesterday.'

'Oh, lovely. Nice to meet you, I'm Natalie. I didn't know there was a place up for sale in the village? Or are you commuting from someplace else?' A small baby began to squirm in the red pram she was holding on to. 'It's OK, princess. It's not your feed time yet.' Leaning over the pram, Natalie's wavy, blonde hair fanned across the pink blanket covering the baby.

'Good to meet you too, I'm Chrissy. We've moved into Corner Cottage, it's just off the High Street.'

'Corner Cottage?' Natalie stood up, tucking her hair behind her ears. 'Wow. I mean, I assumed Mr Lowen had given up on trying to rent that place out.'

Chrissy pulled the strap of her handbag higher up her shoulder and bit her bottom lip.

'I'm so sorry. That must have sounded really rude. I just meant that it hasn't been lived in for so long, I just assumed he wasn't renting it out any more.'

'It's OK. I think, well, actually I know, I was pretty naïve when I signed up for it. It turns out the photos he sent me were from years ago and I was daft enough to sign the tenancy without seeing it.' Chrissy smiled. 'It's my own fault. It's the first time I've ever rented on my own, so it was all quite new to me.'

'I'm sure it will be fine once you've settled your things in. It used to be a lovely cosy place once. It just needs someone like you to give it some TLC and return it to its former glory.'

'I hope so. Now I've cleaned it up a bit and put our things in its looking better already.'

'Natalie, hi. Have you managed to get your parents to babysit for next weekend yet? You're not going to back out on this are you?' A professional looking woman with a black bob bustled up, her hand on her slightly rounded belly.

'Yes, it's all sorted. Please stop panicking, you're starting to make me worry.'

'It's a good job one of us is panicking or you won't even have a wedding. Oh, sorry. Hello, I'm Gina. '

'I'm Chrissy, nice to meet you.' Taking Gina's hand, Chrissy smiled.

'This one here is getting married, on Christmas Eve of all days, so you can just imagine how hectic that's going to be.'

'Christmas Eve? That'll be lovely.'

'It will be, if she starts organising things.'

'Most of it's organised. Plus, as long as I get to marry Graham and I have my family and friends there, I don't really care about the details.'

'You should do. This is your big day. Goodness knows you've waited long enough.' Gina rolled her eyes at Chrissy. 'It took her Graham fourteen years to pop the question.'

'Congratulations.'

'Thanks.'

'Oh, Sophia. What's happened?' Chrissy watched as Sophia and Evie strolled out of class, Sophia's skirt clearly ripped across the front.

'She did it on the climbing frame.' Evie looked across at her sister and then back at Chrissy.

'Are you OK? Did you hurt yourself?' Chrissy rubbed Sophia's shoulder.

'No, I just got something caught on my skirt, no big deal.' Recoiling at Chrissy's touch, Sophia pulled away, looking around the playground.

'Well, at least you're OK, that's the main thing. It's a shame I can't say the same about your skirt, though.

I can't believe you've managed to rip it like that the first time you've worn it.' Bending down, Chrissy picked at the torn fabric. 'At least it's on the seam, I suppose.'

'Leave it, please, Mum.' Taking a few steps back, Sophia smoothed her skirt down. 'I'll just wear another one tomorrow.'

'Umm, you haven't got another one, sweetheart. I could only manage to get one each in your sizes, remember?'

'Oh, yes, because we have to wear stupid navy at this stupid school. If you'd let us stay at our old school, I'd have had tonnes of skirts. I had three grey ones, but, no, you had to make us move here.'

'Sophia, don't. Not here.' Thankfully Natalie seemed to be preoccupied balancing lunchboxes and book bags on the pram and Gina had disappeared. 'So, how was your first day then, girls?'

'It was OK. There's this girl I sit next to who's got the longest hair you've ever seen, longer than Rapunzel's even. Mum, look, she's over there playing on the tyres. Her hair's really long, isn't it?' Evie pointed across to a girl jumping from tyre to tyre, her black plated hair springing up every time she jumped.

'Wow, yes, it is really long. Have you made friends with her then?'

'No, she's really annoying. She keeps shouting the answers out in class instead of putting her hand up.'

'That's not really a reason not to be friends with her though, is it?' Evie had always set her standards high when making new friends. She'd once told Chrissy her list of traits she looked out for in potential friends and Chrissy was sure, if she'd been the same age, Evie would have bypassed her as unsuitable friend material.

'She's said she doesn't want to be friends with her, so just drop it, Mum. We're not desperate.'

'I didn't say you were. So, did you make any friends, Sophia?' Holding her breath, she waited for the backchat.

Sophia crossed her arms, dipping her head to her shoes.

'You OK, Sophia?'

'I just want to go...' Raising her hand to her mouth, she began biting her nail. 'Away from school.'

'Come on then, let's get back to our new home. I've spent the day scrubbing and cleaning the cottage and it actually looks quite nice now.' Placing her arms across Sophia and Evie's shoulders, Chrissy began leading the way out of the playground. 'See you tomorrow, Natalie.'

'Bye, Chrissy. Hope you girls had a good first day?'

Natalie looked up and waved. 'Oh dear, someone's going to be going shopping tonight.' Frowning, she looked at Sophia's skirt.

'It's only a tear, I'll soon get that fixed.' Chrissy grinned, even if she'd had the spare cash, she certainly didn't want to spend their first evening living here, driving around looking for shops.

'Where's the car?'

'We're walking, Sophia. The cottage is only two minutes away. So, girls, how was it really? Can you see yourselves being happy here?'

'It was OK, Mum.' Evie took Chrissy's hand and looked up at her. 'Our teacher seems nice, a bit strict but that's a good thing because there's this boy, Oliver, who is a bit naughty. Isn't he, Sophia?'

'Huh?'

'Oliver, he's a bit naughty, isn't he? He pushed someone at break time. So, I think I like the fact that Mrs Chambers is a bit strict, because I don't want him pushing me or disrupting the class when we're trying to learn.'

'Mum doesn't really care about how school was, Evie.' Sophia kicked a stone with the tip of her newly polished shoe.

'Of course, I do! I care a lot about how you both

got on today. I've been looking forward to picking you up and finding out all about your day.'

'Don't lie. If you cared about us, even just a tiny bit, then you wouldn't have made us move schools in the first place.'

'We've spoken about this already, Sophia.' Wiping her gloved hand across her forehead, Chrissy hoped this wouldn't be the start of another headache.

'She does care, she's told us that we had to move because of selling the house.'

'And whose fault's that?'

'Don't please.' Too late, Sophia had already begun walking ahead, her hands covering her ears. They'd never forgive her for making them move.

* * *

With her ear against the kitchen door, Chrissy listened as Sophia and Evie said their goodbyes to their dad and hung up the phone before she ventured into the living room. 'Everything OK, sweethearts? Has your dad settled into his new home?'

'Yes. He says we can decorate our bedrooms however we like.' Evie reached up from her position curled up on her beanbag and gave Chrissy her mobile.

'Thanks. That's good then. Here, I've made us all a hot chocolate. Budge up and I'll sit in the middle.' Chrissy placed their mugs on the coffee table before throwing down a cushion in the middle of the two fluffy beanbags. 'Shall we watch a film before bedtime?' Lowering herself down, Chrissy squeezed between Sophia and Evie and pulled a throw over their knees.

'OK.' Sophia hugged her mug and leant her head against Chrissy's shoulder.

'Love you, Sophia. You too, Evie.' Chrissy kissed the top of Sophia's head. 'Things will get better, I promise. We've just got to get used to our new life, that's all.' Taking a deep breath in, she hoped they could.

'You never know, Dad might be lonely and decide to come and live with us again.' Evie looked across at Chrissy, hope etched in her eyes.

'Evie, you know that's not likely to happen, but we can be happy here, by ourselves. And we will be, we've just got to accept it and make the most of it. I think it will be lovely living here, in this small village. I was looking at the noticeboard outside the school today and there was a poster saying they have a village Christmas Carol Service at the beginning of December. It sounds as though the whole village meet up on the green and the school join in too.'

'Ooh, that sounds nice.'

'It does, doesn't it? Here, shall we watch *The Santa Clause* film and get into the Christmas spirit? It's only a month and a half away.' Chrissy scrolled to their recorded films, ignoring Sophia's huffing and eye rolling. Yes, this would be their first Christmas, just the three of them, but she was determined that they'd have a good one. She had already started a list of new traditions she thought the girls would enjoy.

4

'Come on, up you get. We don't want to be late for your second day at school.' Chrissy called up the stairs for the third time in the past ten minutes before returning to the kitchen to finish the packed lunches.

'Mum, you've remembered I don't want ham in my sandwiches again, haven't you?' Evie came into the kitchen, rubbing her eyes.

'Drat, no I hadn't. Don't worry, I'll redo them. Do you want cheese instead?' Unzipping Evie's pink butterfly covered lunchbox, she took out the sandwiches.

'Yes, please.'

'OK. Grab yourself some cereal then.' Unwanted sandwiches in hand, Chrissy poked her head around the door and called again, 'Sophia! Please tell me you're getting dressed!'

'She was cleaning her teeth when I came down.' Shaking out the chocolate flakes into her bowl, Evie looked up.

'At least she's awake then. Now, do you want mayo with your cheese or just butter?'

* * *

'Morning, Chrissy. You managed to get a new skirt then?' Natalie joined them on the playground.

'Hi, no. I just fixed it.'

'Really? Wow. Can I have a look? Sophia, isn't it? Do you mind?'

Sophia shrugged and turned so that Natalie could see where the rip had been.

'That's really good.'

'Not really. It was only on the seam so it was pretty easy. I used to be a dressmaker so it's just second nature to me.' Chrissy shrugged. 'Is your boy in Year 5 too?' Chrissy shuffled from foot to foot.

'Yes, he is. I bet you two remember him from yesterday, don't you, girls? He can be a bit loud in class, can't you, Adam?' Natalie rubbed at a mark on his coat. 'I've got Kane too, who's just turned six. He's over there, playing on the tyres as usual.'

'Not really.' Adam rolled his eyes.

'Umm, I'm sure there are a few people who might just be daft enough to believe you.' Laughing, Natalie rocked her pram, shushing the small girl inside. 'I'm sure she has an allergy to this place. The only time she grizzles is when we step foot in the playground, isn't that right, Poppy?'

'Bless her. Right, there's the bell.' Putting her arms over Evie and Sophia's shoulders, Chrissy pulled them towards her and kissed them on the tops of their heads. 'Love you both. Have a great day and try to smile!'

'Bye.' Pulling away, they sauntered slowly into the cloakroom, their rucksacks pulled up high on their shoulders.

'They'll settle in soon enough.' Natalie patted Chrissy's arm.

'I hope so, they've had a lot to deal with recently.'

'Natalie! Natalie! So glad I've caught you. I had to run to the office and thought you'd have gone by the time I got back around here.' Gina rushed up to them, her high heels clicking on the playground. 'We've got problems.'

'Really? I'm sure it's nothing. You should stop worrying about my wedding. You should be thinking of that one, not about me.' Natalie patted Gina's baby bump.

'Believe me, I need something to take my mind off the thoughts of the returning sleepless nights. Plus, Steve does enough worrying for the both of us. Did I tell you he's already painted the nursery and put the cot up? There's only so much organising one baby needs. And, you know how much I'm missing the structure of work. I need to be able to channel my organisational skills somewhere.'

'And I'm the lucky one.' Natalie grinned and laughed before turning to Chrissy.

'Anyway, someone's got to organise your wedding or you'll end up not even getting married and you waited long enough for him to pop the question as it is.'

'You're probably right.' Natalie shrugged and retrieved Poppy's dummy from the foot of her pram, returning it to her waiting mouth. 'Hit me with the drama, then. Have the florists upped their prices again? Because if they have, I'll just tell them I'll go elsewhere.'

'I wish. No, the dressmaker emigrated.' Gina breathed out heavily through her mouth.

'Oh, well, that is a bit more of a problem. Surely

she can't just up and leave when she's halfway through making a custom dress? She's already taken half of the money.' Natalie pushed the pram to a bench at the side of the playground and sat down.

'Yes, well, apparently she can. To be fair, I think her mum has been taken ill so she's had to go to look after her, but that's not the point, it's still unprofessional.'

'What about my dress? And my money?'

'She emailed me yesterday evening so I went round and collected your dress. I haven't looked at it yet though, so I'm not sure how far she got with it.'

'And the money? I've lost that, right? I'll have to buy another one and will only have half my budget left.' Bending her head, Natalie wiped her eyes with the corner of Poppy's blanket. 'This is silly. Why am I getting upset over a dress? All that matters is that I marry Graham, it shouldn't matter whether I'm wearing the most expensive wedding dress on the planet or a bin liner.'

'That's what weddings do to people. Everything becomes more important. And so it should, it's the most important day of your life and one you'll remember forever.'

Chrissy ran her fingers through her hair, yes, it would be one Natalie would remember forever but, well, she certainly didn't agree that it would be the most important day in Natalie's life. After all, a marriage could be wiped out with a couple of small words. Something that 'important' shouldn't be able to crumble so easily.

'Try not to panic. I've been researching this morning over breakfast and there is a discount bridal shop a couple of hours drive away. They promise that they sell the best of the best at reduced prices. We can go over today and check it out if you like?'

'I don't know. I had my heart set on *my* wedding dress. The design has elements of everything that's important to me and my family. One brought off the rail just won't be the same.' Pulling a tissue from her nappy bag, she blew her nose. 'I had wanted to pass this one down to Poppy, to make it into a family heirloom.'

'Right, I'll go and grab the dress and bring it over to yours. We can have a look at it and see how much is left to be done on it. Then we can then start looking for another dressmaker.'

'Do you think another dressmaker would take on a half-finished project though? On half the money?' Natalie shook her head.

'We'll find someone. I've never let you down before, have I?'

'We'll never find someone at such short notice though, especially with Christmas coming up.' Natalie took a deep breath. 'Unless...'

'Unless what?'

'Chrissy?' Natalie looked up at Chrissy.

'Yes?' Maybe she wanted her to go. Chrissy looked down at her hands, she hadn't known whether to go or if that would have looked rude so she'd hung around, thinking that Natalie and Gina would either include her in the conversation or make it obvious to her that she should leave. She had never been good at reading people, at knowing what the social norms were. She'd always felt quite clumsy in these situations. She was too boring, she knew that. Even Andrew had always gone off and left her on her own on the rare occasions they'd managed to get a babysitter and she'd gone alone to one of his friend's get-togethers. He'd always preferred to go off and talk to one of his mates, leaving Chrissy twiddling her thumbs and wishing she had stayed at home. She hadn't bothered going out with him for a couple of years now, there had been no point. She'd obviously outstayed her welcome here too. Looking across at the gate out of the playground, Chrissy shrugged. It didn't matter.

'You probably think I'm being really rude here, but...' Natalie looked down at her shoes and then back up at Chrissy. 'You said you used to be a dress-maker? Would you be able to finish my dress for me, please? I'd pay you the going rate, obviously.'

'Umm.' Chrissy could feel her stomach churning. Her, working on a wedding dress. Just after she'd split up with Andrew too. Oh, the irony. 'I only used to make alterations, nothing much. I don't think...'

'Will you at least look at it? Please?' Natalie looked up, her mascara shadowing the skin under her eyes.

'I guess I can look at it, but I haven't done any proper dressmaking since before the twins were born.'

'Thank you. Thank you so much.' Standing up, Natalie pulled Chrissy towards her, wrapping her arms around her shoulders. 'I really appreciate this.'

'Let's go then.' Gina took Natalie's pram and began pushing it towards the gate.

'What? Now?' Chrissy pulled a loose thread on the sleeve of her coat.

'No time like the present. As long as you're free, that is...' Gina called back over her shoulder.

'Yes, I guess so.'

'You're a life saver. My house is only a five-minute walk away. It's one of those Victorian terraces on the High Street.' Natalie smiled at her.

'This is lovely.' Chrissy stepped into Natalie's hall-way, the tall ceilings boasted the original cornices.

'You've kept the Victorian floor tiles. They're beautiful.'

'Thank you.'

'I love all the old features, it really brings character to a place, doesn't it?'

'It certainly does. Go through to the kitchen, if you like. I'll just get Poppy out of her snowsuit and I'll join you.'

'OK.' Making her way through the living room, Chrissy noticed they'd managed to keep the original fireplace with intricately detailed flowered tiles flanking the grate.

'Ignore the mess! The boys refused to tidy up last night and when they finally went to sleep I was too tired to do anything.' Natalie called from the hallway.

'It's fine.' Picking her way around pieces of Lego and superhero figures, Chrissy pushed the door to the kitchen open. What would have once been a galley kitchen had been opened up into the dining room creating a large family room.

'Take a seat. I'll stick the kettle on.' Natalie bustled in, placing Poppy in her bouncy chair and waving Chrissy towards a brown leather sofa at the far end of the room. 'Tea or coffee?'

'Tea, please.'

'Here you go.' Natalie handed Chrissy a blue mug

just as a sharp trill sounded through the house. 'Ah, that'll be Gina. She always seems to be able to hear the kettle boiling. Can you just keep an eye on Poppy while I answer it, please?'

Nodding, Chrissy took a sip, the hot liquid burning the roof of her mouth. Placing her mug on the coffee table to her right, she put her hands on her knees, pressing down hard to try to stop them jiggling. Gina would have the wedding dress with her, which would only mean one thing, that the conversation would loop back to weddings.

'Here, we are. Hello, again, Chrissy.' Gina marched in, a large white box in her arms.

'Pop it on here.' Swooping her arm across the table, Natalie pushed various pieces of paper, pens and Play-Doh tubs to one end. 'I'm so nervous, I think I might actually throw up.'

'Let's just have a look first.' Lifting the lid off, Gina revealed ivory fabric. 'Go on, Natalie, take it out and have a look.'

Pushing herself to standing, Chrissy joined them around the table as Natalie lifted the dress delicately out of the box, revealing an ivory gown with a silk bodice and tulle underskirt.

'Thank goodness for that. The actual dress is

done, it's just the detail, oh, and the hem, by the looks of it. It's not finished at all, is it?'

'It's a lot more finished than you were worrying about though, isn't it? Why don't you go and try it on and then Chrissy can take a proper look, if that's OK?'

'Of course.' Forcing a smile, Chrissy nodded.

Five minutes later, Natalie swanned back into the room. Chrissy could see the extent of the work that needed doing now. The strapless, silk bodice was too loose and the skirt lacked shape, hanging loosely around Natalie's hips, the edges of the train crudely cut with threads swooping across the floor behind her. Crystals had begun to be sewn below the heart-shaped neckline, but apart from them, no other detail decorated the plain gown.

'Look at it.' Natalie rasped, her voice catching around her words.

'Don't cry, Nat. You'll get mascara all over it. Chrissy, do you think you can finish it?'

'I... umm.' An image of Chrissy's own wedding dress, a strapless, satin bodice gown with a heart-shaped neckline too, refused to be pushed to the back of her mind. Could she really fix up Natalie's dress when her own marriage had fallen apart a few short months before? She swallowed hard. 'Can I just use your toilet, please?'

* * *

Leaning across the sink, Chrissy stared into the plughole, watching as the soapy water twirled around and around before escaping. She'd thrown her own wedding dress, the tiara and veil too, in the wheelie bin the day after Andrew had said he wanted to leave her. The moment he had told her was still as clear as though it had happened yesterday, a cruel memory which refused to fade.

He'd just got home from work, late as usual, and she'd been warming his dinner in the microwave when he'd come into the kitchen.

'Chrissy, we need to have a conversation.' She could picture the way he'd leant against the sink, his arms folded against his pale blue work shirt.

'OK, love.' She'd looked around and switched the kettle on. 'Do you want a coffee?'

'No, thank you. Can you stop?'

'What?'

'Just stop what you're doing and listen to me for once.'

Chrissy had laughed. It had seemed so ironic, him asking her to listen. Normally it was her having to wait until the adverts in between rugby games to try to catch his attention. 'I can indeed.' She'd turned to face him, swinging the tea towel over her shoulder.

'Come and sit down for a minute.'

Chrissy had followed him to the kitchen table and slid into the chair opposite him. It was then that she could see the bags under his eyes, his brow furrowed uncharacteristically. She remembered that the night before that conversation he had been tossing and turning until the early hours. She had thought it was due to a new client his firm had taken on.

'Things haven't been right for a long time now.' He'd clasped his hands in front of him.

'What do you mean? You're not ill, are you?'

'No.' She still remembered the look he'd given her, she remembered thinking that he'd thought she was stupid. 'Between us.'

'Us?' She hadn't understood. 'What's wrong with us?'

'We've grown apart.' He'd begun tapping his fingertips on the placemat in front of him. That had always irritated her, but she'd swallowed her annoyance.

'We haven't. Not really. But I understand where you're coming from, I think we do need to spend some more time together. We need to make an effort to spend time with just the two of us. Maybe your sister will babysit? We could go for a drink at the weekend.'

'That's not what I meant.'

'OK, I guess we could ask her if she'd have them overnight so we can have some quality time over the weekend. We could go up to that place you wanted to go on holiday last year. What's it called? The place with the lighthouse? I can see it in my mind's eye, but can't think of the name.' Much to her own disgust, she had begun to tap the placemat in front of her too, trying to remember the name of the place.

'You don't understand. We've grown apart. A night out, or a weekend away even, isn't going to fix that.'

'Well, not fix it but it would help. You've been putting in so many hours at work recently that it's only natural you're feeling down. You need a break. Why don't you see if you can take a break? Sod it, we could always just take the twins out of school for a week and properly get away.'

Andrew had shifted in his seat, loosening his tie. She'd later found out that those late nights at work hadn't been what they had seemed. Yes, he had been at work so, as he pointed out, he hadn't technically been lying, but he had been spending the time with his childhood sweetheart who had begun working in the same office. 'It's over. Our marriage is over.'

'What? What do you mean?' Every time this scene ran through Chrissy's mind, she could still taste the bile that had stung her throat and risen to her mouth. She still forgot to breathe. That second, the second that she had learnt her marriage was over, was etched into her memory as though it had been a physical strike.

'I want out of the marriage.'

His words had pierced the silent fog shrouding her. 'What? No. Why?'

'We've grown apart. We've changed. We've been together now twelve years. When we started dating we were young, we've both grown up, changed, and now, well, the marriage is over.'

'That's not a reason. Other people stay together longer. Other people change. Give us a chance, please?' She'd felt as though her world had stopped spinning, she had waited for her new reality to change. Everything suspended on Andrew's answer.

'I'm sorry. I don't love you any more.'

She'd looked down at his hands then, spread out in front of him, palms up on the table. It was then that she noticed his wedding ring had gone. He had already taken it off. When? She hadn't noticed before. How long had he given up on them?

* * *

Looking up to the mirror, Chrissy wiped her eyes and focused on her reflection. Her rushed messy bun had sprung strands of hair escaping around her pale face. The bags under her eyes were deepened by the worry of the girls settling at school and fears over how they would survive financially when the small amount of savings from the equity of the house had been swallowed up.

The irony of the fact that Andrew had used the excuse that they had changed because they had known each other so long as the reason their marriage had failed, but she'd later found out he had actually been having an affair with his childhood sweetheart at that exact time, hadn't escaped her.

Could she really help Natalie fix up her wedding dress? Practically? Yes, easily. Emotionally? Well, that was the problem. She'd be signing herself up to staring at a wedding dress for hours on end. Shaking her head, she just didn't know if she could do it.

But then again, they did need the money. She had enough to pay for bills and food up until Christmas, after which, she had promised herself she'd take the leap and try to find a job. This would be better though, if she could sort out Natalie's dress, maybe word would spread and she'd get more work. It could actually turn into a viable little business, earning enough to keep them ticking over, at least. It would save on childcare and be less unsettling for the children than going to a childminder if she got a job. Even if it didn't lead to more business, it would give them a bit of money to be able to make this Christmas a memorable one, a nice (as nice as it could be anyway) one.

'Come on, mum-up. You can do this.' Chrissy whispered to her reflected self staring back at her. 'I can do this for Sophia and Evie. I can.'

Taking a deep breath, she plastered a smile on her face and opened the door.

* * *

'We'll take it in a little bit here too. Like this.' Taking a pin out from the small red pin cushion, she pinched a piece of fabric together and slipped it through. 'You see, it gives you more definition.'

Natalie twisted one way and the other, looking into the wooden mirror Gina had brought down from upstairs. 'It does, doesn't it? It completely changes the shape of the dress.'

'It shows off your figure.' Gina peered over the rim of her coffee mug.

'Right, let's look at the length next. Have you chosen your wedding shoes yet?' Leaning back on her haunches, Chrissy surveyed her work. It looked better already.

'Yes. Gina, can you grab them, please? They're just behind the sofa.' Natalie turned back to Chrissy. 'It's a nightmare hiding anything from Graham. He's such a big kid, I can never keep anything as a surprise from him. Hence why I have my wedding shoes behind the sofa!'

'Sounds like he's excited about the wedding, then?'

'Yes, he is.' Natalie smiled into the mirror. 'For someone who has spent years telling me he doesn't need a big wedding to show the world how much he loves me, he's really getting into it. He's ordered the transport to the church himself, it's a surprise so I'm just hoping I won't be arriving on a motorbike or something.' Laughing, she knelt down and lifted the turquoise lid off the shoe box.

'They're stunning.'

'I fell in love with a pair similar to these when we first got together. So when I saw them, I knew it was meant to be.' Natalie held up a pair of diamanté encrusted silver stilettos. 'I'm not sure how I'm actually going to walk in them, though. I haven't worn heels like these since before Adam was born!'

'As long as you can totter down the aisle in them, you can take them off at the reception.' Gina took one of the shoes, holding it to the light. 'You should get the photographer to get some close-up shots of these, I saw that in one of your wedding magazines. They looked really effective, and these are absolutely gorgeous.'

'Some people change into pretty pumps after the ceremony. It might be an idea.' Chrissy coughed, a lump catching in her throat. That's what she had done, she'd commissioned some pumps from a local crafter who had painted them with Mr & Mrs and stuck crystals across the top.

'I might just look into that idea.'

'Already on it.' Gina pulled her phone from her handbag.

'OK, slip these on and I'll measure the length.'

Stilettos on, Natalie straightened again.

Bending her head, Chrissy gently pulled the fabric taut, pinning it to the correct length.

'Hello? Anyone home?' A deep voice echoed through the house, followed by footsteps. 'Hey, Nat. You look gorgeous! Hi, Gina, how are you?'

Jerking her head up, Chrissy froze. It was Luke.

'Alright, bro. Do you like it?'

'I love it! Graham will be made up.' Leaning over, Luke kissed Natalie on the cheek.

'Damn.' Chrissy pushed the pin in further than she thought. 'Sorry, did I get you?' She'd never done that before.

'No, I'm fine.' Grinning down at her, Natalie indicated to Luke. 'This is my brother, Luke. Luke, this is...'

'Hey, Chrissy. How's your shoulder?'

'Fine, thanks.' Chrissy lowered her head, she could feel her skin heating up already. It only took a couple of seconds for her to go from pale to bright red.

'You've already met?'

'Yes, Chrissy was the one that broke my dream of making a mint on old Lowen's cottage. She's the brave one that's moved into Corner Cottage.'

'I don't know about brave, I think naïve is more fitting.' Chrissy laughed, despite herself.

'Yes, I wondered what you'd have to say about that when I heard.' Natalie thumped him playfully on the arm. 'You might just have to get a proper job now.'

'A proper job? You do realise I earn more now that

I buy, do up and sell on property than I ever did working in that stuffy corporate office?'

'Even so, it just seems as though you're never doing anything.'

'You're just jealous.' Luke laughed and looked down at Chrissy. 'Anyway, how come you're sticking pins into my sister's wedding dress?'

'Luke, to be honest, it's all been an utter nightmare.' Gina walked across to them, picking a grumbling Poppy up as she went. 'Natalie's dressmaker has upped and left, leaving us with a half-finished wedding dress. Chrissy, here, luckily stepped in and has agreed to finish the job.'

'A woman of many talents.'

'Right, I think that's all done. Did you want to take it off and we can go through the detailing you want? Or we could leave that until a better time?'

'Can we do it today? If you've got some time, of course. Don't worry if you've got somewhere else to be.'

'No, no it's fine. Have you got some paper so I we can sketch some ideas?'

'Yes, I'll grab some from the boy's playroom on way. Gina, did you want to stick the kettle on again, please? I think there might be a packet of biscuits in the cupboard too.'

'Will do. Here, Poppy come and say hello to your Uncle Luke.' Gina passed Poppy to Luke.

'Hello, Popsicle.' Luke stuck his tongue out, making Poppy giggle in his arms.

'Thanks again for your help yesterday.' Chrissy perched on the edge of the sofa.

'You're more than welcome. Have you heard from Lowen about fixing the window yet?' Luke joined her on the sofa, his thigh touching hers.

'Not a sound.' Shuffling across, she made more space for him.

'Ah. I'll get one of my contractors to come and have a look for you, if you like?'

'That'd be great, please? Do you know how much it might be? Roughly?'

'I'm sure I can sort something out.' Luke lifted Poppy up in front of him, her little legs kicking against his stomach. 'Uncle Luke will be able to pull a few strings, won't he, Popsicle?'

'If you're sure?'

'I am. If you're lucky, we might have chance to finish that massage too.' Nudging her shoulder and winking, Luke suddenly pulled away. 'Ooh lovely, a nice cuppa. Thanks, Gina.' Luke sat Poppy on his knee, gently leaning her back against him and took the mug with his free hand, being careful to hold it out of Poppy's short reach.

'Thank you.' Chrissy wrapped her hands around her mug. Was he flirting with her? Or was he being genuine? Shaking her head, Chrissy laughed at herself, why would someone like him flirt with someone like her? No chance.

'Are you guys OK budging up?' Natalie, back in her signature jeans and jumper, slid onto the sofa into the small gap between the arm and Chrissy, forcing Chrissy and Luke closer still. 'I've got the paper.'

'OK, great.' Taking the paper and a pencil, Chrissy began to sketch a silhouette of the wedding dress. 'Why don't you talk me through the design you had made up with the dressmaker and we'll see how we can go forward with it?'

5

'Alright, Star. Let me get in first.' Shaking the rain from the umbrella, Chrissy slipped into the hall, shutting the door firmly on the dark clouds outside. She was glad she'd made the twins take their coats to school, despite Sophia complaining that hers was too tight over her blazer.

'Come on then, let's get you a treat.' Slipping her boots off, she pushed the living room door ajar just as the doorbell rang. 'Or not.'

With Star circling her legs, Chrissy made her way back to the front door, pulling it open. 'Luke, hi. What are you doing here?'

'Thanks for the nice welcome. There's nothing better than feeling wanted.' Laughing, he picked up a pane of glass leant against his shin. 'I've come to fix your window.'

'Sorry, I didn't mean it like that. I was just surprised to see you. I thought you were sending one of your contractors over.' Tucking her hair behind her ears, Chrissy smiled apologetically.

'Nah, they were all tied up today and what with the storm supposed to be hitting on Friday, I thought I'd best come and get it sorted.'

'OK, thank you. Here, come in out of the rain.'

'Thanks.' Shifting his tool bag on his shoulder, he lifted the sheet of glass up before following her into the living room. 'How's it going with my sister's wedding dress, then?'

'Well, as you know, we've got the designs all done. I'm going to pop into the next town to get some supplies and then I'll get started.'

'You think you can transform it into how she wants it? It all sounded a bit complex to me.' Luke pulled at the plywood covering the hole in the window. 'Have you glued this on?'

'Yes, I found some old wood glue in the shed.'

'Right.' Luke closed his eyes, trying not to laugh and grabbed a chisel from the bag. 'It's a good job I have the muscles to prise it off then, isn't it?'

'In my defence, I needed to cover it quickly and I couldn't find any nails.'

'No worries. I'll sort it. So, the dress?'

'Oh, yes. Yes, I should be able to sort it for her. It's not as complicated as it sounds, just some detailed embroidery and beadwork. It'll be time-consuming but it's doable.'

'That'll please her, then. I don't know why they're bothering to get married now, to be honest.' With one last tug, Luke pulled the plywood off and began lining the metal window frame with putty.

'Why not?' Chrissy lowered herself to a beanbag and pulled her knees towards her.

'Well, they've been together for so long now, what difference is it going to make? Why now? I don't know, they've got a young family and better things to waste their money on, if you ask me.'

'I don't know.' Chrissy shook her head. 'I'm probably the last person you should ask. My idea of marriage isn't all that great at the moment.'

'How do you mean?' Luke looked back at her over his shoulder, his pale blue eyes meeting hers.

'It doesn't matter.' Chrissy shrugged, it didn't feel right, her taking money from Natalie to finish her wedding dress while at the same time belittling the whole concept of marriage, but it'd be even worse telling her brother that she agreed with him and felt, no knew, that marriage was just a piece of paper, something that could be eliminated with a few words. She couldn't tell him that she felt that buying a house together was more of a tie than getting married. It had certainly taken her and Andrew longer to sell the house than for him to emotionally walk out on their marriage.

'It sounds like you have some pretty strong views on it.'

'Yes, well. I'm sure Natalie and Graham are doing it for the right reasons. And maybe they're the ones doing it right, waiting all this time to get married. At least they know each other properly now. Maybe that's the successful way to go into marriage.'

'Maybe.'

'Anyway, I'll go and grab you a cuppa.' Pushing herself to her feet, Chrissy escaped to the kitchen before he could ask her any other difficult questions.

* * *

'There you go. What do you think?' Luke wiped the last of the excess putty from the frame and turned towards Chrissy.

'It looks great. Thank you so much.'

'Now, shall I finish that massage for you?' Luke grinned.

Chrissy shifted from foot to foot and counted to three, the time it took for the warm glow to travel up her neck and across her face, knowing that it would colour her skin, filling the gaps between her freckles. 'Is that your phone?'

'Drat. Yes.' Bending down, Luke rummaged through his tool bag before pulling out his mobile. 'Sorry, it's one of my contractors. I'll catch you later?'

Nodding, Chrissy held the door open for him. Not sure if she was disappointed or relieved that he had to go. There was definitely chemistry between them, but this probably wasn't the right time in her life to get into anything new with anyone, even if it was just casual.

* * *

'Mum?'

'Yes, Evie?' Chrissy twisted around, potato peeler in hand.

'Dad rang.'

'OK. Has he settled into his new place?' Is this what her future would be like? The twins relaying a conversation they'd had with the previous love of her life, the person she'd thought she'd be with forever? Would she always be tempted to ask questions to try to get a glimpse of his new life? Would the simple fact that they had been able, allowed, to talk to him always sting, always feel as she'd been kicked in the stomach, been disregarded and forgotten?

'Mum, he said that the woman we met the other week will be there when we go on Friday night.' Evie's lips trembled.

'Come here.' Taking the few short strides towards Evie, Chrissy wrapped her arms around her, Evie's small shoulders shaking as she began to cry. 'What woman? What did he mean, sweetheart?'

'When he took us out to the farm park the other week, when we were still living together but you stayed home, one of his work friends came with us. Daddy told us it would be better if we didn't tell you. So we didn't. I'm sorry, Mummy. We should have, shouldn't we? I wanted to, but Daddy had said that it didn't matter.' Evie pulled away, looking up at Chrissy, her eyes welling with tears.

'It's OK. Was she blonde?'

'Yes.' Evie nodded before burying her head back in Chrissy's cardigan.

'It was Susan.' He had introduced his mistress to the twins and made them lie to her. Taking a deep breath, Chrissy stared at a small crack above the doorframe.

Evie's head bobbed up and down. 'Yes. And now she's at his house.'

'Is she living there?' Chrissy's voice was barely above a whisper. He wouldn't have moved her in, not so soon. Surely? He would have told her. He would definitely have told her if he was planning on living with his mistress.

'Yes, she is. He said that she's his girlfriend. That's not true, is it? You and Daddy are supposed to be getting back together. He doesn't really have a girlfriend, does he?'

'Oh, darling. Yes, I'm afraid he does. Susan is his girlfriend now.' Kissing the top of Evie's head, Chrissy cursed Andrew. They had agreed that they would leave it a few months before they told the twins about him and Susan. They had both agreed that the girls needed to settle into their new life and new routines before they had any other big changes to process. 'But he still loves you, you know that, don't you?'

Evie nodded. 'That's what he said. He said to tell you that he's going to pick us up on Friday at six. But I don't want to go. I don't want to meet Susan again. It won't be the same.'

'I know, sweetheart. It will be different, but you want to see Daddy, don't you?'

'Yes, I want to see Daddy, but I don't want to see her. I don't even know her, how can I spend the weekend with a stranger?'

'I think you need to give her a chance, Evie. I'm sure she'll be lovely. Your Daddy wouldn't be with someone who isn't nice.' Why was she sticking up for him? And for the woman who had destroyed her marriage? Chrissy bit down on her bottom lip, what else was she supposed to do? If she had her way, she'd let the twins stay with her, she'd rather they didn't have any contact with their cheating father or his mistress, but for them, she knew she had to put her feelings aside. He was still their father, even if he was only her husband until the divorce came through.

'OK, I will if you want me to.' Evie lifted her head and wiped her eyes with the palms of her hands. 'But I would rather stay with you.'

'I'd rather you stayed with me too, Evie, but he's your Daddy and he loves you so much.' The all too familiar lump appeared in her throat. This weekend would be the longest she'd ever spent away from the twins but she had to be strong, for them.

'Why don't you go into the living room and you and Sophia can choose a film for us to watch?'

'She's not in the living room.'

'Oh, where is she?'

'She locked herself in the bathroom after she put the phone down on Daddy.'

'Oh, OK. Well, why don't you go and choose a film while I see if I can coax her out?'

'OK.'

'Evie?'

'Yes, Mummy.' Evie paused by the door.

'I love you and I promise everything will be OK. Things might feel a bit weird at first, but they will be OK.'

'I love you too, Mummy.'

***

'Sophia.' Chrissy knocked gently on the bathroom door. 'Sophia, it's Mummy, open up please.'

'No.'

'Oh, darling. Please open up.'

'Go away.'

'Sophia, I'm not going anywhere. Open up so I can talk to you, please?'

'I said no, now leave me alone.'

She leant her forehead against the cool wood of the door before lowering herself to the floor, her back against the bathroom door. 'Evie told me what Daddy said.'

'I don't want to talk about it.'

'OK, just listen then.' Chrissy ran her fingers across the wooden floorboards, tracing a scratch in the varnish. 'You know Daddy still loves you, don't you?'

'Why are you asking me questions? You said I just had to listen!'

'I'm sorry. I did.' Chrissy leant the back of her head against the door. 'He's still your dad. I know it will be strange with her living there, but he wants to spend time with you two.'

'It's not fair though, Mum. We're his family, not her. Why is he living with her when he left us?'

'Oh, darling. He didn't leave you, he left me, not you and Evie. He still loves you both exactly the same as he did when we were all living together.'

'No, he doesn't. We would still be living in our old house, all together, if he cared about me and Evie.'

'Sometimes adults fall out of love with each other and so they don't want to live together any more. But they still love their children, exactly the same. It's just the other adult they are moving away from, not their children. Do you understand?'

Straining to hear through the door, only silence met her ears.

'You know I love you, don't you? You know how much I love you. Sophia?'

'Yes, I know.'

'Right, well, it's the same, isn't it? Me and Daddy have split up, but you know I still love you and it's the same with Daddy. He still loves you too.'

'Umm.'

'He does, darling. You'll see that at the weekend. You'll understand that he still loves you. Now, why don't you open the door?' Hearing soft footsteps as Sophia crossed the lino, Chrissy stood up.

Sophia opened the door. Her tear streaked cheeks pale, the end of her nose red.

'Oh, Sophia. Come here.' Pulling her towards her, Chrissy hugged her small frame tightly before running the pads of her thumbs across Sophia's cheeks, wiping the tears away. 'I love you, sweetheart.'

'I just don't like it.'

'Like what?'

'This. All of this. I want you and Daddy to get back together.'

'I know you do.'

'But you won't, will you? That's what I've been telling Evie, that you won't, because I don't want her getting her hopes up and feeling sad all over again. But I want you to.'

'I know you do.' The number of arguments Chrissy had had to field over the past few weeks, some of them louder than others, some of them involving the twins lashing out at each other, and they had all been Sophia trying to protect her sister. Chrissy kissed the top of her head. 'It's going to take a bit of time, but we will all get used to our new lives. And you'll get used to Daddy being with Susan too.'

'I don't want to.'

'I know, but you will. Just because me and Daddy aren't together any more, it doesn't mean that we can't be happy again. We will be.'

'Is Evie downstairs?'

'Yes, she's choosing a film for us to watch. Do you want to go and help her?'

'OK.'

Watching Sophia walk downstairs, Chrissy pulled her cardigan tighter. Sinking to the floor, she let her own tears flow. She wrapped her arms around her knees and rocked. That was it then. Her marriage was definitely over. Andrew had completely moved on. Was that why he'd moved Susan in so quickly? To tell Chrissy in no uncertain terms that there was no going back?

6

'Daddy's here! And he's driving the van!' Evie jumped up from the window ledge where she had been perching, ran to the hall and threw the front door open.

'Mind the road.' Chrissy came through from the kitchen, peering out of the window as Evie ran down towards the van. Automatically, she scooped her hair up into a messy bun. She should have put that deep conditioning hair mask on last night. Not that it mattered anyway. Who was she fooling? Andrew didn't care what she looked like, he didn't love her any more regardless.

She could see him coming up the path, Evie jogging excitedly next to him, hanging on to his every word, no doubt. Picking up Sophia's abandoned notebook from the floor, Chrissy wished she'd been able to sleep better last night, she knew she looked like a washed-out mess. She'd had visions of looking radiant when he came. She had wanted to raise a little doubt in his mind as to if he had made the right decision. She put the notebook on the coffee table, she was being completely daft, she knew she was, but she still wanted him to think she was doing OK, better than OK, on her own without him. Still, today wasn't about her and Andrew. Today was about the twins. They were her priority.

'Chrissy.'

'Hi, Andrew.' Biting her bottom lip, she forced herself to ignore the fact that he had come into the living room wearing his shoes. She was no longer the nagging wife, not that she had been, but taking shoes off at the door had always been one of their family rules. She would not say anything. She would not. She would make him think she was laid-back about it. Plus, he was probably only keeping them on to annoy her. She looked around the room. Evie was trying to stuff her soft toy mouse into her rucksack and Sophia was nowhere to be seen. She had more important things to worry about than dirty floorboards. She knew that.

'Can I have a quick word?'

'Yes, come into the kitchen.' Chrissy led the way, standing by the sink as he shut the kitchen door. She knew what was coming.

'You deserve to know something.' Looking at his feet, he shuffled from side to side.

'I know. You've moved Susan into your new place.' Much to her disgust, she couldn't stop her voice from rasping, from catching around the word 'Susan'. She'd never get comfortable saying that woman's name. Not now, not ever. She'd planted the missile that had blown her family apart.

'Not quite. I've moved into hers. We thought it was the easiest thing to do. She owns her own home, you see. It made more sense than me renting.'

'You've moved into hers?' Her voice, barely a whisper, seemed to echo around the small kitchen. 'I don't understand.'

'As I said, we just thought it would be easier.'

'But you told the girls she'd moved into yours?'

'I know. I just got flustered and didn't know what to say to them.'

Turning around, Chrissy stared at the sink, dish soap suds still clung to the metal sides, slowly dispersing down the plughole. Taking a deep breath, she turned back to face him. 'If you were going to move in with her anyway, why didn't you do it earlier? Why did you carry on with us all living to-gether at home, our old home?' It didn't make any sense.

Shifting his gaze to the bottle of squash the twins had left out on the work surface, he moved it an inch to the left and then back again, clearing his throat as he did. 'We... I didn't think it would be respectful.'

'Respectful? Nothing about this is respectful. Sleeping with your mistress behind my back for good-ness knows how many months, isn't respectful.' Chrissy curled her index fingers, making quotation marks. 'Why start being respectful now?'

'I guess, I wanted the twins to get used to the fact that we were splitting up before I left.'

'I don't know why. I think it probably was pretty darn obvious to the poor little mites that something was up when you introduced them to your mistress behind my back and told them to lie to me about it. You got our girls to lie to me, their own mother. You know how I feel about lying and secrets.' Chrissy shook her head.

'Not lie. I asked them not to say anything to you, that's completely different.' Andrew looked at his feet.

'Omitting the truth, lying, it's all the same and you know it. Don't you ever dare make them lie to me again.' Looking up, she looked him in the eye. 'Andrew, are you listening to me? I promise you, if you make my girls lie to me again...'

'Please don't start.' He held his hands up, palms facing her.

Chrissy took a deep breath in, don't start! How dare he? She wasn't starting anything, she was merely telling him to stop making their children lie to her! Plus, she had every right to 'start' if she wanted to. She shook her head, it wasn't worth it. He wasn't worth it. Not any more. 'Did you bring the sofa and beds?'

'Yes. Can you come out and help me?'

* * *

With the sofa in position in the living room and the mattresses and bed frames in piles in the bedrooms, Andrew stood at the front door.

'Are you ready, Evie?'

'I will be in just a second.' Evie glanced up at Chrissy and back at her dad.

'OK. I'll wait in the van. Chrissy will you send Sophia out soon. I've got to get back.'

Chrissy nodded and watched him retreat to the van. 'OK, are you all set, Evie?'

'I guess so. It's not going to be the same it being Susan's house and not Daddy's though.'

'It's still Daddy's new place.'

'I guess so.' Leaning her head against Chrissy's chest, Evie wrapped her arms around her waist. 'I love you, Mummy.'

'I know you do. I love you too, sweetheart, more than you will ever understand.' Holding Evie's face gently in her hands, Chrissy kissed Evie on the cheek. 'Right, you go and jump in the van and I'll hurry your sister up.'

'OK.'

Chrissy watched as Evie walked down the narrow path to the van, stopping and waving back at her.

After blowing her a kiss, Chrissy turned and made her way up the stairs. 'Sophia, darling. Are you ready?'

'I'm not going.' Sophia's muffled voice floated from her bedroom.

'Hey, Sophia.' Lowering herself to Sophia's airbed, Chrissy felt around until she found Sophia's back under the duvet and rubbed it. 'Daddy's waiting for you.'

'I'm not going.'

'Don't you want to go and check out Daddy's new house?'

'I don't care about his new house. I'm not going. Ever.'

'Why not, Sophia?'

'Because he's chosen her over you.' Sophia sat up quickly, pulling her duvet down to reveal her tearstained cheeks.

'Oh, darling. He can't help the way he feels or who he falls in love with.' She stopped herself shouting that yes, he had chosen the wonderful Susan over herself and he could help who he fell in love with, especially when he was married and shouldn't have been looking in the first place. He should have been in love with his wife, with her. 'And, he's still your dad.'

'I don't care who he is. It's not right. Why can't anyone else see that?'

Chrissy pulled Sophia in for a hug, enveloping her small body with her arms. She wanted to agree with her that, yes, she could see how wrong he was, but she couldn't. She knew she had to put on her mum-face and be strong for the twins. She knew she had to try to guide them through this life-changing nightmare as best she could, hoping they'd come through with as little scars as possible, hoping they'd keep their innocence and positive outlook on life. 'Your dad made a choice, yes, but he didn't mean to hurt you.'

'He meant to hurt you though.' Sophia ground her teeth together, a habit she had had when she got angry since she was a baby.

'I don't think he meant to hurt me. Not really... he just fell in love again and didn't think about the consequences. He's just trying to be happy, which everyone needs to do.'

'Is he happy now? Happy with her?'

'I hope so.' Mentally she crossed her fingers, she hoped they were arguing every day, she hoped he was being condescending and unsupportive like he had been with her, but Sophia didn't need to hear that. 'Now, why don't you get a wriggle on? Daddy's waiting to see you.'

'Chrissy! Can you ask Sophia to come down here now! I need to get going.' Andrew called up the stairs.

'One minute.' Chrissy tried to keep her voice steady and light. She could tell from the edge in his voice that he was getting irate.

'I don't want to leave you on your own. It's not fair, you haven't done anything wrong.'

'Thank you for worrying about me, but honestly, I'll be fine. I'm going to put the beds up and make your bedrooms all nice for when you get back. I might even pop out for a nice coffee somewhere too.'

'Are you sure you'll be OK?' Sophia clasped Chrissy's hand.

'Yes, I promise. You can always ask to borrow Daddy's phone and ring me if you want to.'

'OK.'

* * *

Standing by the gate, Chrissy waved them off, blowing them kisses as the van pulled away and pretending to catch the ones blown back to her. She stood still, watching as they rounded the corner. Gripping the cold metal of the gate, she stopped herself from running after them, from yelling at Andrew to stop and telling him that he'd chosen this new life for them and didn't deserve to tear the twins away from her.

Slowly, she turned her back on the empty road and walked back up the garden path to the cottage. She pulled at a stinging nettle growing near the front step, watching as white spots emerged, covering the skin on her fingers. Trying to focus on the pain in her fingertips, she tried to block out the pain in her heart.

'Come on, Star, back in.'

* * *

Standing at the kitchen sink, Chrissy let the cold water wash over her fingers, numbing the sting. Was this really happening to her? Had he really taken the twins away from her for the whole weekend? What was she supposed to do?

Bringing her hands to her face, she covered her mouth, a rasping sob escaping. This was her new reality. This was her life now.

Twisting around, she sank to the floor, the cold from the tiles seeping through her jeans, the water from her hands mixing with the tears running down her face. She'd done nothing wrong. She'd always supported Andrew, both with his work and with his hobbies. Yes, she'd used to complain when he got home from work only to go straight out to rugby or to meet clients for dinner, but that was only because she'd wanted him at home. She'd wanted them to have some time together as a family.

Shaking her head, she pulled Star, who had come to lay next to her, onto her lap. She'd never stopped him from going out, from pursuing his goals in work or in rugby. Maybe that's what had led them here. Maybe he'd felt unwanted, unloved. Maybe she should have been the wife who stamped her foot and demanded he stay home. Maybe then, he would have known how much he was loved. He would have felt needed. Maybe she had brought this all on herself.

Well, he must feel needed now, loved and needed. He must actually love this Susan woman. Maybe he always had and maybe it was Chrissy's fault for not realising earlier and doing something about it. When she'd started work at Andrew's office he had told Chrissy that he had known her at school, that they had gone out when they were in secondary school and at university. Chrissy should have realised that she was trying to weave her way back into Andrew's life. She should have put a stop to it. She should have made him fire her or relocate her, or something. Instead, she'd laughed it off, after all, her Andrew would never cheat on her. Chrissy laughed, she'd been so stupid. So naïve, so trusting.

And what was this about him moving in with her? If he'd planned on moving in with her, why hadn't he just gone when he'd broken off the marriage? Why would he have wanted to spend eight unbearable months, walking on eggshells and trying to avoid each other stuck in a small three-bedroom house while it was on the market? It didn't make any sense. It just didn't. Plus, if he'd left, Chrissy and the twins could have stayed in the house. It would have been less upheaval for the girls. They could have stayed on at their school, could have had the support of their friends.

Chrissy pulled Star closer. Unless? No, Andrew wouldn't be so callous, so uncaring, not towards his own children, his own flesh and blood, would he? No.

But that was the only logical explanation. He had stayed on in the house, pretended he didn't have anywhere to go, so that they had sold meaning that Chrissy couldn't have stayed there. He had, hadn't he? That's what he had done. He'd wanted his share of the equity.

Burying her face in Star's soft fur, it hit Chrissy that she didn't really know Andrew at all. She'd fallen in love with him, lived with him for eleven years and promised her life to him, but she didn't know him. At all. He wasn't the loyal, family orientated man that she had believed he was. He was a stranger. A devious, uncaring stranger who could cheat on his wife for months until he decided that he wanted to wrench his family apart so he could move in with his mistress.

He was a cold-hearted, heartless stranger who was happy to see his own children be dragged forcefully from a school they were happy at to face an uncertain education and go through the trauma of trying to fit in, trying to make new friends in an unfamiliar school miles away from where they had been happy.

He was a money-grabbing, unfeeling stranger who would prefer his children end up in rented accommodation rather than let them stay in the home they had grown up in, a home where they would have the security of knowing they could live there throughout all of their childhood.

She didn't know him at all. And, in truth, she didn't like the real him, this him. He wasn't the man she had married. Not any more.

Pressing the heels of her hands against her eyes, she tried to push the ever-increasing dull ache away. The weekend stretched before her, the hours, minutes and seconds endless until she got her girls back, until their new tiny family unit was back together again. How was she supposed to survive without them?

She pulled herself up and splashed water on her face. That's what she'd do, she'd go into town and get them a cheap mobile to share. That way they'd still have contact and they would be able to ring or message her if they needed.

7

Chrissy ran the hairbrush through her wet hair before switching the kettle on. The bed frames were put together and the beds were made. The twin's rooms were actually looking like proper bedrooms now rather than just an empty space to sleep. She pulled the sleeves of her pyjama top down to her wrists, it was getting cold. Maybe she could light the wood burner. What was the point though, it would be a waste of logs, heating the house just for her?

Placing her coffee mug on the coffee table, Chrissy pulled her legs up underneath her on the sofa and flicked through the TV channels again. There was nothing on. At all. Hitting the power button, Chrissy drummed her fingers against the side of the sofa. She should make a start on Natalie's wedding dress, but she just couldn't bring herself to, not today.

'That's it.' Pushing herself to standing, Chrissy downed the rest of her coffee. She needed a drink, a proper drink. There was the pub at the end of the High Street. She'd pop in for a quick drink, hopefully it would quieten the thoughts hammering in her mind.

* * *

Narrowly missing a puddle, Chrissy shoved her hands in her pockets, she'd never done anything like this before, she'd never been into a pub or even a café on her own. Not once. What would people think of her? New to the village and drinking alone? Who cared? Chrissy had enough of her own problems to think about, she didn't need to start worrying about what people thought of her. Plus, it wasn't as though she was going in there to get drunk. She'd just slip in, grab a drink and find a quiet table. Nobody would even know she was there.

Taking a deep breath she pushed open the heavy wooden door. Pausing, she let the door close quietly behind her, bent her head and weaved through the tables to the bar.

'Evening. I've not seen you here before. Are you the young lass that's moved into Corner Cottage?' A rosy-cheeked, balding man approached her, smiling kindly.

'Yes. Can I have a gin and tonic, please?' Chrissy slid onto a bar stool and quickly looked around. Most of the tables were occupied. She could either walk through the entire pub to the back room to find a table or just sit at the bar. She'd probably be less noticeable if she just stayed where she was.

'Of course.'

'Thank you.' Chrissy nodded as he put the glass down in front of her, slipped her coat off and took a sip. The sharp tang of the tonic water bubbling on her tongue was a welcome relief. A few more of these and the alcohol might even dull the constant 'what if's' in her head.

Downing the last of the liquid, Chrissy held her glass up. 'Can I have another one, please?'

'Coming right up.'

Her mobile pinged. Fishing in her coat pocket, Chrissy pulled out two tissues, her bunch of keys, and a strawberry lollipop until she got to her mobile.

Andrew: You ok if I bring the twins back at 6.15 on Sun

instead of 12? Going to a Family Fun Day at Rugby Club.

Seriously? The first time the girls are away from her for any length of time and he changes the time he was meant to return them? Who the hell did he think he was?

Chrissy: If you have to. How are they?

Andrew: Fine.

Fine? Was that all she got back? He was obviously having such a great time with his new little family that he couldn't even spare her two minutes to reply to a text properly. Throwing her mobile down, she watched it bounce precariously close to the edge of the bar.

'Another one, please? Make it a double.' Holding up her glass, she caught the bartender's eye.

'Everything OK, love?' The bartender, Bill, or so Chrissy could just about make out on his name tag, slid her another glass.

'Fantastic. Absolutely fantastic.' She took a sip, the double strength of the gin hitting the roof of her mouth.

Picking up her mobile again, she checked to see if Andrew had replied with anything of substance, before putting it back in her pocket. Picking up the tissues and sticky lollipop, Chrissy stuffed them back in her pocket too. Taking another sip, she fiddled with the keys. Two for the cottage, front and back, her car keys and then she gently moved the remaining two keys, pulling them away from the main bunch. They were her old house keys. She'd left them on. Clutching the bunch, she squeezed them tightly, letting the keys indent into the palm of her hand. Letting the pain of the metal marking her flesh dull the pain in her heart.

She downed the rest of her drink. 'Where are the toilets, please?'

'Down that way, through the back room.' Bill pointed towards the back of the pub.

'Thanks.' Standing up, she gripped hold of the side of the bar, the room spinning with the sudden movement. She hadn't drank properly since, probably since, no, she couldn't remember. She hadn't been out drinking in years. It felt good. 'OK, this way.' Grinning, Chrissy pointed with both her index fingers towards the back room.

'That's right, love.'

* * *

Running her fingers through her hair, Chrissy stared at the frizzy-haired woman looking back at her from the mirror. At least she had a bit of colour in her cheeks now, even if she knew she'd have a banging headache in the morning.

She pushed away from the sink and pulled open the heavy door. She'd get one more gin and tonic and then she should probably head back.

'Chrissy! Chrissy, over here!'

Standing still, she put her hand out, leaning against the wall as she scanned the room. She was sure she'd heard her name. It didn't make any sense though, she hardly knew anyone in the village. Unless it was someone she knew from her old hometown? That'd be great, wouldn't it? Someone reporting back to Andrew that he'd turned her to drink, that she couldn't even go a few hours without seeing her girls. Imagine how she'd be at the end of the weekend, they'd say. Maybe they'd even tell him she wasn't fit to be a mother. What if he kept them?

She couldn't see anyone she recognised from her former life. She was probably being paranoid. It served her right, she'd drank too much. Shaking her head, she pushed herself away from the wall and began heading back towards the bar.

'Hey, Chrissy.'

Stopping again, she focused on the person standing in front of her. 'Luke! Luke, it's you.'

'I believe it is. Come over and join us.' Luke waved his arm towards a table in the far corner.

'Us?'

'Yes, me and my mates, Phil and Richie.'

'OK, why not?'

'How many have you had?' Luke held out his arm, letting Chrissy link hers through his.

'Not many. Four, three. I'm not sure, I just haven't drunk in ages.' Chrissy grinned, letting herself be led towards the table.

'Richie, Phil, this is Chrissy, she's moved into Corner Cottage.'

'Ah, yes, Luke told us about you. You've broken his heart, you know.'

'More like his wallet.' Chrissy laughed and slipped onto the bench to the side of the table.

'Right, same again, lads?' Phil stood up. 'Chrissy, what's your poison?'

'Are you sure? Gin and tonic, please.'

A few minutes later, Phil returned, a tray in hand.

'Here we go. Beers for you, Luke and Richie. A gin and tonic for you, Chrissy. And tequilas for us all.'

Luke leant towards Chrissy. 'We're celebrating. Phil, here, has been promoted. Although, fortunately, he doesn't work Saturdays, which is a good thing considering how many tequilas we've had!' Sitting up straight again, Luke passed a tequila to Chrissy and took one himself.

'One, two, three.'

Tipping the small glass up, Chrissy shuddered as the fiery liquid hit the back of her throat. 'Congratulations on your promotion, Phil.'

* * *

An hour, two more tequilas and a conversation about the perils of living in a small village with no late night takeaway, and Phil and Richie said their goodbyes and took a taxi home.

'Time for another one?' Leaning back, he rested his head against the wall.

'Time? I have until 6.15pm Sunday.' Chrissy leant her head back next to his.

'6.15pm Sunday? That's very specific.'

'Yes, well, that's my ex, Andrew, for you. A very specific man.' Leaning forward, Chrissy laughed. The fact that Andrew was so specific in his timings suddenly seemed funny.

'I'll go and get the drinks then.' Pushing himself to standing, Luke staggered back against the leg of the table and grinned.

'You're drunk.' Pointing her index finger at Luke, Chrissy narrowed her eyes, bringing his face into focus.

'It takes one to know one.' Luke pointed back.

'I will have you know, I am not drunk. I am merely a little tipsy.' Chrissy held her thumb and index finger an inch apart and watched him make his way to the bar. She finished her glass and smiled, she was glad she'd ventured to the pub. It had been fun meeting up with Luke's mates. And Luke, well, he was a good laugh.

'A gin and tonic for the lady.' Luke placed the drinks on the table before looking around. 'I'm not sure where she went though!'

'Oi.' Slapping his hand, Chrissy pulled her drink towards her.

'Oh, and I found these abandoned belongings at the bar, Bill told me they were yours.'

Catching her coat as he threw it towards her, she laughed. 'Oops. I'd forgotten all about this.'

'You'd have soon remembered when we got

outside.'

'Who's supporting who?' Chrissy gripped hold of Luke's arm as he stumbled over a pothole.

'Me. I'm supporting you, of course. My Auntie Mary would be so proud of me if she could see me, walking a young lady like yourself home.'

'Oh no, can't she see you then? Has she passed away? I'm so sorry.' Covering her mouth with her hand, Chrissy stopped walking and looked at Luke.

'What? No, she's just probably in bed. Here, come this way.' Luke pulled her in the opposite direction. 'She can see me if you like, she lives just over there. That house with the pond in the front garden.'

'Ah, sure she does.'

'She does.' Cupping his hands around his mouth, he raised his voice. 'Auntie Mary! Auntie Mary, look, I'm being a gentleman.'

'Shhh, don't!' Reaching up, Chrissy put her hand over his mouth before doubling up laughing.

'You're probably right, we shouldn't wake her. She'd only bring us in and make us drink coffee.'

'Nooo. Quick this way.' Chrissy dragged him away and led him towards Corner Cottage.

* * *

'Hello, Star.' Chrissy shut the front door behind them and knelt down to fuss Star. 'Did you want a drink?'

'Me or the dog?' Luke knelt next to her, letting Star sniff his hand before he stroked her.

'You.' Chrissy grinned.

'Have you got anything alcoholic?'

'Umm no. Funnily enough, being as I only moved in less than a week ago, alcohol wasn't on the top of my priority to buy list. I wish it had been, though.'

'Me too.'

'Coffee, then?'

'Are you trying to sober me up?' Luke grinned. 'I'm good, thank you.' He stood up, holding Chrissy and pulling her up with him.

'May I?'

'You may.' Leaning forwards, she let Luke kiss her. To her surprise, it didn't feel weird. It should have done. After all, she hadn't kissed anyone apart from Andrew for the past twelve years, but it didn't, not at all.

8

Throwing back the blanket, Chrissy jumped up from the sofa and looked out of the window. It was them! They were back.

Yanking the door open, she pulled them both into her arms. 'Hi, girls. Sophia, Evie. How's your weekend been?'

'I'll see them the weekend after next, then. Same time.' Andrew piled their rucksacks just inside the door and retreated quickly back down the driveway.

'I missed you so much. Let's go into the living room. I've got the wood burner on, so it's super toasty in there and you can both tell me all about your weekend.' After shutting the door firmly on both Andrew and the cold, Chrissy led the way through to the living room.

'It looks nice in here. Like a proper home. I like the rug.' Evie sat down on the floor, running her hands through the rug. 'It's really fluffy.'

'Yes, I went to the shops yesterday and found it in the sale. I thought it would give the place a bit more of a cosy feel.' Lowering herself down next to Evie, she held her hand out indicating for Sophia to join them. 'Come join us, Sophia.'

'OK.' Sophia sat down, crossing her legs and digging her fingers into the grey pile of the rug.

'So, how was it?'

'It was OK. Daddy's new house is huge, isn't it, Sophia? Like, proper big.' Evie held out her arms, emphasising how big it was. 'We've got our own bedrooms and there's a room downstairs that Daddy says we can turn into a playroom. The garden's big too. And we might even get a swing!'

'That sounds exciting.' Chrissy smiled at Evie. However much it hurt, she wanted to hear about it, about all of it. She wanted to know as much about this part of her daughters' lives as she could. She would never be part of it, she would never share any of the experiences they would have in this other part of their lives. It just wasn't right. Parents and children were supposed to have shared experiences, grow together. Parents were supposed to know all about the lives of their children, be involved, not be shut out of half of their world. Closing her eyes momentarily, Chrissy forced herself to smile that bit harder. 'Did you like it, Sophia?'

Sophia shrugged and nudged a bit closer to Chrissy.

'So, the house sounds wonderful. What did you do? Did you enjoy yourselves?'

'On Friday night we just got a takeaway and watched a film. It was about these kids whose dog had been stolen. Don't listen, Star.' Evie pulled Star towards her and covered her ears. 'So they had to go on a secret mission to get him back. First of all they...'

'She doesn't want to hear about the stupid film, Evie. And it wasn't that good, anyway.' Sophia punched her sister on the arm.

'Hey, Sophia, don't hit. And I do want to hear about it. It sounds really good.' Chrissy leant over and rubbed Evie's arm. 'You OK?'

'Yes, it didn't hurt much. This is what she was like at Daddy's house too. All moody and taking things out on me.'

'Aw, Sophia, come here.' Chrissy pulled Sophia in towards her, wrapping her arm around her shoulders.

Shrugging Chrissy's arm away, Sophia moved away from her.

'Anyway, I'll tell you more about the film when Sophia isn't listening.' Evie looked sideways at her sister before continuing. 'Then on Saturday we went shopping at some massive shops on the retail park and we were allowed to choose some stuff for our bedrooms. I got a unicorn duvet, unicorn lampshade and unicorn lamp. The lamp's really cool, the light changes colour, all sort of unicorn colours really, like light blue and light pink and light green. And I got a unicorn rug and a massive unicorn teddy. My room looks all cosy now.'

'That sounds lovely.' Of course, Andrew now had two full-time incomes coming into their house. Plus, he didn't have the worry of buying uniform, clothes, shoes and all of the boring but necessary things a growing child needed seemingly constantly. But the girls wouldn't see that, would they? They were too young to fully understand. They just saw that their dad was treating them. 'What about you, Sophia? What did you get for your room?'

Sophia stared into the wood burner, the light show reflecting against the glass.

'She didn't get anything.'

'Didn't you, Sophia? How come?'

'She didn't want anything. Then, we went back to the house, super quick, and unpacked everything and made my room all unicorny and cosy, then we went to the pub for dinner. Like, a proper pub, with all of Daddy and Susan's friends there. There were loads of us, there was Darren, Charlotte and their kids, Gabi and... I can't remember all of their names.'

'Gabi and Ryan?' Their names caught in her throat. So they had accepted Susan as Andrew's new partner, then? All of the times they'd gone out, first on double dates and then, when they'd had their children, on family day trips to farm parks or soft play areas, all of these times had been forgotten. She was just a distant memory now. Obviously, despite what she had thought at the time, they had just tolerated her for Andrew's sake, they hadn't been her friends at all. Susan had slotted so perfectly into Andrew's social group, and Chrissy had so conveniently been forgotten.

'Yes, Gabi and Ryan. How did you know, Mummy?'

'They used to be my friends too when me and your dad were together.'

'Really?' Evie looked up at Chrissy.

'Did Gabi and Ryan's children come too? Did you play together?'

'Yes, they came. We played loads, well, I did.

Sophia didn't really join in. Why had we never met them before if they're your friends too?'

'You have met them before. We used to all go out to the farm park sometimes. Just not in the last few years, that's probably why you don't remember them.' They hadn't done much together as a family for the last few years, let alone done anything with other families. 'Daddy said you were going to go to a Family Fun Day at the Rugby Club today, was it good?'

'Yes, it was really fun. They had a disco and some stalls and even a bouncy castle.'

'Why tell her about the bouncy castle? They closed it because it was raining so we didn't even go on it.'

'Oh, that's a shame. It was good apart from that, though?'

'It was OK.' Sophia shrugged.

'I've got so much more to tell you, but I really really need to go to the loo.' Evie jumped up and bounded up the stairs.

'You're very quiet. Come here.' Holding her arms out, Chrissy breathed a sigh of relief as Sophia leant into her. 'Are you OK, sweetheart?'

Sophia nodded.

'Did you have fun at Daddy's too?'

'It was OK. I just don't want to talk about it.'

'It's OK to talk to me about it. I'm glad Evie had a lovely time, and I'll be happy if you did too. As long as my two girls are happy, so am I.' Chrissy kissed the top of Sophia's head.

'It just feels weird talking to you about it all.'

'Hey, please don't feel weird about telling me things you do with Daddy. I'm not there, am I? So, I only get to find out what you did if you tell me. And I'd rather know.'

'OK.'

'Why didn't you let Daddy buy you anything for your new bedroom there?'

'There's no point. I'm only there, like, every other weekend anyway.'

'It would still be nice to have nice things there and to make it your own, wouldn't it?'

'Maybe.'

'I bet if you ask Daddy, he'll take you shopping when you go next.'

'OK.' Yawning, Sophia rubbed her eyes.

'Are you tired?'

Sophia nodded. 'Yes, on Friday we didn't get back from the pub until about half past eleven. We had to get a minibus to fit everyone in and Daddy and Susan were a bit drunk so they couldn't drive. Then I couldn't get to sleep last night.'

'How come?'

'I don't know. I missed you. And Daddy was asleep so I couldn't even ring to talk to you.'

'Oh, darling. Well, I was going to tell you when Evie gets down, but I've got you a mobile to share so you can take that with you next time. That way you will be able to ring or message me any time you want to. Day or night, it doesn't matter. Even if you wake up at three in the morning, I'll be here. OK?'

'Really?' Sophia sprang from the rug and ran up the stairs. 'Evie, Evie. Guess what?'

9

'Mum! Sophia! Quick, wake up! Look outside.'

Chrissy stirred, pulling her duvet down, the chill in the air jolting her awake. 'What's the matter, Evie?'

'Look.' Grabbing Chrissy's hand, she pulled her mum towards the window. 'It's snowing!'

'Oh, wow, it is. It looks as though it's been snowing most of the night too, judging by how deep it is.'

'Wow. It's mega deep.' Sophia joined them at the window, pressing her nose to the glass.

'Is it deep enough for sledging? Can we go?'

'It's certainly deep enough. That's if we can get out of the house.' Chrissy laughed.

'Are we snowed in?' Evie asked, her voice high pitched, a cross between excited and nervous.

'No, no, I'm just joking. Although, if it carries on like this, we might be.'

'Can we go now?'

'You're eager, Evie. Let's get dressed and I'll make some pancakes first, and then we'll go out.'

'OK, come on Sophia! The sooner we get dressed, the sooner we can have breakfast and go out.'

* * *

'Does Star really have to stay here?' Evie wrapped her scarf around her neck and looked at Star who was sat next to the front door.

'Yes, I'm afraid so. She gets snowballs in her paws and if you want to stay out for a while she'll just get cold. We'll take her out for a quick walk when we get back.' Grabbing her gloves from the radiator shelf, Chrissy stuffed them in her pockets. 'Are we all set? Sophia, have you got your gloves? That's it, pull your scarves up to cover your chins.'

'Have you got the shed key, Mum?'

'No, thanks for reminding me, Sophia. We'll get the sledge out on the way.'

* * *

'My turn now!' Sophia stopped, the sledge coming to a standstill beside her.

'OK. I'm going to see how fast I can run pulling you.' Jumping out of the sledge, Evie waited until Sophia was settled in it, gripped hold of the string and pulled. Running as best she could in the thick snow, Evie overtook Chrissy.

Taking her gloves out of her pockets, she pulled them on. She hadn't seen the girls laugh this much since she and Andrew had sat them down and told them they were splitting up. It was lovely to see them so happy and carefree and actually getting on.

'Which way, Mum?' Evie came to a stop, the sledge sliding along and catching her on the ankle. 'Ow!'

'You OK, Evie?' Chrissy trudged through the snow until she came to them.

'Yes. I'm fine.' Evie rubbed her ankle. 'Which way?'

'Umm, let's go right. There's that big field that slopes down just outside the village.'

'Yes! That'll be great for sledging. Come on, Evie, see if you can go a bit faster!'

'I can see it!'

'Not far now. Come here and we'll cross over.'

'I don't think there's going to be any cars coming down here today, Mum.' Sophia said, laughing.

Looking up and down the road, Chrissy laughed too. 'You're probably right, Sophia. It's just automatic.'

'How do we get in?'

'Up here. Look. We just need to climb over the stile.' Chrissy climbed over and held her hand out. 'Here, pass me the sledge.'

'Aw, can't I carry it over?' Sophia hauled it up over her shoulder, holding Chrissy's hand and clambered over the style.

'Careful. Right, your turn, Evie.'

Evie jumped up and over. 'How quick was that, Mum?'

'Very quick. Race you to the top! On your marks, get set, go!' The three of them raced up the hill as fast as they could, their wellies sinking into the snow which was even deeper here than it had been down in the village.

* * *

Stamping her feet, Chrissy wriggled her toes. They must have been out for at least an hour now, the twins happily taking it in turns to sledge down the hill.

'Did you see how fast I went that time?' Sophia ran back up the hill, the sledge bobbing along behind her.

'I did! You went so fast that time.'

'Look. Is that Adam over there?' Evie shielded her eyes from the snowflakes which were still falling, and waved her arm. 'Adam! Adam! Over here.'

'Why are you waving him over? He's a boy.' Her eyes wide, Sophia looked down the hill and shook her head. 'Actually, maybe we could race him and Kane. Girls against boys!'

'Good idea.' Evie ran down the hill towards Adam. 'Adam. Do you want a race? Girls against boys. Best of three goes?'

Chrissy watched as Evie, Sophia, Adam and Kane trudged back up the hill to find a good starting point. Some distance behind Adam and Kane, she could just about make out Natalie, flanked by two men. Standing and watching them coming closer, she soon realised that one of the men was Luke. The other must be Natalie's fiancé, Graham.

Running her fingers through her hair, Chrissy hoped her hair wasn't too flat from wearing her hood. She straightened her scarf, she hadn't seen Luke since the morning after their drunken night together last weekend. It wasn't that she hadn't wanted to see him, but more that she felt awkward. She wasn't sure where she stood. Had it just been a one-night stand or was it the start of something? Not that Chrissy felt ready for another relationship, and she probably wouldn't for a very long time. She tucked her hair behind her ears. It would be nice to have someone to go out with, to spend time with though.

Shaking her head, she shoved her hands in her pockets. If it had been anything, then Luke would have made sure they'd run into each other during the week. Yes, Chrissy had avoided going to Natalie's house or anywhere she thought she might see him, but that wasn't the point, he knew where she lived. Things had been fine on Saturday though, they'd spent most of the day together recovering from their hangovers by watching back-to-back comedies and eating take away pizza, so maybe she wasn't being silly. Maybe he was giving her the brush off.

She looked over to the children who had made it to the top of the hill and were now drawing a start line in the snow. There was no point second guessing what was going on in Luke's mind. It didn't matter anyway, she was making a new life for herself and the twins, she didn't need any complications.

'Hi, Chrissy. How long have you been here? Oh, this is Graham, by the way.' Natalie indicated to the tall man standing next to her sporting Poppy in a baby carrier on his front.

'Nice to meet you, Graham. Going by how numb

my toes are, I'd say we've been here about an hour already.' Chrissy grimaced.

'You must be freezing.' Natalie shoved her hands in her pockets, quickly pulling out a navy-blue glove. 'Excuse me. Kane! I've got one of your gloves.' She began trudging up the hill towards him, waving the glove in one hand.

'He's always trying to get out of wearing his gloves.' Graham rolled his eyes. 'And I'm sure he gave me his other one. Somewhere.' He felt in his own pockets before pulling out the matching glove and following Natalie up the hill, waving the one he had.

'What are they like?' Luke laughed. 'So, have you been trying to avoid me or have you turned into a hermit?' Luke nudged her shoulder playfully.

'It takes two to avoid.' Chrissy stamped her feet, trying to recover some feeling in her toes.

'OK. I guess that's true. But in my defence, I wasn't sure where I stood after Friday night and I thought I'd run into you anyway.'

'Well, that was kind of why I was avoiding you too, because I didn't know where I stood.' Was this what relationships were like nowadays? Complicated?

'In that case, I guess we have two choices then.'

'We do?'

'Yep. We either rack it up as a one-off or we decide to see where it goes.' Luke turned to look at her.

She returned the look, his blue eyes reflecting the brilliant sunlight bouncing off of the snow. 'I guess we do.'

'I don't know about you, but I'd quite like to see where it goes.' He lifted his hands, palms facing Chrissy. 'No pressure though, I completely under-stand if you want to write it off as a one-off. I know you've not long split from your husband.'

'I'd like that. We'll go with the flow and see what happens.' Chrissy smiled.

'Deal. Well, in that case, to celebrate, I think we need to test the course before the little darlings end up crashing into a tree.'

'What? No. No, I'm fine standing right here, thanks.'

'No, you're not. You've already said you're cold. The best medicine for that is a sledge ride.' Luke grabbed her hands and began pulling her towards the starting line.

'No, seriously. I haven't been on a sledge in years.'

'That definitely needs rectifying then.' Dropping her hands, he turned towards the children. 'Kids, me and Chrissy are going to test the course out for you.

Girls, your mum's feeling a bit shy, come and give me a hand, will you?'

'Mum, are you really? Are you really going to have a go on the sledge?' In her excitement, Evie ran head-first into her, knocking her back a little.

'Come on then, Mum.' Sophia started pulling her up the hill. 'This is going to be epic!'

Knowing she was trapped, Chrissy shook herself, winked at the girls and turned towards Luke. 'OK, you're on. But beware, Luke, you're going to lose.'

'Don't be so sure about that!'

At the top of the hill, Chrissy tipped the sledge on its side and knocked the snow from it before lowering herself onto the cold plastic.

'Are you both ready?' Evie squealed. 'Sophia, you go that side and we'll make sure they go at the same time. No cheating, Mum, OK? Luke, no cheating for you either.'

'Hold on, Kane. Quick, let's get down to the bottom. We can be the referees and see who wins.'

'Good idea, Adam.' Evie called after him as Adam and Kane trudged quickly down the hill.

'Ready?' Sophia looked at Evie and they both shouted at the top of their voices. 'On your marks. Get set. Go!'

Chrissy pushed off from the snow with one hand,

while gripping the rope with the other. The sledge, slow at first, built up speed quickly. Clinging onto the thin white rope with both hands, Chrissy laughed as she bumped over mounds of snow and fallen branches, her hair flying out behind her.

'Faster, Mum, faster. Luke's catching up with you.'

'Quick, Mum. You can do it.'

The twins ran ahead of them at first, until the sledges picked up speed and flew past them, leaving Evie and Sophia running behind.

'Catch my snow, I'm coming past.' Luke's blue sledge flew ahead of her, spraying up a thin sludge of melting snow behind him.

Leaning as far back as she could without her head touching the snow behind her, Chrissy's sledge sped up.

'Uncle Luke, you're going the wrong way! Quick, steer it back towards us.' Adam screamed at Luke as his sledge went off course and headed towards a copse to the side of the field.

'I'm trying! I think the steering wheels broke.' Luke's voice cracked between laughter.

'There's no steering wheel, Uncle Luke! Use the rope.' Kane jumped up and down and began running in the direction Luke's sledge was heading.

'Quick, Mum, you can win!'

'I'm trying.' Chrissy twisted her neck, glancing back at Sophia and Evie as they ran, their boots sinking into the snow with every footstep. She hadn't seen them both look so happy in such a long time.

Up ahead of her, Adam waved his arms, indicating to her to slow down. Sitting up and pulling back on the thin rope, Chrissy turned the sledge, snow spraying into her face as she brought the sledge to a stop.

'That was brilliant! You won, Mum! You won!' Running towards her, Sophia and Evie wrapped their arms around her neck.

'Yay! I can definitely say that's the first time I have won a sledging ride for a very very long time!' Laughing, Chrissy let herself be pulled to standing. 'Where did Luke get to?'

'I'm here.' Luke waved as he trudged towards her, Kane running alongside pulling the sledge.

'Mummy beat you!'

'She sure did, Evie. Here, come here for a celebratory hug.' Luke held his arms open.

'Aw, are you needing some consolation after your mega loss?' Chrissy laughed and walked towards him, allowing herself to be drawn into a tight hug.

'I'm fine, thanks, but you won't be!' Luke gripped

her with one hand and shoved a fistful of snow down the back of her neck with the other.

'Noooo!' Jumping back out of his grasp, Chrissy bent her head, trying to get the icy snow out of her coat. 'You're horrible!'

'Just a bad loser, that's all. Now, kids!'

Chrissy ducked and squealed as snowball after snowball plummeted her. Running away, she bent down, rolling a quick snowball in her hand before launching it back at Luke. 'Sore loser! Girls! You should be on my side!'

Pausing, Evie and Sophia laughed before launching a fresh batch of snowballs, this time aiming them at Luke, Kane and Adam.

* * *

'I'm sorry about the snow fight. It was Kane's idea.'

Chrissy glanced at Luke as they trudged back up the hill, the children running ahead eager to race down the hill. 'Umm, why do I not believe you?'

'OK, it was my idea and a particularly brilliant one, I thought.' Grinning, Luke stumbled on a half-hidden tree root, grabbing hold of Chrissy's arm to steady himself.

'Do you think that root was trying to get you back

for ploughing a sledge into one of its kind?' Laughing, Chrissy smiled back at him.

'I think you might be right. OK, sensible faces on now, we need to pretend to be proper adults in front of my sister and Graham.' Luke straightened his face and cleared his throat.

'I'm sure they know exactly what you're like.' Chrissy laughed.

'And what would that be?'

'Umm, childish, a very sore loser... Shall I go on?' Chrissy ticked each point off on her gloved fingers.

'I think you mean gorgeous, an absolute catch, kind, considerate...'

'I think you've certainly shown your true colours there! Putting freezing cold snow down someone's back is not considerate.'

'Ahh, I can explain. That was not what it seemed. That was a celebratory tradition. All the top, professional sledge racers do that to the winner.'

'Is that right?'

'Absolutely! Here, you've got snow in your hair.' Pausing, he reached out, gently brushing snow from her hair.

'Thank you.' She could feel the warm flush creeping up her neck.

10

'Girls, can you come in and make a start on your homework, please? It's got to be in tomorrow.' Holding the back door open, Chrissy shivered against the cold wind gushing into the small kitchen. 'Hurry up, you're letting the little heat we do have escape.'

'We're going to freeze tonight if we run out of logs.' Evie shook her boots off, sludge spraying across the tiled floor.

'No we won't. Not if we keep the heat in anyway. Plus, we do have radiators! I know they're not very good, but they're better than nothing. Come on, Sophia. You can finish your snowman later.'

'Do we really have to do our homework?' Sophia closed the door behind her. 'School will probably be closed tomorrow anyway. Especially if it keeps snowing like this, won't it?'

'It might be, but you still need to get your homework done in case it's not. Hang your coats on the back of the chairs to dry and go and get your homework books out, please?' Turning back to the sink, Chrissy began peeling the potatoes. She couldn't wait until she could start making a proper Sunday roast again, until then, meat cooked in the slow cooker with mash and veg instead of roast potatoes would have to do. Mr Lowen still wasn't answering her emails, so she'd started scouring the social media selling sites in the hope that a second-hand cheap oven would come up. Hopefully, she'd manage to get one before attempting Christmas dinner.

'Urgh, there's tonnes of it.' Sophia slapped her book onto the small table pushed against the wall.

'Best make a start then. Let's have a look.' Placing her hand on Sophia's shoulder, she peered at the homework.

'It's not that much, Sophia. We've only got spellings, maths and a reading comprehension.' Evie slipped into the chair opposite, a pen already in her hand.

'Why don't you make a start on the maths? Get that out of the way and then do the reading comprehension. You can always copy out your spellings later, they won't take you long anyway, will they?'

'There are twelve spellings, Mum. It will take forever.'

'You'd better make a start then. You can do it.' Chrissy turned back to the potatoes.

'Ooh, I like these. Look, Mum, we've got short multiplication. I love doing these, they're so easy!' Evie grinned, bent her head and began, her tongue sticking out in concentration.

'Well, I don't like them! How can anyone love maths anyway? You're just weird, Evie.'

'I'm not. And I can like maths if I want to, can't I, Mum? You don't have to like the same things as me just because we're twins.'

'Yuck, don't remind me. I feel sick every time I think about sharing a womb with you.'

'Girls, girls. Come on, be nice. Here, let me finish peeling this potato and I'll come and help you, Sophia.'

'I don't need your help. I'm not thick, you know.'

'I know you're not. You're a very bright girl, you both are, but maybe if I explain again it might help a bit.'

'Come on, Sophia, we were doing these on Friday.

I'm on my third one already. I can show you, if you want?'

'I don't need anyone's help. I just don't want to do it.' Sophia pushed her homework book across the table and slumped her head into her arms.

'Oi, stop kicking me, Sophia!' Evie pushed her chair back an inch from the table. 'Mum, she's kicking me.'

'Sophia, don't kick, please. Here, I'll go through it with you.' Chrissy placed the half-peeled potato back into the sink and dried her hands on the tea towel.

'Can I go and finish it in my room, Mum? She keeps jogging the table and I've already made a mistake.'

'Yes, of course you can, Evie.'

Balancing her homework book, pen and drink in her hands, Evie left the kitchen.

'Hey, Sophia. I know it's difficult when maths seems so easy for Evie and you need to think about it a bit more, but you can do it. You just need to set your mind to it. Plus, you're both really good at different things, aren't you?' Chrissy rubbed Sophia's back.

'I don't want to do it and I don't need your help.' Sophia squirmed away from Chrissy's touch.

'OK, well, just shout if you change your mind.'

'Hello?' Luke poked his head around the back

door, a sweep of his ash blonde hair peeking out from under his black beanie hat. 'Hi, sorry to let myself round the back but I've got some more logs for you. Shall I put them in the shed?'

'Oh, wow. Thank you. Yes, that'd be great, please? Could I have some in here too, please? We've almost run out.'

'Of course you can.'

'Thank you.'

Luke shut the door again before returning five minutes later.

'All done. Where do you want these?' Luke nodded at the pile of logs balancing in his arms.

'Oh, I'll take those. Thank you.' Chrissy unloaded Luke's arms. 'How did you know we were running out?'

'It was a wild guess.' Grinning, Luke blew on his hands.

'Here, come in and warm up for a bit, if you like? I'll pop these down and get you a coffee.'

'I was hoping you'd say that. It's freezing out here, and apparently, it's going to get colder overnight. No doubt the snow will be frozen solid come the morning.' Luke stamped his boots before coming in and shutting the door behind him.

'Does that mean the school will be closed then?'

Sophia looked up. 'I can leave my homework until to-morrow then, can't I, Mum?'

'It might well be. I know most of the kids are from the village but at least two of the teachers drive in from the nearest town. I guess, if they can't get in, it probably will be.'

'Yes!' Sophia pumped the air with her fist and scraped her chair back.

'Where do you think you're going, miss?' Chrissy lay the logs down by the wall, knowing full well that if she disappeared into the living room, Sophia would have left her homework by the time she got back. 'You can still finish it now, or at least get the majority of it done. I don't want your homework spoiling our snow day if we get one.'

'Urgh, I told you I don't want to do it.' Slumping back in her chair, Sophia threw her pen across the table.

'And I've told you, I'll help you.' Sitting down next to Sophia, Chrissy pulled the homework book to-wards her.

'I don't want your help.' Grabbing her homework book, Sophia snatched it from Chrissy's grasp.

'Sophia!'

'I used to hate homework too, but you may as well get it out of the way like your mum says, or else it will just spoil tomorrow. Plus, on snow days, most of the children in the village go to the big hill and have massive sledge rides. You wouldn't want to miss making the most of the snow before it goes, would you?' Peeling off his wet gloves, Luke laid them on the kitchen side.

'No, but I don't get it.'

'Let's have a look then. Maths? I always found maths hard when I was your age, but I didn't let it beat me. I worked it out, usually with a bit of help, and just kept practising. Now I use maths all the time in my job, pricing up materials, working out profits and I enjoy it too.' Luke slipped into the chair Chrissy had been in and looked at the dreaded homework.

'I'll just go and check on Evie.' Chrissy slipped out.

* * *

Back downstairs, Chrissy paused in the kitchen doorway and watched as Luke explained to and encouraged Sophia, pointing with his finger at the sums. Catching his eye, Chrissy mouthed, 'Thank you.'

'How's it going?'

'Good.' Sophia raised her head and smiled. 'Sorry I yelled.'

'That's OK, sweetheart. Luke, did you want to stay

for dinner? I've got loads. I always seem to do too much.'

'Ooh, yes please?'

* * *

'Alright, Star, we all heard the doorbell, we don't need you barking too.' Reaching across Evie to the coffee table, Chrissy put her hot chocolate down and stood up.

'Hello?'

'Evening. Sorry to intrude, but I was just wondering if Luke was still here? Only I saw him carrying some logs through earlier.'

'Yes, he's here. Come in out of the cold and I'll get him. Sorry I didn't catch your name?' Chrissy stood aside to let the elderly man into the hall.

'I didn't introduce myself, did I? Colin, Colin Thompson. I live next door.' Colin pushed his hood down, revealing a shock of white hair. 'I must say it's nice to see Corner Cottage being occupied again, and by a young family too.'

'Thank you. I wasn't expecting it to be so run-down when we got here, but I think we've begun making it quite homely.'

'Good, good. That's just what this place needs, a bit of care and attention.'

'Come through, he's just in the living room.' Chrissy opened the door, letting him through first. 'Girls, this is our next-door neighbour, Mr Thompson. Mr Thompson, this is Evie and this is Sophia.'

'Nice to meet you, Sophia and Evie. And please, just call me Colin. After fifty years of teaching, I'm fed up of hearing myself being referred to as Mr Thompson.' Colin smiled.

'Colin, how are you?' Placing his mug on the hearth, Luke stood up from his spot in front of the wood burner and wiped cream and chocolate dust from his lips with the back of his hand.

'I'm fine, thank you. A little too cold with this weather, though.' Colin took Luke's hand and patted him on the back. 'Which is why I'm here. I was wondering if I may ask a favour please?'

'Of course. How can I help?'

'Gladys has an emergency doctor's appointment in an hour's time. We've got a taxi booked but they're refusing to come into the village because of the conditions of the road, so I was going to ask if you could possibly take her, please? I know you have your four by four... If it's too much trouble don't worry...'

'I'd be happy to help. My old heap will make light work of this snow anyway.'

'Are you sure? I don't like to ask, but she's had a bit of a reaction to some of her new meds and if this snow continues the whole village really will be shut off by the morning.'

'It's absolutely fine. I need to pop to the super-market before it closes anyway to get some milk and bits for Natalie and Chrissy.' Luke grinned. 'I'll come over to yours in about half an hour, that should give us enough time.'

'Thank you. I really appreciate it.' Colin looked at Luke before glancing over at Chrissy. 'This one's a good'un. Always there to help the ladies.'

'See you in a bit.' Luke saw Colin out, warming his hands in front of the wood burner when he came back in. 'Right, can you make up a shopping list of bits you need, please? I need to make Colin think I was going into town anyway or else he'll feel awkward and try to pay me back somehow.'

'OK. Well, if you're paying, I'm sure I can think of a few things.' Chrissy looked at him out of the corner of her eye. What had Colin meant by Luke being there to help 'the ladies'? Had he meant he was a ladies' man, a womaniser?

'Oooh, can I write the list? I'll have a laptop, a

trampoline and a new bike, please? Sophia, what are you going to order from Luke?' Evie tried her best to keep a straight face, her shining eyes giving the game away.

'I'll have a tablet, please?' Sophia grinned at Luke.

'Whoah, I was only going to pop into the supermarket.' Luke held his hands up and laughed. 'I'd better run over to Natalie's and see if there's anything she needs. Thanks again for dinner and, of course, for the hot chocolate you both made, Evie and Sophia.'

'I'll see you out.' Chrissy stood up, following him to the front door.

'Seriously, thank you for asking me to stay for dinner. It's been really nice spending some time with you all.' Leaning towards her, he kissed her on the cheek before pulling his hood up and disappearing into the snow.

Chrissy shook her head, trying to get Colin's words out of her mind. He had only been teasing Luke, so why couldn't she shake the niggle of doubt away?

11

'Love you both. Have a lovely time.' Chrissy pulled Evie and Sophia towards her, landing a kiss on their heads. Flinching, Chrissy looked up as Andrew sounded the horn again. It wouldn't hurt him to actually walk to the door to collect his children rather than summoning them to the car and disturbing all of their neighbours with his impatience. 'You'd better get a wriggle on.'

'OK. Love you, Mummy.' Evie leant in for a quick hug before running down the path towards her dad.

'Hey, Sophia. You OK?'

Looking at the floor, Sophia nodded.

'Look, try to enjoy yourself, OK?' Cupping Sophia's cheeks, she kissed her on the forehead. 'I know it probably feels a bit strange still, but he's your dad and he loves you.'

'You'll be on your own though.' Glancing up, Sophia mumbled.

'Don't worry about me. I'll be fine. Of course, I'll miss you but I'll keep myself busy and this weekend will just fly right by. I've got to go and see Natalie about her wedding dress anyway, so I won't be on my own.'

'OK.'

'Now go and enjoy yourself. Have fun. You've got your mobile to ring or text me if you want to as well, so you know I'm always at the end of the phone.'

'Love you.'

'Love you too, sweetheart.' Chrissy smiled, her cheeks hurting, as she watched Sophia trudge down the path and get in the car next to her sister. She waved and blew them kisses as Andrew drove them away.

Standing on the doorstep, she watched as Andrew's car disappeared around the corner, taking her two girls miles away from her for the weekend. Taking them back to Susan's house where they could play happy families, two adults and two children, just as they had been, should still be doing.

Slowly shutting the door behind her, Chrissy let

her smile fade and wiped the tears as they spilt down her cheeks.

It wasn't fair.

It wasn't fair that overnight she'd become a member of a part-time family. A family where she had to be apart from her children every other weekend. It was unnatural, and downright wrong. All she'd ever wanted as a child was to become a mother herself, and now, now she had that role stripped from her twice a month.

This was how life would be from now on until the girls were old enough to decide what they wanted to do, she'd be everything to them for two weeks and then nothing for a whole weekend, absolutely nothing. She'd be no one. She had no purpose when they were at Andrew's house. They were her purpose.

What if they preferred Susan to her? What if Andrew's mistress was a better mother figure to them? What if they wanted to go and live with them? What then?

Digging her fingernails into the palms of her hands, she walked into the living room. She needed to get out of here. Needed to get away from Sophia's half-full glass of milk on the coffee table and Evie's pens and colouring book scattered across the rug. She needed to get away from the reminders of what they should still be doing if Andrew hadn't taken them for the weekend.

She would go to Natalie's. She didn't really need to, she'd only wanted Sophia to think that she'd be busy, but she would go. She had to ask her opinion about some crystals she'd ordered for the bodice anyway. She'd ordered two different sizes because Natalie hadn't been sure at the time, so she'd pop over and ask. It would get her out of the house for half an hour at least anyway.

* * *

Opening the front door, Chrissy stamped the snow sludge off her boots before entering into the hall. Most of the snow had melted, but there were still mounds of sludge frozen where it had been scraped away from pathways and driveways.

Natalie wanted the bigger crystals sewn around the rim of the bodice with the smaller ones scattered across. It should look lovely, even if it would take a long time to achieve the look Natalie wanted.

Taking her coat off, the chill in the house seeped into her already cold bones.

'Damn.' She must have forgotten to leave the heating on. Taking the two short steps towards the thermostat, she checked the setting. That was strange, it was set to twenty-one Celsius, there was no way it was as warm as that in the house. Breathing out, she could see the condensation as her warm breath met with the icy coldness in the air. It definitely was not twenty-one Celsius. She twisted the thermostat all the way down and then back up again, listening for the pop from the boiler as it kicked into action. Nothing. It must have broken. That was all she needed.

Laughing a hollow laugh, she realised Mr Lowen would not be in the slightest bit interested or inclined to get it fixed, and she didn't really want to have to dip into the limited savings she did have. She'd budgeted their monthly outgoings for the next six months and there wasn't really anything spare. She shrugged, she'd have to get it fixed, there was no choice. She'd have to use the money Natalie was paying her for finishing her wedding dress.

Slumping onto the sofa, she stared at the wood burner. She should light it, but even then it would take a while to heat the room. And what was she supposed to do? She was bored. If she was honest, she was lonely. She didn't want to rattle around the cottage all weekend but it wasn't as if she knew many people from the village, not well enough to just drop in for a chat anyway.

There were her old friends, but she hadn't seen her proper friends, the ones from before Andrew, for so long it would be weird to contact them out of the blue. She and Andrew had always met up with his friends, not hers. Whenever a social event involving her old friends had come up, he'd always made some excuse or other, they didn't have enough money to waste it on a meal out or he wanted to spend some time as a family, even though he'd inevitably still hidden in the kitchen whilst she'd tried and failed to put the twins to bed before he sloped off upstairs leaving her with two grumpy children.

So, now she was left with no one. His friends had sided with him. She didn't blame them, they had known him long before her, but it would have been nice if at least one of them had thought to contact her, to check she was OK. And her friends, well, she was probably just a distant memory to them.

Chrissy pressed the heels of her hands into her eyes, focusing on the bright speckles that appeared. She'd just have to get used to doing things on her own. She'd been fine going down the pub by herself. Yes, she'd met Luke there but that hadn't been until nearer closing time. She'd spent most of the time on her own.

That's what she'd do, she'd go to the pub. Maybe

she'd even get something for her dinner there. Yes, it was a waste of money, money she shouldn't be spending, but if it kept her sane, it would be worth it. Plus, she'd only get a bowl of chips or something equally cheap and a couple of drinks. She didn't want to get drunk and show herself up like last time.

***

Opening her sketchbook, she took a chip from the bowl to her left and looked out of the window. It really was a pretty little village. If they really could make their lives here, it would be a nice place to live and to bring the girls up.

She took another chip. She'd show Andrew. She'd show him she could cope and make a nice life here for the twins and herself.

'You're looking all melancholy.'

Jerking her head up, Chrissy smiled at Luke who was towering above her.

'Hi. No, not really. Just thinking. How are you?'

'Tired. I've just got back from travelling up and down the country on a wild goose chase after this old hotel which was supposed to be super cheap.' Luke looked down at the two glasses he was holding and nodded towards the seat opposite Chrissy. 'Can I join you? I've got a gin and tonic with your name on here.'

'Yes, of course. Thank you. I'll get the next one.'

'You're welcome.' He pushed the glass across the table.

'Chip?' Sliding the bowl across the table, Chrissy closed her notebook.

'Lovely.'

'So this hotel you went to see, was it not what you were looking for?'

'No. A mate of mine tipped me off about it. He said it had been standing empty for years and so was going to auction. Anyway, I thought, great, another one I can renovate and sell up making a tidy profit. So I drove all the way up north to go to the auction just to find it had been pulled out at the last minute.' Luke took a chip, dipping it in tomato sauce before eating it.

'It was a wasted trip then?'

'Yep. Never mind. These things happen, don't they?'

'They sure do. Have you got any other houses lined up?'

'Not really. I'm still working on one anyway, so I'll probably wait until that's finished before I go to another auction, it was only because the one up north was supposed to be a steal.' Luke wiped his brow with the back of his hand and took a long gulp of lager. 'Never mind, let's drown our sorrows and think about nicer things.'

'I'll drink to that.' Holding her glass out, she clinked it against Luke's.

'So, tell me, what's in the notebook?' Taking another chip, he pointed it at Chrissy's sketchbook.

'That's got your sister's wedding dress design in, among other things.'

'Can I?' Leaning across the table, Luke slid the sketchbook towards him.

'Will she mind? She's not keeping the final design a surprise or anything?'

'Nah, she won't mind. She showed me the first design anyway. The one that the runaway dressmaker drew for her.'

'OK then.' Shrugging, Chrissy took a long sip from her drink. Natalie liked her design so she wasn't sure why it mattered what Luke thought. Although, for some reason, it did. It mattered a lot. She took another sip and rested her elbows on the table, leaning across, trying to gauge a reaction from him. 'So?'

'It's great. Really detailed, much better than the one she had drawn out for her before.' Luke tilted the sketchbook up. 'Yes, it's beautiful. You've got a real talent for fashion and design, haven't you?'

'Hardly! Look at me.' Standing up, Chrissy twirled around, her faded jeans had a hole in the knee from where she had tripped over a few months ago, and her dark green jumper had seen better days, the threads hanging from the sleeves were a constant distraction which she frequently fiddled with.

'Oh, I don't know. I think you look rather sexy.'

'Luke!' Laughing, Chrissy sat back down.

'Too much?' Flicking through the rest of the sketchbook, Luke paused and looked back up. 'What's this?'

'Oh, ignore them. They're just some silly sketches I did.' Waving her hand dismissively, Chrissy took a gulp from her drink, hoping the icy alcohol would cool the flush creeping up her neck.

'They're not silly. They're actually really good. 'Chrissy's Creations', 'Speedy Dressmaker', 'Chrissy's Tidy Tailoring'. These are good, and I love the way you've got the needles with the thread writing the name on this one.'

Reaching across, Chrissy pulled the sketchbook back to her, closing it and setting it to the side. 'As I said, they're just some super quick sketches.'

'Are you thinking of going into business properly?'

'Yes, I think so. I need to start earning some money to support us and this way I could work from home and be there for the girls. Plus, that's what I used to do. It was only when I had the girls, and with them being twins everything was twice as manic, I just didn't have the time. And then when they started school, Andrew, my ex, didn't want me working.'

'Why not?'

'I don't really know, really. He said it would be too much hassle, that it would take up too much of my time.'

'When are you going to start up your business then?'

'I'm not sure. After Christmas maybe. I'd like to get everything in place, you know, do it properly. And I want to finish your sister's dress before I take on anything else anyway.'

'I think it's a great idea.'

'Thanks.' Chrissy took a final swig from her glass and stood up. 'Same again?'

* * *

'Shhh, you're such a loud drunk.' Clinging onto Luke's arm, Chrissy laughed as she stumbled down the kerb.

'Here, let me be a gentleman, even if I am a loud one, come on this side before you get run over.' Holding on to Chrissy's hand, Luke pulled her across to the inside of the path before linking arms with her again.

'Oh yes, careful, look at all the traffic.'

'No need to be sarcastic. You never know, we once had a herd of sheep roaming the road. Now, they were dangerous, they sneaked up on the tipsy people as they were chucked out of the pub.'

'A flock, not a herd.' Laughing, Chrissy leant her head against his shoulder. 'And if tonight is anything to go by, I bet you were more than a little tipsy.'

'Maybe a tiny tiny bit.' Luke squeezed his thumb and forefinger together.

'Here we are.' Chrissy stopped outside Corner Cottage, and threw open the gate, watching as it bounced off the hedge and shut itself again. Shrugging, she looked at Luke. 'Are you coming in for a coffee?'

'I was rather hoping you'd offer something a little stronger.'

'I do actually have a bottle of wine this time, if that will tempt you? It's red wine though and I'm normally rubbish at knowing which one to get so it may taste of vinegar.'

'I think I'm brave enough to take my chances.' Luke swung the gate open, holding it for Chrissy as she stumbled through.

'Oops.' As the keys clattered on the concrete step at her feet, Chrissy glanced across at the neighbours. They were safe, there was no twitching of curtains or lights being turned on.

'Step aside, madam.' Luke cleared his throat, bent to retrieve the keys and opened the front door.

'Thank you.'

'Bliming heck, it's freezing in here!' Following Chrissy inside, Luke wrapped his arms around his middle. 'Can we have the wine on the doorstep? I'm sure it was warmer outside.'

'Drat. I forgot, the heating's broken.'

'Did you leave the wood burner on? Please tell me the wood burner's on and it's toasty and warm in the living room.'

'Umm... no. I didn't want to waste the logs.'

'I can't believe you.' Luke laughed and pulled her towards him, holding her hands and making her wrap her arms around him.

Throwing her head back, Chrissy laughed. 'What are you doing?'

'Trying to take all of your heat. If I'd known you were leading me into a house colder than an igloo, I would have insisted we trekked the extra half mile to my house.'

'Aw, poor Luke. We can always go there now if

you're too much of a wimp to withstand the temperature in my house.'

'Nope, we're here now. I'm not risking going out into the night again, those sheep are probably prowling the streets by now.'

'Come on then, come through. I'll light the log burner now.' Chrissy unwrapped her arms and pulled him through to the living room.

'No, you find the wine, I'll tackle the matches.' Rubbing his hands together and breathing warmth onto them, Luke walked over to the mantelpiece to get the matches.

'OK.'

* * *

'Here, budge over.' Placing the glasses and bottle on the coffee table in front of them, Chrissy joined Luke on the sofa, pulled the pink checked throw from behind them and laid it across them both.

'Warm enough?'

'No, it's still freezing.' Chrissy shivered under the blanket.

'The wood burner will soon start throwing some heat out.' Leaning towards her, Luke rubbed her leg through the blanket.

'Do you want to try this wine then?'

'The vinegar? Why not?'

Reaching forwards, Chrissy took hold of the glasses and watched as Luke poured the red velvety liquid, filling them to the brim.

'Cheers.'

'Cheers.' Taking a deep breath, Chrissy tentatively took a sip. 'It's not that bad, actually.'

'No, it's not. You're more talented at choosing red wine than you give yourself credit for.'

'Well, thank you very much.' Chrissy laughed and leant her head back against the sofa.

'How are you finding living here?'

'It's OK. I quite like the village life and I'm warming to the cottage.' Chrissy laughed at her own joke.

'It does take a little bit of getting used to, doesn't it? Living in such a close-knit community, everyone knows everyone's business.'

'I guess. I like it though. How long have you lived here for?'

'I grew up here. In the house that Natalie and Graham live in. Our parents passed away when we were in our early twenties, one after the other. My dad got ill and then after he'd gone, my mum just seemed to give up.'

'That's awful.' Chrissy laid her hand on Luke's arm.

'It was. Natalie and Graham had just found out they were expecting Adam, so it seemed like the right thing for them to stay living in the house. And me, I hate to admit it, but I had to get away. I went travelling for a year to clear my head.'

'And then you came back?'

'Nope, I met my ex-wife, Meredith. We were back-packing through the Philippines at the time.'

'I didn't know you had been married.' Chrissy traced Luke's name on his forearm with her index finger.

'Yep. It lasted all of nine months.'

'What happened?' She glanced up at Luke. 'You don't have to tell me if you don't want to.'

'No, it's fine. Nothing horrible. When we finished travelling we both landed jobs up near Leeds and re-alised that we didn't actually have that much in com-mon. She started seeing someone else and I came back down here for a bit.'

'Sorry to hear that. What makes some people think that cheating is OK?'

'Beats me. Natalie said your ex cheated on you? Is that right?'

'Yes. With his childhood sweetheart!' Chrissy let out a hollow laugh.

'That must have been difficult.'

'It was. Especially since we had to carry on living together until our home was sold. Don't get me wrong, our marriage was far from perfect. For the last couple of years we had almost become strangers living in the same house, trying not to piss the other one off. But, it was still hard. It was hard seeing how it affected the girls too. How it still affects them.'

'I guess at least I had somewhere to come to get away when I found out what Meredith had been up to.'

'I guess.' Twisting around to face Luke, she pointed at him, her wine sloshing perilously close to the rim of the glass. 'Do you know what really hurts? It's not just the fact that my husband, sorry, ex-husband, views our marriage, the life we had together as worthless but it's also the way that I have been totally ostracised from his family and friends. We used to get on really well, really well. My ex-mother-in-law used to say that she viewed me as a daughter. And now, nothing. Nothing at all. They don't speak to me, they don't ask me how I am. I am nothing. I have been well and truly, totally replaced by perfect Susan.'

'Is she the mistress?'

'Yes, the mistress. I bet she'll be sat around the table chatting away for hours after Sunday lunch with the in-laws. Yuck, yuck, yuck.'

'You're not over him, are you?'

'Andrew? Oh yes, I am totally over Andrew but I still feel let down by them. By those people who were supposed to be my family.'

'I guess I can understand.'

'But I am totally, totally over Andrew. I hate him now. I hate the way he waltzes in and takes my kids away every other weekend. I mean, that's not right, is it? It was him who broke our family up. Not me. I should get to keep them, shouldn't I?'

'Well...'

'Ssshh. Don't answer that.' Chrissy held her finger to Luke's lips. 'I'm sorry, red wine always does this to me. It makes me cross and sad, I shouldn't have had any. But I promise I am over Andrew, it's just that everything carries on, there's always more drama. I'm always going to be tied to him. I'm always going to be reminded of what he did to me and what we should have had.'

'But would that have been better? Being with him still if you were living like strangers?'

'No, no it wouldn't. It all went so wrong a long time ago but it shouldn't have, we were good together, years ago and we should have had a different future.'

'People change though, don't they?'

'I know. It still doesn't stop me feeling as though I've lost something. I know I need to get used to the idea that my future is now going to be different. I guess, I didn't ever think I'd become a single mum, scrimping and saving to pay the bills.'

'You won't be for long, scrimping and saving, I mean. You've got a solid business idea. You start that, and you'll see, it'll be a success.'

'I hope so. And I know I've got a lot to be thankful for since splitting up with Andrew, that I wouldn't have otherwise. I don't need to walk on eggshells in my own home for the first time in at least three years. I'm in control of my finances. I'm not in debt.' Chrissy raised her glass, red wine dribbling down the sides. 'If I was still with him I'd still be paying for food and petrol on my credit cards while he went to play rugby every week, drinking and eating a meal out after every match. I can follow my dreams, do what I want to do, like the business. But, most importantly, my girls aren't growing up in a home full of arguments.'

'See, that sounds positive.'

'It is. I am so so much happier than when I was with him. I really am. And, of course, I wouldn't be able to have cosy nights in with a gorgeous property developer.' Leaning forwards, Chrissy kissed Luke, his lips warm against hers.

'Now, that's a bonus for me too.'

'I'm sorry, I've rattled on too much about my ex. You probably didn't want to hear me whittling on about him.' Slumping back into the sofa cushions, Chrissy downed the rest of her wine before slamming the glass on the table.

'It's OK. I like to know what I've got to live up to.'

'Very funny. So, who have I got to live up to then? You must have had more than one ex. I don't believe for one second that you've been single since Meredith.'

'You're right, I haven't.' Luke shifted his position and wrapped his arms around her, pulling her back towards his side. 'I admit I have a few stories to tell.'

'You mean you slept around?' Closing her eyes, Chrissy snuggled against Luke's warmth.

'Yes and no. I spent a couple of years as a tour rep in Ibiza and, yes, I probably had a few too many holiday flings, but when I came back to England I met up with a group of people I used to go to school with and me and this girl, Laura, started seeing each other. Things got pretty serious and we ended up moving to London together.'

'What is it with men and old friends from school? Are you literally all the same?'

'No, I wasn't seeing anyone at the time, so I am most definitely not like your ex.' Luke kissed the top of her head. 'And besides, I didn't used to go to school with her, she was tagging along with an old friend. She'd just split from her fiancé and I was the rebound. Or so I found out five years later when she dumped me because she still had feelings for her ex. Who, I might add, had strangely enough just moved to London, to the same borough we were living in.'

'She cheated on you? Just like Meredith did?'

'No, no it wasn't anything like that. She split from me first and then three months later I saw a post of hers on social media announcing that she was in a relationship with her ex. She didn't cheat, I'm a hundred per cent certain on that, but I do think I was just rebound material. Whether she knew that or whether she did think she loved me at the time, I'll never know.'

'That's rubbish. What is it with us? Do you think we're too trusting or just thick?'

'I'll go with us being too trusting!'

'I'm sorry, I have made a complete fool of myself tonight. You're just so easy to get drunk around. And I'm not a pretty drunk.'

'You are a very pretty drunk and you haven't made a fool of yourself. Plus, I'll add the fact that I'm easy to get drunk with to my list of many talents. Of course, I could argue that you are easy to get drunk around too.' Twisting his neck, it was his turn to kiss her. 'I can think of a way to keep us warm.'

* * *

'Wakey, wakey. Breakfast time.'

Chrissy lifted her eyelids, immediately closing them again against the bright sunlight streaming in through the thin curtains. 'What time is it?'

'Nine o'clock.'

Forcing her eyes open again, Chrissy pushed herself up on the pillows behind her.

'Breakfast is served. I hope you don't mind me helping myself to your food?' Placing a tray of toast and scrambled egg on her knees, Luke perched on the edge of the bed.

'Mind? Not at all. Help yourself to food every day of the week if this is how you treat me. I haven't had breakfast brought to me in bed since... nope, I can't remember. Thank you.'

'You're very welcome.'

'I apologise for my ramblings last night. Please don't ever let me drink red wine again.'

'You were fine. It was quite nice to get to know you a little better.'

'It was nice to get to know you too.' Chrissy smiled at him. It was nice, what they had together. Luke made her feel wanted and worthy as a person, which she hadn't been made to feel in a very long time.

12

Holding Star back by the collar, Chrissy opened the front door.

'Hi, Mum.'

'Hey, Evie.' Bringing her in for a hug, Chrissy kissed the top of her head. 'Did you have a nice time? Where's your sister?'

'She's coming. Yes, it was nice. I just need to go to the toilet and then I'll tell you all about it.'

'OK.' Standing aside, Chrissy watched Evie kick her shoes off before running through the living room, heading to the stairs. Turning back, she furrowed her brow as Sophia came tearing down the garden path, her rucksack dragging along the path behind her. 'Soph...'

Pushing past her, Sophia ran into the house.

'Chrissy.'

Hooking her thumb through Star's collar, Chrissy pulled her through to the living room and shut the door before straightening her back. 'Andrew. Is everything OK?'

'Just sort your daughter out before they come next time, will you?'

Taking a step back, she took a deep breath, she hadn't heard him speak so gruffly before, not about the girls anyway. 'I beg your pardon.'

'You heard. Sophia's a disgrace. She needs to sort her attitude out before she gets herself into trouble.'

'What the hell do you mean?' Pursing her lips, Chrissy narrowed her eyes. What was Andrew on about? What had happened with Sophia? And how dare he speak about her, their, daughter in such a way?

'Ask her yourself. I'm off.'

'Don't you talk about one of our children like that, Andrew!' Scowling, she watched as he retreated quickly down the path, waving his hand out to her. That was it, she was dismissed. Slowly she closed the door. Obviously, something had happened.

* * *

'Sophia, sweetheart. Let me in.' Gently tapping on Sophia's bedroom door, Chrissy raised her voice trying to be heard above the music. Shrugging, she turned away, maybe she just needed a bit of space to calm down and then she'd be ready to talk about it.

'Evie, sweetheart, why is Sophia so upset?' Back downstairs, she lowered herself next to Evie on the sofa.

'Oh, she's been really grumpy all weekend. And then she had an argument with Susan.' Evie put the book down that she was reading and turned to face her mum.

'I thought she was going to try to enjoy it?'

'She was, but then when we got there she asked Daddy if she could go and get some things for her bedroom. You know, like the things I told you I got last time we went?'

'Yes, I remember. Sophia had told me that she was going to ask.'

'Well, Daddy said yes and then when we were putting our shoes on to go, Susan spoke to him in the other room and he came back out and told us she couldn't get the stuff. He said that she had chosen not to get it all when he had offered and that she was being ungrateful.'

'What happened next?'

'Sophia cried and said that she was sorry but she hadn't felt comfortable getting the stuff to make her room homely last time and that she felt more ready now. But he just said that he was the adult and went into the kitchen with Susan.'

'Right, OK. And what did Sophia do then?' Had he really listened to Susan's parenting wisdom, or lack of it, and taken her side over his own daughter's? After Sophia had poured her heart out to him explaining how she had been feeling? Sophia and Andrew had never been particularly close and it must have taken a lot for Sophia to have spoken to him so openly and that was how he repaid her? Chrissy bit down on her bottom lip. 'And how was it for the rest of the weekend?'

'Not nice. Sophia spent most of the Saturday up in her room, she didn't even come down for breakfast or lunch on Saturday.' Evie picked at a fingernail.

'Did Daddy have to take it up to her then?'

'No. He said that she had to come down for it and that she'd come out of her room if she was hungry.'

'Oh.' Starve her out. Yep, I'm sure that's not neglect. Chrissy focused on a crack above the window. She knew she had to sit and listen, to find out what had happened, but all she wanted to do was get in the car and drive to Andrew's place and give him a piece of her mind. And that was if she could control herself.

'Don't worry, Mummy. I took her up half of my sandwich and a carton of juice.' Evie looked up at Chrissy.

'You're a good girl. Thank you for looking out for her.'

'That's what we do. At school, at clubs, wherever. We make sure the other one's OK. Sophia would never admit it, but I know she looks out for me too. Like that time I got pushed over at our old school? Sophia tripped the boy up who had pushed me. Though I don't think he meant to hurt me but... Sophia looks after me and I look after her.' Evie looked down at her hands.

'You're going to make me cry. I'm so proud of you. I'm so proud of the way you both look out for each other.'

'You told us to.'

'I did, didn't I?' Chrissy smiled, even though the twins always seemed to fight against each other, re-pelling to find their own identities, she guessed their twinness was still strong.

'Anyway, she came down after lunch and we went to the park on our bikes.'

'OK, so everything was OK after that? Why did she

come home in such a foul mood then?' Something didn't make sense. Unless, of course, Sophia was worried that Chrissy would tell her off for behaving the way she had at her father's. She wouldn't, obviously. The way Andrew had treated her by not letting her get some things to make her bedroom her own, especially after saying she could, was downright cruel. She didn't blame Sophia for the way she had behaved, not at all.

'Yes, things were OK until just before we left.'

'Why? What happened?'

'We were getting ready to come home, you know, packing our rucksacks up and Susan went into Sophia's room. I crept out on the landing and sat outside listening. She told Sophia that she should show Daddy more respect and do as she's told because Daddy was the adult and he'd got upset when Sophia had locked herself in her room.'

'Really? She said that?' Who the hell did Susan think she was? How dare she try to step into the parenting role? She was no one to the girls. Apart from, of course, being the woman who broke up their parents' marriage. She had no right, no right whatsoever.

Evie nodded. 'Are you cross?'

Clearing her throat, Chrissy tightened her arms

around Evie and kissed the top of her head. 'I'm glad you told me. How did Sophia react?'

'She shouted at Susan.' Evie drooped her head, a deep blush spreading across her cheeks. 'She swore at her and told Susan that she had no right to talk to her about respect because she hadn't respected you when she'd got together with Daddy.'

'Oh.' Was it bad that she felt touched by the way Sophia had stuck up for her? It probably was. 'I bet that didn't go down very well?'

'No, Susan just walked out. I saw her come past me and she was crying. She then just left, slamming the door on her way out.'

'Oh dear. Did Daddy tell Sophia off?'

'No, he was just really really quiet all the way here.'

'OK. Thank you for telling me, sweetheart. I'm going to make you both a hot chocolate now and take Sophia's up to her so I can have a chat with her, OK? Why don't you pop the TV on and have some chill-out time?'

'OK. I love you, Mummy.'

* * *

'Sophia, I know what happened. Let me in.' Holding a mug of hot chocolate in one hand Chrissy tapped on the door. 'OK, I'm letting myself in.' Twisting the handle, Chrissy paused in the doorway, letting her eyes adjust to the darkness and her ears to the loud music blasting from Sophia's iPod.

'Go away.' A muffled shout came from under the duvet.

'Nope, I'm not going anywhere. We need to talk, sweetheart.' Flicking the lights on and the music off, Chrissy then sat down on the bed.

'Why can't I get any privacy? Most people my age have locks on their doors so they can shut their parents out. I want a lock.' Throwing the duvet aside, Sophia stared at her mum, her eyes swollen and red.

Chrissy shook her head, that argument could be stored for another day. 'Hey, Evie told me what happened over the weekend. You could have rung me if you were upset you know.'

'I didn't want to ring you, I wanted you there. I wanted everything to be like it used to be, with you and Daddy getting along and being together. Us all being together.'

'Oh, Sophia. Come here.' Chrissy set the mug down on the bedside table before twisting herself round and sitting next to Sophia, her back against the headboard.

'I missed you. I miss all of it.' Wiping her eyes with the sleeves of her green hoodie, Sophia moved closer and leant against Chrissy's side.

'I know, but things weren't so rosy when me and your dad were together. You must remember that?' Pulling Sophia into a hug, she leant her chin on the top of Sophia's head.

'It was.'

'Don't you remember all the arguments and shouting that used to happen?'

'Only when Daddy was home and he was always at work.'

'There you go then. You're right, your dad was out the majority of the time, so surely that should make this easier? You were used to not having both of us around.'

'Yes, but I knew you were together. Whereas now, I know you're not.'

'But we were always arguing and that wasn't right, arguing in front of you and your sister.'

'So it was our fault you two split up.'

Chrissy felt Sophia's shoulders stiffen. 'What? No, not at all. It wasn't. It wasn't right that we argued in front of you both, but that wasn't why we split up. We split up because we argued and because we'd grown apart. We just didn't love each other in the end.'

'Are you sure it wasn't anything to do with me or Evie? Well, me, because it's always me that loses my temper, Evie's always good.'

'Hey, you're good too. No, it definitely, definitely was not to do with either of you. Grown-ups fall out of love sometimes and sometimes, well, there's nothing that can be done to change that.' That and the fact that your father was having an affair. Biting her tongue, Chrissy held her breath, she would not say that. She would not tell Sophia the truth about her father. She didn't need to know what he had done to her, to them. Plus, Sophia was obviously upset that he had moved on so quickly, she didn't need to know how long his relationship with Susan had really been going on.

'I was a bit mean to Susan.' Looking at the end of her sleeves, Sophia picked a loose thread.

'It's OK, we all get cross sometimes.'

'It was her fault that Daddy changed his mind about letting me get some things for my room.'

'Susan hasn't got any children, has she?'

Shaking her head, Sophia took a sip of hot chocolate, immediately wiping the cream from her lips.

'Well, I wonder if she just doesn't know how to behave properly around you two yet. I wonder if she's trying to come across as the parent, trying to teach you right from wrong but is coming over as too harsh. She's probably just as worried about all the new changes as you are. I mean, she's gone from having to only worry about herself to suddenly having you and Evie over every other weekend. She's probably just finding it really tough to know how to behave in front of you both.'

'Do you think?'

'Yes, I do.'

'Do you think I was too harsh on her then? She told me that I wasn't showing Daddy any respect so I said that she wasn't showing you any because she'd started going out with Daddy so soon after you both splitting up.'

'No, I don't think you were too harsh. I think you were probably cross at the way your dad and her had let you down about buying those things and you took it out on her.'

Sophia looked into her mug. 'I think I shouted, like really loud, in her face.'

'I'm sure it will all be forgotten about by the time you go again.'

'It's not really Susan that I'm angry with.'

'No?'

'It's Daddy. I actually feel like throwing up when I think about what he's done. When I'm there, at his new house, with her, my tummy hurts and I can't stop feeling like I'm going to cry.'

'Oh, sweetheart. It will get easier. It will all get easier. Just give it a bit of time and before you know it, going to Daddy and Susan's house every other weekend will feel normal.' Pulling her in tighter, Chrissy kissed the top of Sophia's head. Her hair smelt different, she must have showered using Susan's shampoo. Straightening up, Chrissy used her other hand to squeeze at her temples.

'It won't. He's gone and replaced us with a girlfriend and soon, you'll do the same.'

'He hasn't replaced you. You're his girl, he'll never replace you. He's just moved on from me, that's all. And we want him to be happy, don't we? He'd be rather lonely living most of the time by himself otherwise, wouldn't he?'

'I guess so.'

'And what do you mean, I will too?'

'You'll get a new boyfriend and then things will change around here too. It won't just be the three of us.'

'Hey, if I do ever meet someone new, they wouldn't change what we have. I might love them, but nowhere near what I feel for you and your sister. And I certainly wouldn't move anyone in here, not until after a very long time.'

'It would be weird if you met someone though, wouldn't it? I mean, we'd end up living with a total stranger.' Sophia looked up at Chrissy, her eyes glistening with tears. 'You won't, will you? You won't meet someone else, not for a very long time at least, will you?'

'Hey, nothing and nobody would ever come between us. We're the three musketeers, remember?'

Nodding, Sophia rested her head against Chrissy's side. 'I don't have to apologise, do I?'

'No, by the sounds of it things were blown out of proportion and it wasn't fair the way they both changed their minds about letting you get some things for your room. Don't even give it all a second thought. Daddy and Susan have probably forgotten all about it already.'

'OK.'

'But if you do get upset again, for any reason, just ring me. I'm always at the end of the phone, whether it's during the day or three o'clock in the morning, I'm your mum and I'll answer. And I can even come and pick you up if you want me to, OK?'

'OK.'

'Now, why don't you get in your pyjamas while I go downstairs and make you a fresh hot choccie and then we can snuggle down on the sofa and have a film night?'

With both Evie and Sophia upstairs getting changed, Chrissy stepped out into the garden, pulling her cardie tight around her against the cold. Taking a deep breath, she pressed the call button.

Three rings and he picked up. 'Chrissy. What do you want?'

'I think you probably know exactly why I've rung, Andrew.' Keeping her voice steady, she was determined not to get drawn into an argument.

'Is this about Sophia? Honestly, I don't know what's wrong with that girl, she was out of control here. Her behaviour has really deteriorated since you've moved there.'

'Seriously? She's a ten-year-old child whose parents have recently split up and she's been dragged from the only home she's ever known and been made to join a new school away from a secure friendship group. To be honest, I think she's coping pretty well.'

'Yes, well, it's no excuse. You can't let her act out like this. She'll turn into one of those unruly teenagers and then things will be even harder.'

'She had an outburst, that's all. And by the sounds

of it, you asked for it. They've told me that you went back on a promise to take her out to buy some bits for her room.'

'Yes, I admit I should never have said yes in the first place and, yes, I did go back on a promise but that was only because she should have got some things when I offered and when Evie got them. She'd been in a mood that weekend too.'

'She's a child. A child who is trying to get to grips with her new reality of having to have split homes. You've got to give her time to adjust. You might be settled and all happy with the situation, but then again, we all know that you've been planning this probably since you started your affair with Susan. The kids don't know that you were seeing her behind my back, they think you've only just got together with her. You need to give them time to adjust.' How many times did she have to say it?

'Maybe.'

'Maybe? Definitely. And the poor thing poured her heart out to you by telling you how she'd felt that first weekend. I just don't understand how you could have been so callous, so uncaring, towards your own daughter.'

'I am not callous or uncaring. I love them both very much.'

'Then start showing it, Andrew, before you damage your relationship with them by trying to impress your mistress.' Leaning her forehead against the glass of the back door, she let the icy cold begin to dull her throbbing head.

'That's not fair.'

'Isn't it?' Why couldn't he see what was happening? 'I understand it must be difficult for you, and her, but you both need to show a bit more understanding towards the kids. They didn't ask for this. They don't deserve to be caught up in whatever is going on between you two.'

'What do you mean by that?'

'Like I said, you trying to impress her and her trying to work out how to have two ten-year-olds around the place. Just sort it out before they come again and, for goodness' sake, let poor Sophia get a few bits to make her bedroom at yours more homely. It's not fair on her.'

'For your information, Susan and I have already decided that we'll take her shopping for some things next time they come, but it's still no excuse for her shouting at Susan the way she did.'

'OK. I'm going to go now. I'm glad you've sorted it.' Pressing the end call button, Chrissy drew in a sharp breath of icy cold air. What had happened to him?

She shook her head, she could see why Sophia had felt that he was putting Susan before her. Chrissy wouldn't let them get hurt. Well, any more hurt anyway.

Returning to the kitchen, she let the warmth envelop her and switched the kettle on. Her mobile pinged, announcing a text. Andrew always had had the habit of having to get the last word in. She supposed it made him feel as though he'd won the argument somehow.

Slowly, she spooned the hot chocolate powder into their mugs and watched as the boiling water poured from the kettle, dissolving the tiny granules and turning the water a rich, velvety brown. Only after she'd sprayed the cream on top, twirling the can around and around to make perfect little peaks did she relent and take her mobile out of her back pocket. She wouldn't give him the satisfaction of replying, but a part of her wanted to know what he'd written.

Chrissy straightened her back and leant against the work surface. It wasn't Andrew. It was Luke.

Luke: Fancy meeting for lunch tomo?

Pinching the bridge of her nose, she slumped her shoulders.

Chrissy: No. Sorry

She shook her head and joined the girls in the living room.

* * *

'All ready?' After pulling the throw up higher around them, Chrissy pressed play, the familiar Christmas tunes signifying the start of their favourite festive film. This was what life was about, her and her girls. No one else.

Luke had been a good distraction, and, yes, she had felt something for him, but she needed to focus on her girls now. They needed her, and by the way Sophia had spoken earlier, Chrissy getting a boyfriend would just make things harder for them.

Reaching forward and placing her now empty mug on the coffee table, Chrissy wrapped her arms around Evie and Sophia's shoulders. She had probably meant nothing to him anyway. Colin had hinted that Luke was a bit of a womaniser and he himself had said he used to sleep around. No, there was nothing going on between them anyway. There couldn't be.

13

'Did you both have a good day at school?' Smiling, Chrissy rubbed her hands together, she should have brought her gloves.

'It was OK.' Sophia shifted her rucksack higher onto her shoulders and Evie nodded. 'Can we watch a film when we get home?'

'Later, you can. But we're going to pop by the cottage to chuck your bags in and pick up Star. I've been working on Natalie's wedding dress so I've not had the chance to take her out yet.'

'Do we have to? We've been at school all day.' Sophia dragged her shoes on the ground as they walked out of the playground.

'I'm afraid so, Sophia. We can just pop to the green

and play ball with her for a few minutes, that'll tire her out anyway.'

'Good idea, Mum. We can take her new ball, can't we? She's not seen that yet!'

'Evie, she's not going to take any notice of a new ball. It's just the same as her other ones anyway.' Sophia rolled her eyes.

'Yes, she will. It will smell new so she'll be able to tell.'

* * *

'That's it, Star. Good girl.' Bending down, Evie retrieved the soggy tennis ball from Star's mouth and threw it again. 'Oh, look. There's Adam.'

'So what?' Sophia glanced across at him as he emerged through the narrow gateway, almost entirely hidden by conifers.

'So he's got a basketball, he might be going to play. Mum, can I go and join him?'

'Yes, that's fine. Come on, Sophia.' Chrissy linked arms with Sophia and followed Evie.

'Hey, Adam!' Waving her arms, Evie tried to catch his attention. 'He's got Kane and Luke with him. Do you think Luke is going to join in too? He was so funny when we went sledging.'

'So he has.' Looking down at her feet, Chrissy plastered a smile on her face. She couldn't very well retreat now.

'You like basketball, Sophia. Why don't you go and join in?' Chrissy watched as Evie ran towards Adam, immediately trying to take control of the basketball. 'Look, it's one against two. Go and give your sister a hand.'

'OK.' Sophia trudged towards the court, pushing her shoulders back as she got closer. She enjoyed basketball. In their old home, she'd begged Andrew to put a hoop up in the back garden. He never had. Now they had this basketball court just around the corner from them maybe they could come and play regularly.

'Hi, Chrissy.' Luke sidled up to her.

'Hi.' Shielding her eyes from the low winter sun, Chrissy watched as Sophia took charge of the basketball and shot a hoop on her first try.

'She's good, isn't she?'

'She sure is. She loves basketball.' Chrissy smiled.

Luke cleared his throat. 'How come you stood me up for lunch?'

'Sorry, I just had loads to do. I've almost finished sewing the crystals on to Natalie's bodice though.' She stretched her fingers out, they were still painful from sewing for five hours straight.

'That's OK then. I thought you were getting cold feet.' Luke glanced at her and smiled.

'What do you mean?'

'I mean, I thought we were at the beginning of something good.' Luke nudged her and grinned.

'Right.' Momentarily closing her eyes, Chrissy bit her bottom lip. So she *had* meant something to him then? And she couldn't deny how much her feelings were developing for him. She shook her head. It didn't matter anyway. Sophia needed to get used to how things were now before she could even think about starting a relationship with anyone. She looked at Luke, he deserved to know what was going on, but not here, not in front of the kids.

'Come on then.'

'What?'

'You may have beaten me at sledging, but I'll buy you a whole gallon of gin and tonic if you beat me at basketball!' Grabbing her by the hand, Luke pulled Chrissy onto the court. 'OK, kids, boys against girls?'

* * *

Leaning over, her hands on her knees, Chrissy panted. Why was she so unfit? She had been more active since moving to the village.

'Chrissy, are you struggling? I told you I'd beat you at this.' Patting her on the shoulder as he ran past, Luke laughed at her.

'Come on, Mum. You're making us lose. You keep giving the basketball away.' Sophia pointed to Adam as he threw the ball through the hoop again.

'Tell you what, girls, I'll go on your team and your mum can slow Adam and Kane down.'

'Yay! With Sophia, we'll win now!'

'Thanks, Evie.' Standing up, Chrissy ran after Sophia who was now in possession of the ball. 'The game's not over yet!'

'Go on, Sophia! Score!'

'Yay! Well done.' Luke high-fived Sophia as they watched the ball bounce on the tarmac after flying through the hoop. 'I'm going to take Adam and Kane to the pub for dinner later, did you want to join us?'

'Yes, OK. Why not?' Just because there couldn't be anything serious between them, at least until the girls had settled into their new life, it didn't mean she wasn't allowed friends. 'Is Natalie and Graham coming too?'

'Nope, Graham's working late and Natalie has gone swanning off with Gina to finalise flower choices or something.'

* * *

'Here you go, kids.' Returning from the bar, Luke slid a tray full of bowls of ice cream onto the table.

'Ooh, that looks good.' Chrissy helped him dish them out.

'And we have sprinkles, marshmallows, chocolate chunks and sauces to customise them with.' Grinning, he placed bowls and sauces in the middle of the table.

'That's awesome!' Sophia leant over, peering into the bowls of toppings. 'I'm going to make the best ice cream ever!'

'Shall we have a competition? We could all create our own ice creams, and Mum and Luke, you two can be the judges.'

'Yes, great idea, Evie.' Adam clapped his hands together.

'I'm happy with the job of being a judge. As long as I get to taste them all, that is.' Chrissy laughed.

'Same here.' Luke smiled across at Chrissy and winked.

Returning the smile, Chrissy wrapped her hands around her hot chocolate. He was so good with Sophia and Evie. He seemed so natural around them. Chrissy watched as he helped Kane squeeze strawberry sauce into his bowl. She knew he had a lot of experience with Adam and Kane, from what he'd said he babysat them regularly and he was equally good with the twins.

She looked up and caught his eye. It was just too soon. Far too soon. Not for her, she and Andrew had hardly spent any time together in the same room, let alone touched for months before he announced his affair, but for the girls and, in particular, Sophia, it was. She'd made that clear when she'd got back from Andrew's house. Chrissy wouldn't put her feelings before her daughters'. And if that meant that Luke decided she wasn't worth waiting for or found someone else in the meantime, then so be it. It would be their Team of Three against the world. She had to, and would, put her girls first.

* * *

'It's OK, I'll get these.' Luke put his hand over Chrissy's purse as they stood at the bar.

'No, thank you, but no. I'd rather get mine and the girls'.'

'Are you sure?'

'Yes. Thanks for inviting us though, they've had fun.' Looking back at the table, Chrissy watched as the children all finished eating their ice cream, adding the leftover topping to their melted concoctions. She laughed as Evie looked around the pub before holding her bowl down to be licked out by Star. 'There you go, even Star has benefited from us coming out.'

Laughing, Luke touched her hand. 'Are you free tomorrow for lunch? I've got to go to a couple of house auctions in the morning but I should be back by about one or half one at the latest.'

'I can't tomorrow, sorry. I'm going round Natalie's for a fitting.' She bit her bottom lip, she had to tell him that they had to cool it off, but she really was busy tomorrow. 'Maybe later in the week?'

'Already looking forward to it.'

The children ran on ahead, Star running alongside them, barking excitedly every few minutes.

'I might be able to help you out with that heating, if it's still not working? I've organised for my mate, Brian, who's a gas engineer to come and service Natalie and Graham's boiler so I can ask him to pop by yours after, if you like?'

'OK, that'd be great, please?'

'OK, I'll speak to him then. He owes me a favour.'

'Thank you. I really do appreciate it.' Chrissy looked up at him, his ash blonde hair had fallen forward, half covering his left eye. She reached up and flicked it back. 'Are you growing it?'

Running his hands through his hair, Luke grinned. 'Why? Do you like it a bit longer?'

'I think it looks nice either way.' She wasn't going to tell him that he could shave it all off and tattoo his scalp and he'd still look just as gorgeous.

'I might do. It would save me bothering with the barbers anyway. Right, I'd better get these two home before Natalie thinks I've abducted them.' Luke paused at the end of Chrissy's lane.

'Yep. We'd best get back too. See you.' Walking towards the green where the children were now playing, Chrissy looked back at Luke.

'Hey, wait up.' Running the short distance, Luke caught up with her. 'I have really enjoyed this evening.'

'Me too.' Looking across at him, she smiled and cleared her throat. 'Right, come on, girls. Time for home.'

'OK. See you at school tomorrow, Adam. Bye, Kane.' Evie ran towards Chrissy, Star trotting by her ankles and Sophia sauntering just behind.

After waving their goodbyes, Chrissy and the twins turned down the lane towards Corner Cottage.

'Did you have fun, girls?' Ramming her hand into

her pocket, Chrissy located the key and hoped the wood burner was still going strong.

'Yes, it was great. I really liked making our own ice creams.' Kneeling down, Evie petted Star as she waited for Chrissy to open the front door.

'How about you, Sophia? Did you enjoy playing basketball with the others?'

'Yes, Adam's pretty good at it actually and it was funny when Luke swapped with you to come on our team.'

'I still maintain it was the cold that made me so rubbish. I couldn't shoot the ball through the hoop properly because my hands were so cold.' Laughing, Chrissy held the door open, waiting for the twins and Star to slip through before she followed and shut the cold out. She slipped her coat off, the wood burner must still be on. She'd have to check there were enough logs on it. If it went out, the cold would quickly creep back in and once it was in it was hard to warm the thick walls of the cottage again.

'Mum, where's my blanket?' Evie popped her head around the living room door.

Hanging up Star's lead, Chrissy turned around. 'On your bed. Why don't you get changed while you're up there and I'll make us a hot chocolate.'

'OK.'

'Evie, can you ask Sophia to get in her pyjamas too?'

'Will do.' Twisting around, Evie ran back into the living room.

Opening the front door, Chrissy bashed the twins boots together, clumps of mud flying off onto the cracked path. She looked up, the stars were really clear here, not like in their old place which, at the time, she had thought were pretty clear. But here, the sky was like glass, the stars as bright as the crystals she'd painstakingly sewn onto Natalie's wedding dress. They should get a map of the sky and learn what the names of the constellations were called. Maybe, when it got warmer, they could get some garden chairs and sit outside in the evenings, seeing how many constellations and stars they could name.

Glancing up the lane towards the road, she watched as a car slowly drove past, its headlights highlighting the empty street. It was idyllic here. The people all seemed to be welcoming, although they were probably just glad that someone had eventually rented out Corner Cottage instead of it standing empty. The girls were settling into school, even if Sophia liked to remind her what a cruel mother she was for taking her away from her friends at regular intervals throughout the week. She, herself, had actually made a few friends, most were just other parents at the school gate that she could practise her small talk on, but Natalie and, even Gina, were becoming more than just casual acquaintances.

And Luke, well, maybe there could be something there. Sophia had said he was 'fun'. Maybe if they just kept it quiet, which she'd want to anyway, things could work out. She didn't want to introduce them to anyone unless she was completely sure there was a future there and a long future at that. So if they kept it quiet for six months or so, Sophia would probably have gotten used to the idea of her getting a boyfriend. Plus, if they met up with Luke when he was looking after Kane and Adam like they had tonight, then hopefully things would naturally just fall into place. The twins would get used to him being around as a friend and so if they announced they were seeing each other it wouldn't seem so strange.

Placing the boots down and pulling the front door behind her, she made her way down the path and tugged the gate shut. She was sure Star wouldn't wander off, but if she saw a cat there was still that chance.

She shook her head and pulled her cardie tighter around her. She'd panicked when Sophia had come back from Andrew's so upset about him living with

Susan. Luke wasn't Susan, Luke hadn't broken their marriage up and the twins could just view him as a family friend for now. If they still hadn't come round to the idea when they told them after six months, then that would be it. The girls always came first.

Maybe she should give him a call when the girls had gone to bed, let him know that, yes, she did want more but to keep it under wraps until they were sure there was a future? Yes, she'd call him later. At least that way she could find out what was going on from his point of view too.

14

'I don't know what to say, it's stunning. I love it.' Natalie clasped her hands in front of her as Chrissy unzipped the gown bag hanging on the doorframe.

'The crystals and beading make all the difference, don't they?' Gina ran her fingers over the bodice.

'Do you want to go and put it on and then we check to see if there are any other alterations that need doing?' Chrissy breathed a sigh of relief, she'd hardly slept a wink last night and when she'd managed to snatch an hour here or there, she'd woken up in a cold sweat, images of Natalie crying because she hated it or in her most extreme vivid dream, Chrissy had woken up convinced that Natalie had burnt the dress right in front of her, insisting that she had asked Chrissy to dye it black.

'You try and stop me!' Standing on her tiptoes, Natalie gently unhooked the hanger and made her way out of the family room.

'It really is beautiful, Chrissy. You've got a real talent there.'

'Thank you. I just hope it fits OK.' Chrissy smiled and looked down at Poppy who was kicking away in a Winne-the-Pooh bouncy chair. 'Are you all ready for when your little one makes an appearance?'

'We've got most of the big things stored in the loft from Olivia, so I think we're pretty much set. Or we will be when the new flooring for the nursery is fitted. Although I have started to look at prams. I had convinced myself that I didn't need a new one but my old one is so plain, so I think we might get a new one.' Gina rubbed her bump.

'At least you've already got most of what you need.'

'Yes. It's certainly easier the second time around. Here she is. Oh, wow, Nat, you look gorgeous.'

Turning around, Chrissy watched as Natalie walked towards her. She did look gorgeous, the ivory gown fitted her like a glove, clinging to all of the right places, the crystals and glass beads shimmered under the lights, emphasising the beautiful cut of the heart neckline. The train flowed behind her, the flowery lace overlay adding just enough detail.

'Chrissy, I completely, absolutely love it! I don't know how you've done it, but you've turned that shapeless, plain gown into the dress I've been dreaming of for so long. Thank you!' Holding Chrissy's shoulders, Natalie kissed her on the cheek before stepping back and slowly twirling around.

'So how does it feel? Is the length OK? Is there anything you want me to add or change?' Kneeling down, Chrissy pulled the fabric taut before letting go. The length looked good, any shorter and Natalie's shoes would be visible, any longer and it would catch on the heels.

'Nothing. I wouldn't ask you to change anything at all. It's lovely as it is.'

'The length looks fine. Are you sure you're happy with it?'

'More than happy!'

'OK, brilliant.' Stepping back, Chrissy folded her arms. She had done a good job, even she, as self-critical as she was, could see it was a vast improvement from the dress it had once been.

'I'm going to go and change again and then I'll make us a cuppa.'

Grinning, Natalie made her way back out of the room.

* * *

'Here you go, Chrissy, Gina.'

'Thank you.' Taking the hot mug, Chrissy shifted across, making room for Natalie on the brown leather sofa.

'OK, I need to ask you a favour. Well, another one that is, Chrissy, please?'

Chrissy lowered her mug and nodded.

'I got the bridesmaid dresses back in, when was it, Gina? About March time I think and they were all fitted and were fine, but one of my bridesmaids has recently been on a diet and been hitting the gym and, well, it just hangs off her. I've not actually seen her wearing it for ages now, but from what she says it just doesn't fit properly any more. So, I was wondering, and say no if you don't want to, but would you be able to alter that too please?'

'Yes, I should think so.'

'Really? I know it's really short notice and it's only another few weeks until the wedding but obviously, I'd pay you for it.'

'Honestly, it's fine. I'll be happy to.' Chrissy smiled,

the more work she did, the better it would be for her business when she got around to setting it up.

'Whose dress is that? I thought your old dress-maker got them all altered before she went?' Gina curled her legs up under her on the sofa and took a biscuit from a plate Natalie had placed on the footstool.

'It's Laura, since she split from Phil she's been spending all her spare time at the gym. I've not seen her for a few months now, since the last fitting for the bridesmaid dresses, but from what she's said she's lost a lot of weight and the dress isn't fitting any more.'

'I didn't think she had any weight to lose anyway.'

'No, she didn't really, but since Phil left her, she seems to have something to prove.'

'I wish the same could be said of me.' Laughing, Chrissy pinched her belly. 'Ever since me and my ex split, I've been cramming the comfort food down.'

'I'm the same, I mean, I was before I met Graham.' Natalie slid onto the floor, shaking a toy above Poppy's head.

'I bet Luke's happy that she's single again.' Gina laughed and rubbed her bump.

Natalie glanced at Chrissy and back down to Poppy. 'I don't think he's interested any more. It was a long time ago now.'

Chrissy took a biscuit, what did Laura have to do with Luke? She shook her head, they probably knew each other, especially if she was one of Natalie's old school friends or someone she had known for a long time, Luke would have met her.

'I guess it was, but the way he was after she'd dumped him. Do you not think he'll want her back now she's split from Phil?'

Of course, Laura, Chrissy was sure she'd recognised the name. Laura was Luke's ex, the one he'd moved to London and lived with. They'd been together for, what, five, six years, she couldn't remember now, but it had been a serious relationship and then she'd left him for her ex, possibly this Phil bloke.

'No, he's over her.' Natalie looked at the floor.

Taking a bite from her biscuit, Chrissy caught the crumbs in the palm of her hand. Natalie thought Luke still liked her, that was obvious. But he didn't, did he? She knew that he wanted to be with her, not Laura or anyone else. When she had rung him last night, he had said he wanted them to be serious. To give things a real go. She smiled, he'd been so understanding when she'd explained how she'd wanted to keep their relationship to themselves for six months, until they were sure there was a future for them. He'd even suggested they keep meeting up when he had Adam and

Kane so the girls could get to know him without there being any pressure.

Natalie must have it wrong. Maybe Luke hadn't told her about him and Chrissy. After all, she had said she wanted to keep it between them so the twins didn't hear about it on the grapevine. She'd expected him to tell his sister though. And the way she kept glancing at Chrissy when she spoke about Laura suggested she knew. She shrugged, there was no point reading into signs that probably didn't exist. Luke had told her he wanted to be in a relationship with her, that was enough.

'But she the one that after she dumped him he went a bit weird, wasn't it?'

'Weird? What do you mean?' Chrissy jerked her head towards Gina, cricking her neck.

'Oh, you probably don't know.' Gina leant forward, getting ready to spill the gossip. 'Luke, Natalie's brother, met this girl Laura, fell in love and moved to London with her. He gave up his job, his house here. Everything. So, of course, when she dumped him a few years later, he came back and stayed with you, didn't he, Natalie? And he became a bit of a recluse for a while. He was really cut up about her.'

'A recluse is a bit of an exaggeration.' Natalie looked across at Chrissy again and seemed to stop before taking a deep breath and carrying on. 'He was young and had given up everything he'd known so he could move to the City and start a new life with her and, well, when her ex, Phil, moved near them, Laura must have fallen for him again and broke up with Luke.'

'Yes, and then he came to stay with you and became a recluse. You wouldn't know it now, he's, like, one of the most outgoing, confident people you'll meet, but she really knocked him off his feet for a while, didn't she, Nat?'

'He was really upset, yes. But he was young and a lot has happened since then. He's completely over her now.'

'I don't know. Does he know she's one of your bridesmaids?'

'Of course, he does. He knows we're still really good friends and he's fine with it. He's been there when a group of us have been out before, so it's not as though he's not seen her for years. He has.'

'But, does he know she's single again?' Gina took a final sip of her tea before placing her mug on the coffee table.

'Yes, I told him.'

'But he's not seen her since she's been single, has he?'

'No, but that doesn't mean anything.' Glancing back at Chrissy, Natalie bit her bottom lip.

'I wouldn't be so sure. Luke is Graham's Best Man and his ex is one of your bridesmaids. And she's fit, not that she wasn't when they were together, but now she's even fitter.' Gina clasped her hands in front of her. 'It might be your wedding, but I bet you and Graham won't be the only lovebirds there.'

'Gina!' Natalie stood up. 'Who wants another cuppa?'

Chrissy cleared her throat. 'I'm going to have to get going, thanks anyway though. There's a couple of bits I need to do before I pick the girls up.'

'OK, I'll see you out. Gina, can you just keep an eye on Poppy for me, please?'

'Sure.' Gina knelt down next to the play mat, taking over Natalie's job of waving toys above Poppy's head, her small hands desperately trying to grasp them.

* * *

'Don't take any notice of Gina. She always gets excited if there's any potential gossip coming her way.' Natalie patted Chrissy's arm as she opened the front door. 'Luke and Laura were over years ago and they're both completely different people now. It's best to just take anything Gina says with a pinch of salt.'

'OK. Well, thanks for the tea and biscuits.'

'No, thank you for finishing my dress for me. It's so beautiful, I don't know what I would have done without you coming to the rescue.'

'You're welcome. I've enjoyed it, to be honest. It's got my creative juices flowing again.'

'Luke said that you're hoping to start up your own business as a dressmaker?'

'Yes.' Looking down, Chrissy hoped the heat filling her cheeks wouldn't show. 'I'm hoping to.'

'I think that's a great idea. Especially being as the only local-ish dressmaker we had has gone over to Spain now, there'll be a good market for it.'

'Hopefully.'

'Hey, I've just thought, are you going to set up a business page on social media? If so, you're more than welcome to include before and after pictures of my wedding dress, and Laura's bridesmaid dress. I've got a photo of what mine was like on me before you worked your magic and I can get Gina to take some of me now if I pop it on again, if you like?'

'That's a great idea. Are you sure you don't mind?'

'Of course not. I'll send you the photos later.'

'OK thanks.' Smiling, she stepped outside, immediately plunging her hands into her pockets against the bitter cold. She'd have to remember to pick up her gloves from off the radiator before she did the school run.

'Bye.' Natalie waved before shutting the door.

At the bottom of the driveway, Chrissy paused, she wanted to go and see Luke and ask him how he felt about Laura, but that would just make her look needy. Plus, according to Natalie, he knew Laura was a bridesmaid so he was aware he would be seeing her again soon, and he still wanted to be with Chrissy. He'd made that obvious in the conversation last night. He didn't have to, he could have said he wasn't sure, hedged his bets until he'd seen Laura again.

Chrissy shook her head and turned towards Corner Cottage. She was being silly, she knew she was. Not all men were still secretly in love with their exes. Exes were exes for a reason. She needed to get over the trust issues Andrew had left her with, and quickly, before they spoilt things with Luke.

She knew she was reading too much into this, so why did she still have that uneasy feeling in the pit of her stomach?

15

'Bye, girls. Have a lovely day.' Much to their disgust, Chrissy kissed Evie and Sophia on the tops of their heads and watched them walk into school.

'Hey, Chrissy.'

Twisting around, Chrissy smiled. 'Luke. What are you doing here?'

'Dropping off Adam and Kane. Nat's panicking over her housework.'

'Oh, why? Her house is normally really tidy anyway.'

'She's got one of her bridesmaids coming. Although I've told her, friends who can't see past a cobweb or two, not that she has any, aren't real friends anyway.'

'Of course.' He was referring to Laura. Why didn't he just say her name? Did he not realise that she knew his ex was coming down to have her bridesmaid dress fitted today?

'It's you altering her dress, isn't it?' Grinning, he slapped his forehead as if only just realising.

'Yep.'

'Right.' Luke nodded. 'Did you want to catch a quick coffee before you go?'

'Why not?'

Walking towards Luke's house, they were careful not to walk too closely until they were away from the playground. Once around the corner, Luke linked arms with her.

'It's so difficult not to kiss you when I see.' Leaning across, he whispered in her ear.

'Same here. Thank you for being so under-standing though.'

'It's OK. I think you're doing the right thing. I'd like to think I'd be just as protective if I had my own kids.'

'Do you want children of your own then?' Chrissy twisted a loose piece of hair around her fingers and looked down, feeling a hot blush speeding towards her cheeks. Why had she even uttered those words?

'Sorry, you don't have to answer that. I didn't mean with me, I just meant in general.'

'It's OK.' Laughing, Luke was apparently immune to such personal questions. 'I would, yes. Just not right now.'

'Well, obviously.' Chrissy laughed, trying to make light of the conversation.

'I have thought a lot about it recently. Maybe it's because I'm getting older or spending more time with Adam and Kane, I don't know. But I do know that I'd like to be a dad one day. I just want to get a few more property renovations under my belt so I can be taken seriously in this business. But in a couple of years, maybe.'

'Sorry for the personal question, it just kind of tumbled out after you said about being just as protective over your own kids. I didn't mean anything by it.'

'You mean you don't want my children? I'm deeply offended.' Holding the palm of his hand against his heart, he laughed at her.

'No, I... You're teasing me now.' Taking her glove off, Chrissy threw it at him.

Pulling her into his front garden, he held her in his arms and looked down at her. 'I would love to have your children one day, or more precisely, I would love you to have my children one day.'

'Yes, that might be easier than you being the first man to bear a child. Unless, of course, it's your life's ambition to be a scientific breakthrough?'

'Nah, I'll leave all that childbirth and pain stuff to you. It would be wrong to take it away from women.'

'You'd be too scared, you mean.' Laughing, she wrapped her arms around his neck, standing on her tiptoes until their lips touched.

* * *

'It's such a shame you've got to go to Natalie's. Why don't you tell her you're too busy entertaining her brother to sort her bridesmaid's dress out?' Leaning down to Chrissy as she sat at the breakfast bar, he kissed the back of her neck.

'Believe me, I'd love to but it's the only day Laura's down.'

'Of course, it is.' Straightening up, Luke walked towards the kettle. 'Have you got time for that coffee before you go?'

'Yes, that'd be nice.' Had she imagined it or had he just distanced himself as soon as she'd mentioned Laura's name?

'Here you go, freshly ground coffee, straight out of

the jar.' Grinning, Luke passed her a dark blue mug and slipped onto a stool next to her.

'Thank you. As long as it's strong, that's all I care about.' Smiling, she pulled the steaming mug towards her.

'Aren't you sleeping? Too busy thinking about me?'

'That must be it.' Chrissy laughed. 'I've been sleeping just fine, I think it must be the country air wearing me out.'

* * *

Smoothing her hair down and plastering a smile on her face, Chrissy knocked on the door. She hadn't noticed the bright blue two-seater sports car parked outside before, it must be Laura's.

'Hi, Chrissy. Come on in.' Opening the front door, Natalie jiggled Poppy on her hip.

'Hi. Hello, Poppy.' Stepping inside, Chrissy stroked Poppy's cheek and laughed as she immediately tried to clutch her tiny fingers around Chrissy's. 'You've got a strong grip, haven't you, Poppy?'

'She has, believe me. Only this morning she got hold of a clump of my hair in her death grip. She almost scalped me!'

'Ouch!'

'Here, come on through.'

'OK.' Although Gina's presence always made Chrissy feel a little uneasy and ungainly next to her delicate features and tailored clothes, she was glad she was here today.

'Laura, this is Chrissy.' Laying Poppy on her play mat, Natalie indicated to Laura and back to Chrissy.

'Chrissy! I'm so glad you could make it today. I have been seriously going out of my mind with worry over this dress. I really don't want to let Nat and Graham down by following her down the aisle looking like an oversized strawberry.' Laura stood up from the dining table and turned to face Chrissy, her long glossy blonde hair flicking around with her before dribbling down her back in perfect curls. Her slender, but muscly, figure was shown off under a simple tight-fitting white T-shirt and navy jeans, her lightly bronzed skin shining healthily under Natalie's light.

'Nice to meet you.' Chrissy took Laura's hand, grimacing as she compared her own nails to Laura's pale pink manicured ones.

'Nat showed me her wedding gown, the transformation is magical. I'm hoping you'll be able to do something as inspiring to mine. At the moment I do look awful, it just hangs off me.'

'I'll do my best.' Chrissy bit her tongue, it must be awful, as Laura put it, to have a dress 'hang off' her. As she watched Laura glide out of the room, she pulled on the waistband of her own ill-fitting jeans trying to loosen them a little. She seemed to be putting weight on rather than losing it. She'd hoped she'd lose some weight naturally now that she was using her car less and walking more. She was obviously doing something wrong.

'Here you go.'

'Thanks.' Taking the mug from Natalie, she took a sip and let the hot liquid swirl around her mouth. Laura was gorgeous, there was no other way to describe her, she seemed perfect. She was beautiful and seemed kind too, which was often a rare combination.

'I'm coming in. Please don't laugh at me.' Laura called from the other side of the door before walking in.

Chrissy swallowed hard, the deep red of the dress complemented Laura's pale features, the satin fabric highlighting her curves and svelte body.

'Wow. Laura, you look stunning.' Natalie looked at Gina and whispered loudly out of the side of her mouth. 'Remind me why I chose Laura to be a bridesmaid, she's going to upstage me.'

'Don't, Nat. I know you're only trying to make me

feel better. But look, I look dreadful. It's just hanging in all the wrong places and look...' Pinching about an inch of loose fabric from around her waist, Laura's cheeks reddened, her eyes glistening with tears.

'Laura, don't cry. You do look gorgeous, because you are, but Chrissy will work her magic on the bits you don't like about your dress, won't you, Chrissy?'

'I will indeed.' Placing her mug on the table, she took out her pincushion from her handbag. 'I can see the fabric needs bringing in a bit around the waist.' She began gently holding the loose fabric on both sides of the dress and pinning it. 'How does that feel?'

'So much better already.' Smiling, the redness from Laura's cheeks vanished as she smoothed the dress against her hips with the palms of her hands.

'OK, let's see what else we need to do.' Stepping back, Chrissy surveyed her. The bodice, a sweetheart neckline to match Natalie's, drooped down a little to the right for some reason. Whether the previous dressmaker had only taken it in on the left or whether there was another reason, Chrissy wasn't sure. 'The way the bodice lays seems a little uneven to me.'

'That's what I said to Natalie's previous dress-maker but she blamed my eyes.' Laura shrugged the bodice a little higher.

'It's nothing I can't fix. It may take a little longer

than the waist though because it's a little more fiddly so make sure you're comfortable.' Chrissy began pinning the bodice.

'So, Nat, what have I missed? I feel as though I haven't seen you guys for ages. Last time we met up, little Poppy had only just been born.'

'Not much really, you know how it is. Graham's busy with work, I'm busy with trying to keep on top of this place.'

'And how about Luke? How's he doing?'

Chrissy followed Laura's gaze as she looked at a family photo above the sofa. She'd not noticed it before. It must have been taken a few years ago. Kane was just a baby, even Luke looked a lot younger as he held his youngest nephew up next to a Christmas tree. The way both the boys were clutching presents, it looked as though they had been to visit Santa.

'He's fine. Still living around the corner. He's doing well building his property business.' Natalie picked Poppy up from her play mat where she had begun to grizzle and placed her in her bouncy chair.

'That's good then.' Laura looked down. 'I often wonder how my life would have turned out if I'd stayed with him and not gone back to Phil.'

Stepping back, Chrissy refilled her pincushion. She touched the back of her neck where Luke had last kissed her and ducked her head, hoping to shield herself from the blush she could feel rising. Laura still had feelings for Luke then, Gina had been right. She glanced quickly across at Natalie whose eyes were fixed on Poppy. Natalie knew this too. Did Luke still have feelings for Laura? What man wouldn't? Look at her. She was every man's dream.

'These things happen for a reason though, Laura.'

'I know, Nat. It just feels like the only reason me and Phil got back together was so he could waste some of what should have been the best years of my life, before publicly humiliating me by refusing to marry me when I proposed to him.'

'You proposed to him?' Gina looked up, her gossip radar on full alert.

'I did. I had waited years for him to pop the question and had convinced myself that he just didn't know how, so I took the matter into my own hands. I had planned everything meticulously, I took him to a posh restaurant near where we lived and asked the waiter to put the ring in the fondue. You know, how they do in the movies. Everything was perfect, or it would have been if he hadn't almost thrown up at the idea and stalked out of the restaurant leaving me on one knee and a violin quartet playing the Bridal Chorus.'

Gina passed her a tissue, which she used pat her eyes with. 'That's awful.'

'I know. By the time I got home, naturally after a detour of all the pubs on the way, he'd moved out. He'd taken what he needed for the next few days and left a note.'

'What did the note say?'

'Sorry. Just "sorry". Pathetic really.'

'He's the pathetic one, not you.' Standing up, Natalie wrapped her arms around Laura's slight frame.

'That's what everyone says, but it doesn't stop me feeling the stupid one for not realising something was wrong.'

'Sometimes you just don't notice though. They hide it too well. Chrissy, tell her about your ex.' Gina crossed her legs, settling back against the sofa cushions.

'Not much to tell really. We split up after he had an affair with an old school friend. I didn't know until he said that he wanted us to sell the house because he was leaving me for her. He's moved in with her now.'

'That's shocking.' Laura placed her hand on Chrissy's arm. 'How awful for you.'

'To be honest. I'm slowly realising it was the best thing that could have happened. I'm so much happier now.'

'Really?'

'Yes. It's only now, being apart from him, that I realise what he was really like. He was quite controlling and now, well, *I'm* in control. I decide what we do. I manage the money. It's all down to me, and it's quite liberating really.'

'That's really inspiring. I wish I could feel the same about my split from Phil.'

'It took some time, don't get me wrong. For ages I felt as though my world had been torn apart and shaken, but now, things are good.'

'See, so there is hope, Laura. You just need to believe in yourself a bit more.' Natalie sat back down on the floor next to Poppy's bouncy chair.

'That's what everyone says but I don't know if I'll ever get over how he treated me.'

'You will. Just give yourself time.' Natalie smiled. 'Anyway, we'll find you a new man on Friday night.'

'I don't think I can...'

'Oh, you can make it. All of the wedding party are coming. You'll come too, won't you, Chrissy?' Natalie looked across at Chrissy and smiled.

'Sorry?'

'We're all going out into town on Friday. I've booked out a room at that posh restaurant down the High Street and then we're going to hit the clubs. It'll be a laugh. Most of us haven't set foot in a club since we were teenagers!'

'I'm not sure.'

'Go on, please? I'd be wearing a bin bag to my wedding if it wasn't for you. You must come, your ex has the twins this weekend, right?'

'Yes, but...'

'No excuses then. From either of you.' Natalie looked from Chrissy to Laura and back again.

Chrissy smiled and carried on pinning the bodice. It was nice of Natalie to see her as a friend and include her, but she hadn't been out properly in years, not even to a nice restaurant. She shrugged. She should force herself to go, to step out of her comfort zone. She might actually enjoy herself. Besides, Luke would presumably be going. It would be nice for them to spend some time together.

'Is Luke going?' Laura looked across to Natalie.

Jerking her head up, Chrissy pricked her finger with a pin. Laura did want Luke back.

'Of course, he is her brother!' Gina giggled. 'I take it you want him back?'

'No, I... I just wondered. I haven't seen him in ages and it would be nice to catch up, that's all.'

'OK, whatever you say.' Gina laughed and rubbed her bump.

'Right, that's the bodice done. Is there anywhere else that you want altering?' Stepping back again, Chrissy could see there was no comparison between her and Laura. If Laura wanted Luke back, she'd get him. She'd only have to bat her mascaraed eyelashes at him and he'd be straight back to her. Chrissy bit down on her bottom lip, she wouldn't think about it now.

'No, I don't think so. It looks a hundred per cent better already.'

'Well, if you're happy with it, you can change back, just go careful with the pins, and I'll make the adjustments. If you're back here at the weekend, I'll get it done before then and if you've got a spare ten minutes you can try it on and check you're happy with it.'

'That sounds great, thank you.'

'You're welcome.'

* * *

Chucking another log on the wood burner, Chrissy sat on the rug in front of it and watched the fire dance around the new log before clutching it into the orange flames.

It was probably for the best, Laura wanting to get back with Luke. It was probably too soon for Chrissy herself to be falling for someone anyway. Yes, Andrew had, but he had been having an affair with Susan so obviously the marriage vows they had taken were meaningless to him. Chrissy wiped the back of her sleeve across her face, they had meant something to her. She had never expected to be left as single mum struggling to provide a safe and stable home for her two daughters. She and Andrew had meant to grow old together.

Running her fingers through the long pile on the rug, she let her fingers sink into the warmth of the wool. That wasn't going to happen now though, and if she were honest with herself, the thought of spending any longer in a partnership with Andrew, let alone growing old with him, made her feel sick. No, she was better off on her own. She felt far less lonely than she had when she'd been in a relationship with him anyway. It was just going to take some time to adjust to the fact that what she thought her future had looked like didn't belong to her any more.

And, after Luke met up with Laura again, he wouldn't be interested in Chrissy any more. Laura was everything she wasn't, beautiful, a successful business-woman, independent. When Luke realised Laura wanted to get back with him, he wouldn't look twice at Chrissy. Why would he settle for someone who had just as much emotional baggage as physical baggage? The not-been-cut-for-three-years hair which often got so knotty in the morning she had to tie it up in a loose bun hoping nobody would look too closely, reflected the part of her that believed she was not worthy of spending money on. She was trying to claw her way off of a future on benefits and begin her dressmaking business, but it would never earn her what Laura clearly earnt. And, yes, she was independent, but after years of being led to believe she wasn't capable of filling up the car, driving in the dark or making any decisions, she was still a long way from viewing herself as the strong, single mum she aspired to be.

No, Luke would be daft to choose her over Laura and he clearly wouldn't. Plus, Luke clearly still had feelings for Laura, he'd acted strange earlier when she'd popped round his for coffee and he hadn't wanted to say Laura's name when he'd been talking about the dress fitting.

Standing up, Chrissy grabbed her coat and gloves. Looking in the mirror before she went outside, she patted her cheeks dry. Why did she feel more upset over the thought of losing Luke than she had when Andrew had told her he didn't love her any more? She shrugged, she guessed she'd seen it coming with Andrew, whereas Luke had seemed perfect.

16

'Mum! We're going to be late if you don't hurry up!'

Wiping her mouth with a tissue, Chrissy stood up. 'One minute.'

'Come on.' Even Evie sounded impatient. They weren't usually this eager to get to school.

It was no good, Chrissy leant over the toilet bowl again and heaved. She must have caught a bug, even the smell of the twins' breakfast cereal had sent her to the bathroom earlier. And she'd had to give up trying to make their packed lunches, she'd have to root around for some change for school dinners instead.

* * *

'Love you, Evie. Love you, Sophia. Have a good day.' Waving them into the school office, Chrissy turned and pulled her gloves back on.

'Hi.'

'Luke. Hi.' Looking behind her, she contemplated making up some excuse as to why she had to go back into the office. She shook her head, she recognised the parent stood talking to the receptionist as the head of the PTA, if she did go back in she'd be there ages waiting to be seen. Plus, she couldn't avoid Luke forever. The village was only tiny, they would be constantly running into each other, until he moved back to London with Laura of course.

'Are you OK? You didn't answer my messages last night.' Touching Chrissy on the arm, Luke looked at her.

'Sorry. I've just not been feeling too good. I think I must have caught some bug or something.' Glancing down at her trainers, she looked back into his eyes, the pale blue pulling her closer. He deserved to know what was going on and so did she. 'Actually, have you got a couple of minutes? Can I have a quick word?'

'I've always got time for you, you know that. Here, come back to mine, I want to get your opinion on the suit Graham wants me to wear to their wedding, but don't laugh. It's a bit old-fashioned.' Luke frowned, his ash blond hair momentarily covering his eyes before he blew it away.

* * *

'I want your honest opinion, OK? Don't say it looks nice just so you don't offend me. I'm a big boy now, I can take criticism and I'd rather know if I'm going to be looking a numpty all day than thinking I look like James Bond, OK?' Holding her hand, Luke guided her upstairs and into his bedroom. 'Sit down and get comfy.'

Chrissy lowered herself to his bed, slipping out of her coat. This was going to be so hard, but she needed to know where she stood with him. She picked at a bit of fluff on his navy-blue duvet cover and rolled it around her fingers as he disappeared into the en suite to change into his suit.

'Close your eyes.'

Doing as she was asked, she took a deep breath in, she could smell his distinctive aftershave as he came through the door.

'Now, remember you promised not to laugh, so no going back on a promise. I don't want our relationship to be based on a lie either though, so be honest about how it looks, OK?'

Nodding, Chrissy could hear the suppressed laughter in his voice. She almost found it funny herself, only it wasn't quite so funny when she thought about him choosing Laura over her.

'Open!'

Opening her eyes, Chrissy smiled, the dark grey suit highlighted the blue of his eyes and the red cravat empathised the blonde of his hair. 'You look gorgeous.'

'Even with the top hat?' He balanced a black top hat on his head, the wave of his hair flicking out from underneath.

'Even with the hat.'

'And the tails? The tails are too much, aren't they? I feel like I've just stepped out of a Charles Dickens' novel.' Spinning around, the tails from his suit jacket flapped against the top of his legs.

'No, they're just right. You look really sexy.'

'Then why do you look as though you're worrying about something rather than trying to rip my clothes off?'

Shifting on the bed, Chrissy scratched the back of her neck.

'Chrissy?' Joining her on the bed, he put his arm around her.

'Do you really want to know?'

'I do indeed.'

'OK, well, yesterday I altered your ex's bridesmaid dress.'

'Laura's? So?'

'Luke, it's not that difficult to work out.' Chrissy pulled away from his arm and twisted herself on the bed, bringing her legs up beneath her.

'OK, maybe I'm just being daft, but I don't know where you're going with this.' Holding his hands up as if to surrender, he frowned, his forehead crumpling.

'She's beautiful.' She coughed.

'Yes, she is, but so are you.' Turning around, he looked her in the eyes and smirked. 'Are you feeling insecure?'

'No, of course not. It's hardly serious between us yet anyway. Why would I?' Looking away, Chrissy chewed on a jagged nail, Laura wouldn't have jagged nails.

'Well, that's me told, I guess.' Standing up, Luke loosened his cravat.

'I didn't mean I didn't want it to be. I just meant...' Placing her thumb and forefinger on her temples, she pressed down, hoping it would relieve a little of the tension.

'I know. I get it. You've been hurt before. Your husband left you for his ex-girlfriend. You're probably thinking I'm going to get back with Laura but, if you think about it properly, don't you think I would have got in contact with her when her boyfriend, Phil, left her?'

Chrissy looked at the floor before looking back up at him. 'I guess so. I didn't think about it like that.' But did he know she was interested in him? Should she tell him or would she just be feeding him straight into her hands?

'I'm honestly not interested in her in the slightest. You, on the other hand, I am very interested in and I thought things were getting serious between us? I know we can't tell anyone because of your girls, but I am falling for you.'

'I'm sorry I guess I just said that because I wanted you to feel like you could back out of us if you wanted to get back with her.' Chrissy drew a star with her finger on the duvet.

'I don't want to back out of anything. Now, come here and help me get out of this suit.' Luke pushed her down gently on the bed, kneeling over her.

Swallowing, Chrissy tried to stop the bile rising in her throat. It was no good. Rolling out from underneath him, she ran to the en suite.

* * *

'I'm sorry.' Sinking her back against Luke's chest, she wiped her mouth with a tissue.

'And I thought you said I looked sexy in this suit.' Gently touching her forehead, Luke kissed her on the top of her head. 'You don't feel as though you've got a temperature. Have you got a stomach ache or anything?'

'No, I just keep feeling sick. I'm sorry to kill the mood.'

'Nah, we'll just have to make the most of the suit at the wedding and find a quiet spot somewhere.'

Chrissy smiled, trust him. 'Very funny.'

'Have you had any breakfast? Maybe it's because you've not eaten.'

'No, don't.' Holding her hand over her mouth, she took a deep breath and tried to imagine the rain pelting down outside. 'Even the thought of food... no. I'll be OK. I think I'm just going to go home and have a lay down.'

'Good idea. I'll get changed and walk you back. You need to be on top form tonight for the carol service.'

'Oh yes, I'd forgotten about that.'

* * *

'Off you go to the front then, girls. Just say excuse me please and people will let you through. Love you both.' Standing on her tiptoes, Chrissy watched as Evie and Sophia made their way through the crowds to the stage set up in the middle of the green.

'Hi there, I grabbed you a hot chocolate from the stall over there.' Sidling up to her, Luke held out a Styrofoam cup.

'Hot chocolate? This village certainly knows how to organise a carol service.' Slipping her gloves off, she wrapped her hands around the cup. 'Thank you.'

'Hi, Chrissy.' Natalie and Graham joined them, Poppy strapped to Graham's front in her baby carrier. 'It's always a good show. The kids love it too, especially when the Christmas lights get turned on at the end.'

'Oh, I didn't realise that.'

'Yes, they started it a few years ago now, when Kane was a baby, I think.' Natalie looked across at Graham who nodded in agreement. 'They started off picking someone from the audience to turn them on but now they choose a couple of school kids to do it.'

'Where we used to live they always tried to get some z-lister to turn them on, you know someone who had been on some reality TV show once ten years earlier or something. It's nice that they let the school take charge of switching on the lights, it keeps it as a real village celebration.'

'Exactly.' Natalie turned to Graham, placing her hand on top of Poppy's head. 'Do you think she's warm enough?'

'Are you feeling any better?' Leaning towards her, Chrissy could feel the warmth of Luke's breath on her cheeks.

'Yes, I'm fine now. Sorry about earlier.'

'Don't apologise, I knew that suit was dodgy.'

Twisting her neck, she could see the glint of laughter in his eyes. 'Yes, well, I'll just have to make it up to you another time.'

'I hope that's a promise.'

'Would I lie?' Smiling, Chrissy let him slip his hand into hers.

'They're about to start! The choir teacher always does that funny stretching thing with her arms before they begin.' Natalie looked down at Luke and Chrissy's hands and smiled.

'I told Nat about us, but only Nat, I promise. I hope you don't mind?' Leaning in towards her, his whisper was barely audible above the general hubbub of people talking.

'That's fine. I'm sure I'd tell my sister if I had one.' It really was fine, although it must put her in a funny position knowing that Laura wanted to get back with him. Maybe she'd already told Luke, maybe he knew Laura still had feelings for him and he had truly decided he wanted to be with her. Chrissy shook her head, she didn't know and she certainly couldn't ask Natalie or Luke for that matter. No, she'd just have to take his word that he wanted to be with her.

'There they are.' Natalie pointed to the children climbing the stairs up to the stage and settling in rows.

Straining her neck so she could see above the woman with the bobble hat in front of her, Chrissy smiled, Evie and Sophia stood in the third row back. Waving at them, Evie smiled back while Sophia scowled, obviously deeply embarrassed by her mother's actions in trying to catch her attention.

As the familiar tunes of 'Away in a Manger' washed over her, Chrissy allowed herself to daydream. Maybe next year Luke and her would be holding hands at the front for all the world to see. He'd be great with the twins too, hyping them up for Christmas and joining in with the festivities. She looked over at him as he sung and she knew then that she had totally fallen for him too. She finally admitted to herself that she did actually love him.

When Andrew had broken off their marriage she had just assumed that was it, that she had experienced the only love for a man that she would in her lifetime and yet, here she was, barely months into life as a single mum, and she already felt that rush, that heaviness of security and true love. She took a sip of her hot chocolate. Had she ever felt this way about Andrew? Had he just been a stepping stone to prep her for the all-encompassing love she now felt for Luke?

The applause from the crowd tore her away from her thoughts and she gently tapped her hand against her cup.

'They get better every year.' Luke called above the noise.

She nodded. Evie loved singing. Sophia, on the other hand, had almost had to be bribed to come but she looked as though she was enjoying it now.

* * *

'Ten... Nine... Eight... Seven... Six... Five... Four... Three... Two... One... Go!' A small boy of Reception age pressed the red button, illuminating the green with brilliant white icicles drooping from every available tree and lamppost.

Twisting around, Chrissy watched as light after light flickered to life. In addition to the icicles lighting the green, white stars hung from the lampposts lining the High Street and small lit Christmas trees hung at an angle from the walls above the pub and corner shop.

Turning back to the stage, she could see Sophia and Evie clasping hands and talking, their eyes glistening with excitement and reflecting the lights from the icicles.

'Pretty special, hey?'

Chrissy smiled, how easy it would be to lean in towards Luke and let him wrap his strong, secure arms around her. 'It sure is.'

17

Forcing herself to open her eyes, Chrissy lifted her head from the cushion. She must have fallen asleep.

The trill from her phone rung incessantly. Reaching across to the footstool, she picked it up, hitting the answer button.

'Hello?'

'Hey, Chrissy. You OK? You sound all croaky?'

'Luke. Yes, sorry, I just nodded off for a bit, that's all.' Pushing herself to sitting, she looked across at the plate of toast she'd made for the twins before Andrew had picked them up. The leftover crusts and crumbs jeered at her and laying her hand on her stomach she tried to suppress the all too familiar churning. No, it wasn't working. 'Ring you back.'

Running into the kitchen, her hand cupped across her mouth, she leant over the sink and spat out the bile that had risen. Tearing a piece of kitchen roll off, she wiped her lips. She just couldn't seem to shake this bug. Sometimes she felt absolutely fine, but other times she just couldn't hold anything down and the thought, or worse, the smell or sight of food just made her stomach churn.

Pulling a chair out from the table, she flopped down, her chin resting on her hand and picked up her phone.

'Luke? Sorry, I'm still not feeling great.'

'Have you been sick again?' The concern in his voice made her smile. He really did care about her.

'Yes. Sorry, I don't think I should go out to your sister's meal tonight.'

'OK, well, I'll come over and keep you company. We can snuggle up and watch a film.'

'No, no, you go. She's your sister, you need to be there for her and Graham.'

'They won't mind.'

'No. Honestly, you go. I'll probably just end up falling asleep anyway.'

'OK, if you're sure, but I'd rather stay and keep you company.'

'You go and have a good time.'

'OK. Promise me one thing though?'

'What?'

'That you'll go and see a doctor if you still feel rough on Monday?'

'OK.' She lined up the colouring pencils discarded on the table from the girls earlier drawing session.

'Good. It's not normal for a bug to be going on this long. You've been throwing up all week.'

'I'm probably just a bit run-down after the move and settling the girls in at their new school.' Moving the blue pencil to the top she made a house.

'Even so, humour me.'

'OK. Only if you go and have a good time though.'

'Deal. I'll give you a call later.'

'Bye.' Pushing her pencil masterpiece aside, she rested her forehead against the cool of the wooden tabletop. What had she done? She'd just sent him off on his own to get drunk knowing full well that his ex-girlfriend, who happened to still be in love with him, would be there. Did she trust him? He'd shown no signs why she shouldn't, but then again he was a red-blooded male and Laura happened to be both gorgeous and kind-hearted.

She pushed herself up and sank back against the sofa cushions, pulling the throw over her legs. It was done now. There was nothing she could do. He would either get back with Laura or he wouldn't. Grimacing, she supposed she should be viewing this as a good thing. If Laura didn't tempt him tonight when they would both surely get completely drunk and nostalgic, then she'd know once and for all he was serious about her.

A film and an early night was what she needed now. She needed to kick this bug before the twins Christmas Concert on Thursday. Andrew had said earlier that he was coming, so she needed to be well enough to show him that she was coping with this single mum thing and that they were settling into village life here. She didn't want him to think she didn't have everything under control or that she was struggling.

Pressing 'play' on the remote, she settled back and closed her eyes as the music to her favourite romcom film filled the room.

* * *

Bolting upright, Chrissy reached for her phone. It must be Luke. Was he ringing to tell her that it was over? That he now realised he was still in love with Laura? That he had always been in love with Laura?

'Hi?'

'Mum! Is it true?'

Shaking her head, she tried to focus on the small voice filtering through the smog of sleep.

'Mum? Are you there? Mum?'

'Evie. Sorry, sweetheart, I must have drifted off to sleep while watching a film.' Finding the remote control on the floor, Chrissy turned the TV down. She couldn't have been asleep very long, it hadn't even reached the middle of the film. 'What's the matter? Shouldn't you be asleep?'

'What? No, maybe, but we're not. We're allowed to watch TV in our bedrooms, but I've got a tummy ache and Sophia keeps saying it means I'm going to start my period. Is it true? Will I? I don't want to start it yet, and I definitely don't want to start it here. I haven't got anything and I'm definitely not asking Susan for anything. Mum, can you come and get me if I start my period? It's not far. Please, Mum?'

'Hey, slow down, Evie. Just because you've got a tummy ache it doesn't mean you're going to start your period. Have you tried going to the toilet?'

'Yes, it's not that. It just hurts.'

'When did it start hurting?' Running her hand over her face, Chrissy tried to wipe the sleep from her eyes.

'Earlier, on the way back from the pub.'

'The pub? Did you go to the pub for dinner then?'

'Yes, we went with Carol and David and their little boy, I can't remember his name.'

'Bobby?' Scrunching her eyes tight together, she sat up and circled her shoulders, trying to ease the aching from falling asleep in a funny position. She knew Carol and David well, her and Andrew used to meet to go out with them regularly. Of course, the outings all stopped a couple of years ago, around the time that Susan had begun working with Andrew, coincidentally. Had they known about Andrew's affair? Chrissy shook her head, it didn't matter any more. What was done was done as her grandmother had always used to say.

'Yes, Bobby, that's it. How do you know his name?'

'Me and your dad used to meet up with them quite a bit.'

'Oh, right.'

Chrissy listened to the silence at the end of the phone. It must be strange for Evie to think about Chrissy knowing people that her dad and Susan were so friendly with. She couldn't help but picture Carol, David, Andrew and Susan sat around a table chatting and laughing. She tried to push the thought of them joking about her out of her mind. They probably preferred bubbly and outgoing Susan to meek and mild

Chrissy anyway. She'd always felt on the outskirts of Andrew's big group of friends, as though she didn't quite fit in, that she would never be accepted. Maybe they had known that she and Andrew wouldn't last all along, maybe that's why they'd never fully let her in. 'Evie, are you OK?'

'I just miss you.'

'Oh, sweetheart, I miss you too. I really do, but you're having a good time at Daddy's, aren't you?'

'I guess so, but I still miss you.'

'We'll have a film night on Sunday night when you get back, shall we? I'll get some popcorn and we can all get in our pyjamas and snuggle up under the throw and watch Christmas films. What do you think?'

'I'd like that.'

'Good, have a think about what films you want to watch then and you can ask Sophia what Christmas films she'd like to watch too.'

'OK.'

'OK.' Evie needed a hug, Chrissy could hear it in her voice. She bit down on her knuckle. Her little girl needed a hug from her mum and there was nothing Chrissy could do about it. Oh, she hated Andrew for tearing her girls away from her. She couldn't ever envisage getting used to being apart from her children every other weekend. How did anyone get used to it?

Maybe they didn't, maybe they just learnt to cope with the Friday to Sunday pain.

'Mum? Sophia was just teasing, wasn't she?'

'Yes, she's just teasing you. You're not going to start your period this weekend, but maybe we can pack a few bits in your bag for you to take over next time for when you do, so you don't have to worry?'

'OK.'

'How's your tummy now? Why don't you go and ask Daddy for some medicine for it?'

'No, it's OK now. I think I just needed to pop.'

'Evie!' Chrissy chuckled down the phone.

'I'm going to go and see if Sophia will let me watch TV in her room with her now.'

'That's a good idea. I love you, sweetheart and tell Sophia I love her too, please?'

'I will. I love you too, Mummy. Bye.'

'Bye, Evie.' Chrissy whispered down the already silent phone line and put her mobile back on the coffee table. She gently shifted Star from her legs and sat up. She would sort some bits out for the girls to take to Andrew's in case they started their periods at his. At least then they wouldn't have to worry about telling Susan if they didn't feel comfortable talking to her about things like that.

Pushing herself to standing, she reached down

and grabbed her mug. She'd get herself a hot chocolate and get in her pyjamas. She may as well get comfy if she was going to have a night in front of the TV. She still felt a bit sicky but not as bad as she had earlier, although it seemed to just creep up on her. She'd pick up some orange juice tomorrow, hopefully the Vitamin C would help kick whatever bug her body was trying to get rid of.

* * *

'Come on, Star, do you need to go out in the garden?' Watching Star slip out into the dark, Chrissy took a deep breath and let the cold night air fill her lungs before shutting the door and switching the kettle on.

She piled two, three spoonfuls of hot chocolate powder into the bottom of her mug. The twins had been talking about puberty at school this week, they'd had a letter home the week before to ask permission to take part in the lessons, no wonder they were both thinking about it.

The kettle clicked, condensation rising and settling on the underside of the cupboards. She'd forgotten something, she had that funny feeling as though there was a thought at the front of her mind but she couldn't quite focus in on it. The twins had both taken their toothbrushes, hadn't they? Yes, she had double checked their overnight bags as she normally did before they went to Andrew's, she would have noticed if they had forgotten to pack anything.

She'd told Luke she wasn't going tonight, she remembered that conversation. She'd forgotten to tell Natalie though, she'd meant to send her a text. But there was something else. She couldn't think what. The twins were fine, Luke had been told, Star had been fed. She was sure of that, Star was vocal if she was hungry and she was being good so she'd definitely remembered that.

Her period.

She hadn't had her period since they'd moved in. She stirred in the boiling water, watching the dark brown powder dissolve and colour it. It wasn't any surprise really, her period had always been temperamental, especially when she was stressed. She poured a little too much milk into her mug, it would make her hot chocolate too cool. She'd have to drink it before she went to get changed now.

Shrugging, she let Star back in and made her way back into the living room, perching on the edge of the sofa. She didn't feel stressed. A little stressed that she couldn't shake this sickness bug off, but not stressed enough for her period to stop. They'd settled quite nicely into life here and things had certainly been more stressful when she had been tiptoeing around Andrew and trying to avoid him before the house had sold.

And she couldn't be pregnant, she and Luke had been being super careful. She took a sip of the cool hot chocolate, letting the bittersweet taste sit in her mouth for a while before swallowing. Apart from the first time when they'd both been completely drunk. Had they been careful then? Chrissy shook her head, she couldn't remember. She could hardly remember getting home from the pub that night, let alone anything else.

She picked up her mobile, turning it over in her hand. Would Luke remember? She couldn't very well call him up in the middle of a night out and ask him though, could she? Even if they hadn't been careful, the chances of her getting pregnant from that one time? No, she shook her head, she was being daft. She was probably still stressed from the move, just because she didn't feel stressed, it didn't mean her body wasn't, did it?

Placing her mug on the coffee table, she laid back down on the sofa, pulling the throw up over her and turning the film back on.

It was no good. Sitting back up, she swung her legs

around and stood up. She'd only worry all night and not be able to relax. She needed to pop to the shop to grab some popcorn for Sunday night anyway, she may as well go now and pick up a test. Just to put her mind at rest. She knew she wasn't. There was no way whatsoever that she could possibly be pregnant, but if she got a test then she wouldn't have to worry any more. Her period would probably start as soon as she bought it anyway, just to remind her that she would have wasted ten pounds.

'Right, you be good, Star. I won't be long.' Closing the front door behind her, she shrugged into her coat and looked up at the crystal clear sky. She'd never tire of that view. She checked her watch, it was just gone nine now. The small shop down the High Street would be closed now, she'd have to drive into the nearest town to go to the supermarket. It was probably a good thing anyway, the community was so close-knit here, rumours began when someone forgot to put their recycling bins out.

* * *

Tapping her fingers on her knee, Chrissy watched as the numbers steadily decreased on the timer on her mobile. Shifting her position on the side of the bath, she glanced across at the small plastic stick sat innocently on the sink. She couldn't see the results and there was no point in looking, not until the magic three minutes were up.

'Alright, Star.' Chrissy stroked the top of Star's head as she weaved between her legs before settling at her feet. Why did she feel so nervous? She was just being silly. She knew she wasn't pregnant. She'd know if she was. She'd known almost instantly with the twins. Well, OK, had hoped she was pregnant, and she'd been right. That was another thing, it had taken her and Andrew four months of trying to get pregnant to fall, she couldn't possibly be pregnant after one time of not trying with Luke. It was ridiculous. She was ridiculous.

There was no point in even looking at the test, it would be negative anyway. Now that she was thinking clearly, she knew it would be. It had only been because she had been fuzzy-headed and not thinking straight after falling asleep on the sofa.

Standing up, she walked out of the bathroom and into her bedroom. She shook her head and laughed. She was a grown woman, not a teenager. Things like getting pregnant after a drunken night together didn't happen to women her age.

She picked up Evie's T-shirt from the pile of clean

laundry strewn on the bed from earlier and folded it. She'd get this cleared now and then it would save her a job later when she came up to bed.

The fast beeps of the timer pierced through the silent cottage. Placing another T-shirt onto the appropriate pile on her bed, Chrissy retraced the short distance back into the bathroom and turned the timer off. She'd have to wrap the test up well before putting it in the bin, she didn't want the twins to find it.

Pulling some paper off of the toilet roll, Chrissy picked up the pregnancy test and glanced at it quickly.

Letting the toilet paper flutter to the floor, she blinked. There couldn't be. There couldn't be two blue lines. Shaking the plastic stick, she looked again. They were still there, staring straight back at her.

Could the second one be a condensation line? You hear about it all the time. Women getting false positives from their tests. But it looked so clear and dark. The second line jeering up at her was just as dark, if not darker than the control line.

No, she couldn't be.

She couldn't be.

Leaning over the sink, she threw up, the bitter taste of hot chocolate burning the back of her throat.

She couldn't be pregnant. She had a bug. She didn't have morning sickness. It was a bug. Just a bug.

Running the cold tap, she swilled her mouth out, washing away the taste left behind. It was probably a faulty test. That was it. It was all a mistake.

Sinking to the floor, she held the test in her hands, staring at it, willing the second blue line to vanish. She just needed to give it time, a few minutes and the line would be gone. Maybe she hadn't left it long enough, or maybe she'd left it too long. She picked up her mobile, maybe the timer had broken. Maybe that was it.

Dropping the test and her mobile onto the floor beside her, she sank her head into her arms and held her breath. She was pregnant. What the hell was she supposed to do now? What would she tell the twins? What would she tell Andrew? What would everyone think of her? A newly single mum getting pregnant so quickly.

She couldn't do this. How was she going to cope with a baby? And the twins? They didn't need another upheaval. They'd been through so much recently. They didn't need their newfound stability rocked now.

But what choice did she have? She was pregnant. There was no going back.

And Luke? They'd barely even known each other for a couple of months, not even that. And most of that short time they hadn't even been in a relationship.

Their first time together and they had gotten pregnant. What would he say?

Lifting her head, she grappled for her phone and found Luke's number, pressing 'ring' before she could think about it.

The rings echoed in her ear as she waited for him to pick up. She didn't have a clue what she would say to him. Would she tell him now, over the phone? Or ask him to come round and tell him in person? What would be best? If she waited until he got here she might lose the bottle, might not be able to tell him.

Come on, Luke, pick up.

Nothing. He was out though, won't he? He was out with Natalie and Graham and their friends for a pre-wedding meal and drinks or whatever it was. He was out with them. He was out with Laura.

Pulling herself to standing, she wretched over the side of the sink. She'd told him to go out. He hadn't wanted to. He'd wanted to come round, he'd wanted to spend the evening with her. She'd sent him out to get drunk with his ex-girlfriend, the ex-girlfriend who wanted to get back together with him.

What had she done?

She needed him now. But what if it was too late?

Taking a deep breath, she pushed herself away from the sink and walked slowly into her bedroom. Lifting the laundry from her bed she placed it in a pile on the floor by the wardrobe and sank onto her mattress. Without changing into her nightclothes, she pulled the duvet tight around her, trying to ward off the chill seeping into her bones.

She'd think about it all tomorrow. She couldn't think about it now.

18

'I'm sorry to mess you around. There was nothing else I could do. My parents are away for the weekend and Susan's got this spa day to go to today with some friends.' Andrew jangled his keys in his hand. 'It shouldn't happen again. I'm not on call again until next month, and then I'll make sure I have a backup plan in case I get called out.'

'OK, no worries.' Chrissy pulled her dressing gown tighter around her middle and smoothed her hair back. She must look a sight. It was barely eight o'clock in the morning. Although she'd gone straight to bed after doing the test last night, she'd barely had a couple of hours sleep.

'I'd better go. Bye, girls.' Waving at Evie and

Sophia as they stood in the hall, their overnight bags at their feet, he turned on his heels and headed back to the car.

'Right, let's get you two some breakfast.' Shutting the front door behind her, she swallowed the bile threatening to rise in her throat.

'Can't I just go back to bed for a bit? Dad woke us up at just gone six o'clock.' Sophia yawned and rubbed her eyes.

'Yes, if you want to. Is that what time he got the call from work?'

'I guess so.'

'Never mind. We get the weekend together now.' Chrissy smiled. 'Is your tummy all better from last night, Evie?'

'Yes. Can I have some toast for breakfast, please?'

'Of course, you can. Sophia, you go and have your nap and, Evie, you go and pop the TV on while I get your toast.'

* * *

Spreading the butter onto the hot toast, Chrissy watched as the flick of yellow melted into the warm bread. She had to keep it together. She had to put it all out of her mind and focus on the twins. They had an extra weekend together. They should make the most of it and find somewhere Christmassy to go.

'Here you go, Evie.' Passing Evie the plate, Chrissy sat down next to her, bringing her legs up underneath her.

'Thanks, Mum. I'm glad Susan was busy. I wouldn't have wanted to stay there while Daddy went to work.' Evie bit into the toast, crumbs spilling onto the plate on her lap.

'She's not horrible to you or Sophia, is she?'

'No, we just don't know her, that's all. It would have been weird.'

'I guess it will take a little while to get to know her properly.'

'Yes.'

'You'd tell me if there was anything bothering you about her though, wouldn't you?'

'Yes. I would.' Evie paused to take a sip of juice before carrying on eating her toast. 'What are we going to do today?'

'Well, I've got to go round Natalie's house and take a dress round for one of her bridesmaids to try on, but then maybe we can go over to the garden centre, they've got an ice rink up at the moment.' Closing her eyes, she tried to shut out the realisation that she was going to have to see Laura today of all days.

'Yay. I love ice skating!'

'I know you do.' Smiling, she picked up a couple of stray crumbs from the sofa cushions and put them back on Evie's plate.

* * *

'Will Adam be here? Do you think we'll be allowed to go and play in the garden while you and Natalie do your wedding thing?' Evie glanced up at Chrissy and pressed the doorbell again.

'Probably. I think you've rung that enough now, you don't want Natalie thinking there's a fire or something.' Chrissy gently pulled Evie's hand away from the doorbell.

'Chrissy, hi. Hello, girls.'

'Hi, Natalie. I hope we're not disturbing you, I just wanted to drop Laura's bridesmaid dress off so she can try it on. I wanted to catch her before she left for London again.'

'Of course you're not. Come in. Sophia, Evie, Adam's playing footie in the garden if you wanted to go and join him?'

'Yes, please.'

'Go on then. Take your shoes off and carry them to the back door, Natalie doesn't want mud walked through the house.'

'Honestly, don't worry. The number of times Kane and Adam, well, and Graham come to think of it, plod mud everywhere, I shouldn't worry. I think Poppy's going to grow up with an immune system made of steel. Come through and I'll stick the kettle on.'

Following Natalie through the living room to the back of the house, Chrissy glanced around. She couldn't see any signs to suggest they'd had a heavy night of drinking the day before and Natalie seemed her usual well organised and groomed self. 'Did you have a good time last night? Sorry I couldn't be there.'

'That's OK, Luke said you weren't feeling well. Are you feeling better?'

'Yes, thanks.' Chrissy turned her head away from Natalie, hoping she had been quick enough to hide the deep crimson flushing through her cheeks. 'So, how was your night out?'

'Really good, thanks. Gina's husband is so funny when he's had a bit to drink so he was encouraging everyone to join him. Hence, why Graham's still asleep upstairs. He can't handle his drink quite as well as Gina's other half.' Natalie laughed. 'We ended up going to the nightclub in town. Do you know the one? A rather dingy place with sticky floors and groups of teenagers?'

'No, I didn't grow up around here.'

'Well, you haven't missed anything. Apart from Gina dancing around like she was on something! And she obviously hadn't touched a drop of alcohol because of the bump. Still, she always says she doesn't need to drink, she just gets drunk on everyone else's jolliness.'

'You're not suffering today then?'

'No, I'm still breastfeeding so can't drink anyway.'

'Yes, of course. Where do you want this?' Chrissy nodded to the gown bag in her arms.

'Can you just lay it over the back of one of the chairs, please? I'll take it upstairs in a bit.'

'OK.'

Natalie looked over at Poppy who had begun to cry and kick her legs in her bouncy chair. 'Are you OK just picking her up while I finish these?' She indicated the mugs with the teaspoon in her hand.

'Yes of course.' Walking over to Poppy, Chrissy stood over her before taking a deep breath and picking her up. 'Hello, Poppy.'

'Did you want a biscuit?' Natalie turned, holding an open packet of chocolate biscuits towards Chrissy.

Swallowing hard, she closed her eyes and waited for the nausea to ease before turning towards Natalie. 'No, I'm fine, thank you. I'm trying to be good.'

'You've got more willpower than me then! Even with the wedding just under two weeks away and the constant nightmares about not being able to pull my dress up over my hips, I still cave when it comes to biscuits. Or any food for that matter.' Carrying the mugs of steaming tea, Natalie joined Chrissy and Poppy on the sofa.

'How's the planning going? Are you all ready for the big day?'

'I think so. Although if you asked Gina, I'm sure she'd say something different. She's been an absolute star. She's single-handedly organised more or less the whole thing.'

'That's good of her.'

'It is, although I think she's secretly just happy to be kept busy. She was made redundant shortly after she announced to her work colleagues that she was pregnant again.'

'That's awful. Surely she'll have a legal case against them?'

'You'd think so, wouldn't you? But it was all very complicated. Although she'd worked there as Events Manager for over five years, just after she'd told them she was pregnant the company was taken over. I think they panicked and made her redundant.'

'That's so wrong.'

'It is, but legally she didn't have a leg to stand on because they merged departments or something so it looked as though her job wasn't needed any more. What the bosses didn't realise is that she'd have probably carried on working until she dropped and then she'd have most likely gone back after six weeks like she did with Olivia.'

'Wow, that's quick.'

'That's what she's like, she needs to keep busy. That's why she's been all over my wedding. Which is good for me, obviously. I'm going to have an amazingly well-organised wedding that I quite literally haven't had to lift a finger to pull it off.'

'That's handy then.'

'It certainly is. Are you OK with her for a minute while I see if the kids want a drink?' Standing up, Natalie indicated to Poppy.

Nodding, Chrissy bent down and picked up a fabric doll from the play mat, holding it just within Poppy's reach. 'Are you trying to reach it?'

Holding Poppy on one knee, Chrissy rubbed her temples with her free hand. Was she ready for this? Was she ready to go back to the beginning again? The twins were only a year and a half away from starting secondary school, they were becoming more independent every day. This baby would mean toddler groups, nursery, primary school, everything all over again.

She looked down into Poppy's wide blue eyes. Maybe it wouldn't be so bad starting over again. Plus, the twins were always bugging her that they wanted a baby brother or sister. Or they were before she and Andrew had split up. Now, they'd probably given up on the idea that it would ever happen. Andrew hadn't wanted any more children, and if he had been honest, he hadn't really wanted any. It was Chrissy who had been ready to be a parent, not Andrew.

Smiling, she sat Poppy up on her lap, supporting her neck. Luke wanted children, he had said that. Although he had said he wasn't ready yet. Chrissy leant her head against the back of the sofa. What if he said it was too soon and turned his back on her?

'You OK?'

Jerking her head up, Chrissy smiled. 'Yes, I'm fine thanks. This one's almost trying to sit up on her own, isn't she?' Luke was one of the good guys, he wouldn't turn his back on her, on them.

'She is, isn't she? It's not going to be long. She rolled over the other day too! Admittedly, she got stuck and screamed the house down, but she still rolled.'

'Clever girl. What time is Laura coming by to try her dress on?'

'She's not today. She's had to go away. Sorry, I'm sure her dress will fit though, it looked lovely when you were pinning it.'

'That's fine, don't worry.' Circling her shoulders, she let herself relax a little, at least she wouldn't have to face her.

'Mum, they're going ice skating this afternoon, can you take us?' Adam came in through the back door, followed by Kane, Evie and Sophia.

'I can't today. Sorry, love.' Natalie took another biscuit from the packet.

'How come?'

'Because Gina's coming round to finalise some bits for the wedding. We'll go another time.'

'Can Dad take us then?'

'Your dad, if you hadn't noticed, is still in bed with a sore head. I really don't think he's going to be in any fit state to take you anywhere today, let alone to test his balance on the ice.' Laughing, Natalie brushed some crumbs from her biscuit onto the floor.

'How about Uncle Luke then? He likes ice skating. He can take us.'

'I'm afraid not, boys. The last time I saw your

Uncle Luke he was in an even worse state than your dad and I've not even heard from him today.'

'Oh, Mum. That's not fair.'

'Sorry, kids. Another day though.' Finishing the last of her biscuit, Natalie offered the packet to the children.

He hadn't been in touch with his sister. And Laura had cancelled her fitting today too. Chrissy cleared her throat. It all made sense. Complete sense. Luke and Laura must be together. They must have spent the night together last night.

'Come on, girls. Time to go.' Standing up, Chrissy passed Poppy to Natalie. 'Thanks for the tea.'

'You're welcome, I'm just sorry it was a bit of a waste of time for you.'

'Don't worry. It's fine.' Stumbling over a discarded toy, Chrissy grabbed onto the back of a dining chair to steady herself.

'Are you OK?'

'Yes, sorry, I just didn't see it. Thanks again.' Smiling at Natalie, Chrissy watched as she stood up. 'No, don't worry, we can see ourselves out.'

* * *

Ushering the twins through the front door, Chrissy let the cold winter wind cool her cheeks. That was the end to her fairy-tale ending then.

'Can we go straight away?' Sophia looked up at her mum.

'Where?'

'Ice skating of course.'

'Right, of course. No, let's get home first. I'm not feeling too good.' Looking at her feet, she focused on putting one foot in front of the other. Bile rose into her mouth again and the pain in her head gripped her temples. She needed to lie down for a bit. She needed to stop thinking.

'Mum, you promised we could go.'

'I know, and we will. I just need to get home first. Come on.' Turning down their lane, Chrissy picked up the pace. She couldn't throw up out here, not in the middle of the village.

'We will go though, won't we?'

'Yes, Sophia. in a bit. Quick, in you go.' Holding the front door open, Chrissy let the girls through before letting the door slam behind her and running upstairs.

* * *

'Mum, are you OK?' Sophia's voice floated through the bathroom door.

'Yes, sweetheart, I'm fine.' Splashing her face, she looked in the mirror and tried to pinch a bit of colour into her cheeks.

'Have you just been sick?'

'Only a little bit.'

'Are you poorly?'

'I've just got a headache, that's all.'

'We're not going ice skating, are we?'

'Can I just have a lie-down and then see how I feel?'

'OK.'

Chrissy listened to Sophia padding down the stairs and opened the door. She'd have to get used to coping with the nausea, she had been sick throughout the twins' pregnancy. She couldn't keep hiding away.

* * *

'Mum, Luke's here. Shall I open the door?'

Opening her eyes, Chrissy moved the cold flannel from her forehead. Evie was standing at the end of her bed.

'Luke? How do you know it's him? You haven't opened the door, have you?'

'Of course not, Mum. You always tell us not to open the front door unless you're there. He called through the letter box though and...' Evie ran out onto the landing and back in again. 'And now, Sophia is telling him how you chucked up everywhere.'

'What? She hasn't, has she?'

'No, I'm just teasing you. She's asking him about the rules to basketball or something equally boring.'

'Oh, OK.'

'Come on then. He'll be getting cold out there.'

'Yes, right.' Chrissy pushed the duvet off and stood up. What was she supposed to say to him? Would he tell her about Laura? What was she supposed to say if he did? Or worse, what should she do if he didn't say anything? She couldn't put herself through being in a relationship with someone who was having an affair. Not again. Not after Andrew. And she certainly couldn't tell him about the pregnancy, he'd either run back to London or finish things with Laura and stay with her through duty. She didn't want to share her life with someone who didn't want to actually be with her.

'Come on.'

'I'm coming.' Rubbing her eyes, she followed Evie down the stairs.

'Mum's here now.' Sophia called through the letter box before letting it clatter shut and turning away.

Pausing to look in the mirror, Chrissy smoothed her hair, frizzy from sleep, and pulled open the door. 'Hi, Luke. Sorry about that, I was upstairs.'

'Asleep. She was asleep.'

'Thanks, Sophia.'

'Are you still feeling rough?' Luke's eyes searched hers as he rested his hand on her forearm.

'Just some bug or something.' Dismissing his concerns, Chrissy led the way into the living room. Why would he even care that she was feeling ill? 'Here, come through to the kitchen.'

'OK.'

Holding the kitchen door open for him, Chrissy shut it firmly behind him and leant against the work surface. She was as ready as she'd ever been.

'I missed you last night.'

Chrissy turned her head as he leant in towards her, accepting a kiss on the cheek.

'Are you OK?' Standing back, Luke furrowed his brow.

'I'll be fine. I'm just not feeling a hundred per cent yet, that's all.' She looked down at her feet, one of her socks had a hole in the toe. She'd have to remember to throw it out instead of repeatedly washing it, wearing it and meaning to throw it away. Instead of trying to kiss her and stringing her along, why couldn't he just come out with the truth? Tell her he had been with Laura last night and they'd decided to give it another go?

'You've been feeling rotten for the last few days now, why don't you book a doctor's appointment on Monday?' Stepping forward again, Luke held his arms out, ready to hug her.

With all the willpower she had left, she slid away from him and crossed her arms. If she let herself sink into his strong, safe arms she'd never be able to pull away.

Clearing his throat, Luke stuffed his hands in his pockets. 'I popped in to see Nat earlier, and she mentioned that Adam and Kane wanted to go ice skating with you guys, so I just wondered if you wanted to take them tomorrow?'

'I can't, sorry.' Why didn't he just tell her? What was wrong with men anyway? What gave them the right to think they could keep two relationships going at once? Is that what he was trying to do? Would he move to London for 'work' or something and still expect to come back to the village to visit her whilst being shacked up with Laura in the City? Was that the plan?

She shook her head, she couldn't actually work out who was worse, Andrew for having an affair when their marriage was on its last legs or Luke for firstly getting together with her when he must have known he still had feelings for his ex and then thinking he can have two relationships on the go.

Yes, Andrew had broken their marriage vows which were supposed to be sacred, but they'd both known their marriage had begun to grow holes so large they were irreparable. Whereas, things had been good with Luke and he'd still ran off back to Laura. Did literally no man actually move on from their exes? Was it normal or was she just so repulsive they were desperate to relive loves from their past?

'Are we OK?' He used his hands to indicate the space between them. 'Are you annoyed at me because I didn't ring or pop round last night after going out with Nat and everyone?'

'No, I...'

'I'm sorry. I had meant to, I just got a bit carried away last night. I stupidly tried to keep up with one of Graham's mates and ended up sleeping on his sofa. I couldn't even tell you how I got there, I'd had that much to drink.'

Chrissy turned and straightened the tea towel hanging from the oven door, he wasn't even going to tell her the truth. Didn't she deserve that? At the very least? No, she would not put herself through this again. She couldn't. She turned back to face him, lifting her eyes to meet his. She had to do this now. 'Luke, I don't think this is working.'

'What? Me coming round here? I know you want to keep our relationship quiet from the girls but they know we're friends, don't they? Plus, I was only popping in to see if you wanted to take them ice skating tomorrow.' Luke glanced at the closed door and back to Chrissy.

'Us.' She cleared the croakiness from her throat. 'We're not working. I'm sorry.'

'Us?' Luke stepped forward before thinking better of it, returning to his spot by the table and gripping the top of a dining chair. 'Why? I thought things were going really well between us. I've fallen for you, Chrissy. I was planning on telling you I loved you last night.' He wiped his hand across his face.

Momentarily closing her eyes, Chrissy looked back at Luke and took a deep breath. He was going to tell her he loved her. She bit her bottom lip, he was such a good liar. He was better than Andrew had been. With Andrew, Chrissy had known something was amiss, she'd just not been able to work out what it had been. But with Luke, he even looked as though he was going to cry and she'd never seen him remotely upset about anything before. 'Please just go.'

'Chrissy, please? I don't understand.'

'Luke, go.' Turning around Chrissy smoothed out a kink she'd missed in the tea towel. She knew what he was like, so why was this so hard? Focusing on a yellow stain on the checked tea towel, she listened as he opened the kitchen door and made his way back through the living room.

Turning her head, she heard him answer Sophia's question about how many points you get if you shoot a basketball through the hoop outside the three-point arc and congratulate Evie on getting top marks in her times table test at school. He was being so good with them, even now. She had to keep repeating to herself that he was the one in the wrong for not only spending the night with Laura, but also, and maybe more importantly, not telling her the truth. He was a liar, a very good one.

She waited until she heard the front door click shut behind him before running to the bathroom. Shutting the door behind her, she lowered herself to the floor, bringing her knees up towards her stomach. He was a liar and a cheat. He had lied to her face. He had done this, not her.

Leaning her head back against the cold ceramic of

the bath, she tried to ease the pain searing behind her eyes. Why had she ever let herself think things could have been serious between her and Luke?

Pulling herself up, she splashed cold water over her face. It was probably a good thing that things hadn't worked out with him, she'd have ended up trusting him too and then being let down further down the line. They were all the same, men, all the same.

Sinking her face into the softness of the towel, Chrissy dried her face. This was it. Now, she needed to focus on the three of them. Four, nearly four of them. She could do it. With all the hours Andrew had worked, she'd basically brought the twins up single-handedly anyway. Yes, she hadn't had to worry about money or making the big decisions on her own, but the practical stuff, she'd been there and done that. They'd be OK financially if she built up her dress-making business before the baby was born and didn't take maternity leave. They'd be fine. They'd have to be. It wasn't as though she had a choice.

'Mum, are you coming down yet? You've been up-stairs ages.' Sophia's voice floated up the stairs.

'Just coming.' Hanging the towel back on the rail, Chrissy looked at herself in the mirror and pinched some colour into her cheeks. She could handle this, she could. On Monday she'd go to Natalie's and get that before photo of Laura's bridesmaid dress she'd promised her and she'd start working on advertising for her business. She'd had a lucky escape with Luke. Being on her own would be far better than knowing he was seeing Laura behind her back.

19

'Come on, we're going to be late.'

'OK, OK, I just need to finish this quickly.' Momentarily, Sophia lifted her head from where she was bending over the coffee table furiously scribbling in her homework book.

'Mum, tell her. She should have done her spellings yesterday when I did mine. If we're late I'm not going to be able to do my job. I'm Snack Monitor this week, I need to get there on time and hold the snack basket for everyone.' Stamping her foot against the tiled floor, Evie twisted the handle on the front door, a bitter breeze escaping in through the small gap.

'How much have you got left, Sophia?' Walking

over towards her, Chrissy laid her coat and gloves on the coffee table.

'Two, just two. And it's not such a big deal being Snack Monitor, Evie. It won't matter if you're late, someone else will just do it.'

'I want to do it. It's my turn. You did it last week and I didn't make you late. Tell her, Mum. She's being unfair.'

'I'm done now anyway.' Sophia stretched before standing and slipping her coat on.

'Here, give me your homework book. I'll pop it in your bag while you put your shoes on.' Picking up the book, Chrissy slipped it into Sophia's rucksack. There was no point nagging her or telling her to hurry, knowing Sophia, she'd only go at an even slower pace to annoy her sister.

'Come on.' Grabbing Sophia by the arm, Evie ran to the garden gate, Sophia reluctantly matching her pace. 'Mum!'

'I'm coming.' Twisting the key in the lock, Chrissy jogged towards them. 'Right, let's go.'

* * *

'Quick! They're about to shut the doors.' Evie rounded the wall to the playground and ran towards the class-room door, slipping in just before the door was shut.

'Do you want to go and knock, they might still let you in?' Turning behind her, Chrissy watched as Sophia strolled into the playground.

'Nah, we had a whole assembly about being late last week where they told us that if the door's been shut, they won't open it again. We'll have to go to the office.'

'OK, come on then.' Chrissy shrugged. 'Is everything OK, Sophia?'

'I heard you having a go at Luke on Saturday. What was it about?' Sophia caught up with Chrissy.

'Did you? Oh, nothing really, just a little disagreement.'

'What was it about?'

'It doesn't matter, Sophia. Just adult stuff.' Putting her arm around Sophia's shoulders, Chrissy kissed her on the top of the head. 'Nothing for you to worry about.'

'Were you dating him and you broke it off?'

'What?' Chrissy let her arm flop to her side and paused.

'It sounded like you were dumping him. Evie said

that I'm just being silly, but that's what it sounded like to me. You were talking too quietly for it to be something small.' Sophia turned to face Chrissy, her eyes wide.

Blinking against Sophia's stare, Chrissy cleared her throat. 'That doesn't mean we were breaking up. Adults can speak quietly sometimes, you know.' Smiling, she put her arm back around Sophia's shoulders, pulling her into her.

'It's just that before you and Dad told us you were splitting up, you had all these quiet talks.'

'Really? You heard us?'

'We didn't hear what you were saying, but we knew something was going on. And with Luke, it sounded like that.'

'I'm sorry, sweetie, I hadn't realised.' She had thought her and Andrew had been really discreet when they were having discussions about breaking up, certainly more discreet than the normal arguments they used to have anyway.

Sophia shrugged. 'It's OK. Were you dating Luke then? Before you had the argument, I mean?'

Chrissy swallowed. She didn't believe in lying to the twins. The odd white lie telling them that the music on the ice cream van meant they had run out of ice cream, yes, but real, serious lies, no. 'I'm not going to be dating anyone for the time being at least.'

'That's a shame because both me and Evie like Luke. Anyway, love you, Mum.' Stopping outside the door to the school office, Sophia tilted her face towards Chrissy, waiting for her usual peck on the cheek.

'Love you too, Sophia. Have a lovely day.' Kissing her cheek, Chrissy smoothed Sophia's hair down and smiled at her.

'Bye, Mum.' Waving behind her, Sophia wiped the kiss from her cheek, as was her routine, and pulled open the heavy door to the office.

It had been Sophia who hadn't wanted Chrissy to date anyone, who hadn't wanted her to get into another relationship, and yet, she'd just given her blessing to Chrissy seeing Luke. Pulling her scarf higher up her chin, she bit down on the maroon wool. It was too late anyway. Plus, the Luke that they had been getting to know, hadn't been the real Luke anyway. If he was capable of spending the night with his ex-girlfriend and lying about it straight to her face, what else was he capable of?

Chrissy turned slowly and made her way towards the school gates. She'd go straight round Natalie's and ask her for that photo before she lost her nerve. Luke would have probably spoken to her already and likely told Natalie how awful she had been to him. Obviously, he wouldn't have told his sister he had been seeing Laura behind her back, so it would be Chrissy's fault the relationship was over.

She shook her head, if she could just pop round and ask her to forward that photo, then she probably wouldn't need to see her again, not as friends anyway. She'd more than likely run into her on the school run, but she could always try to avoid her if Natalie got funny with her. She just had to get that photo for her social media business page. Natalie was lovely, she wouldn't not give it to her just because she'd broken up with Luke, would she?

Pausing at the school gates, she held her hand out, resting it on the cold metal and waited until a dizzy spell passed. She should have tried to have something to eat for breakfast. Even if she wasn't hungry, she needed to eat for the baby.

'Chrissy? Are you OK?'

Chrissy felt Luke's strong, dependable hand on her shoulder and bit down on her scarf again before turning around. 'Luke. Yes, I'm fine thanks.'

'You don't look it.'

'Thanks.' Turning around, she looked into his crystal clear eyes, nothing but concern stared back at her.

'You know what I mean.'

'I'm fine. What are you doing here anyway?'

'I offered to take Kane and Adam to school. Poppy had slept in after keeping Nat awake most of the night. And, if I'm honest, I was hoping I'd run into you.'

'You've been hanging around? Waiting for me?'

'Yes.' Looking down at his feet, he cleared his throat before looking back up at Chrissy's face. 'But only because I wanted to talk to you to try to work things out between us.'

Laughing, Chrissy shook her head. Did he really take her to be a complete mug? 'Luke, you know what's happened and you know why we split so stop the innocent act. I'm happy to talk about it, but if you can't even own up to what you've done...'

'What do you mean? I have no idea what I've done or what I'm supposed to have done.' Stretching out his arms, his hands palm side up, Luke looked at Chrissy, searching her face.

'Seriously?'

'Seriously. I thought things were going really well between us, as I told you on Saturday, I was going to tell you I loved you. And I do, I love you, Chrissy. Please, just tell me what it is I'm supposed to have done.'

'You see, that's the scary part, you actually don't

know what it is.' Shaking her head, she shoved her hands in her pockets.

'Things were great between us on Friday when I saw you, weren't they?'

Chrissy looked down at the floor and scraped the toe of her trainers against the fallen leaves. She wasn't going to spell it out. He must realise that she knew what he had done, or if he didn't, then he would soon. He'd work it out.

'Chrissy, please? Things were great Friday and then you finished it all on Saturday. I don't get it, what could have happened in one night. I wasn't even with you on Friday night.'

'Exactly.' For someone who managed his own property development business, he was being very slow at adding two and two together. Or maybe he just didn't see anything wrong with infidelity. Maybe she'd got it all wrong. Maybe they'd had an open relationship all along. She pushed a few of the leaves into a mush pile at her feet. They'd never had the talk about being exclusive, but surely, at their age, exclusivity was expected, was the norm? Maybe she'd completely misunderstood. But still, it didn't make it right.

'Was it because I went to the meal without you? I wanted to stay, it was you who told me to go out. Or was it because I got drunk and didn't ring you? Was that it?' Luke placed his hand on Chrissy's forearm.

'I need to go.' Shaking his hand off, she walked quickly through the gates towards Corner Cottage. She'd go to Natalie's later.

20

Taking a deep breath, Chrissy rang the doorbell. She'd just ask Natalie to forward the photo to her if it was on her phone and then go. She wouldn't even need to go in.

'Chrissy, hi.' Pulling the door open, Natalie smiled. 'How are you?'

'OK, thanks. I'm sorry to bother you and I probably shouldn't have come round, but I just wondered if you could forward that photo you said I could have of the bridesmaid dress before I'd altered it? I completely understand if you want me to just go though.'

'Don't be daft. Just because you've had a bust-up with Luke, it doesn't mean I don't still class you as a friend. Come in.'

'It's OK, I've got to...'

'Come on, I won't take no for an answer. Come in out of the cold.'

'Thank you.'

'You're welcome. I've got to say, I was rather shocked when Luke told me you'd split up though. I thought you were a great couple and I hadn't seen Luke so happy in years.'

'Well, I...' What was she supposed to say? She couldn't very well tell her that her brother had played away, could she?

'Hey, look, it's between you and Luke, not me.' Natalie held up her hands to stop Chrissy from saying any more. 'Come through.'

Following Natalie through to the family room, Chrissy smiled. It was nice that Natalie was staying neutral, it would make things easier.

'Cup of tea?' Natalie pointed to the kettle before handing Poppy, who was happily kicking her legs in the bouncy chair, a teething ring she had dropped.

'Could I just have a water, please?'

'Are you sure?'

Chrissy nodded and perched on the edge of the sofa.

'Here you go.'

'Thanks.' Taking the glass, Chrissy took a long sip,

the chilled water hitting the back of her throat was a welcome distraction to the fact she was now sat on the sofa with Luke's sister.

'Luke rang me after he'd dropped the boys off at school to tell me Kane had forgotten his lunchbox.' Natalie rolled her eyes. 'Typical Kane, he's always forgetting something and just when I'd thought I'd got out of doing the school run this morning.' Natalie laughed and leant back against the sofa cushions.

'That's always the way, isn't it?'

'It sure is. With him anyway.' Natalie took a sip of the coffee she had resting on the coffee table. 'He mentioned you hadn't seemed very well? You do look a bit peaky. Is everything OK?'

'Yes, I'm fine thanks.' She took a cushion from behind her and laid it on her knees. 'I just didn't get much sleep over the weekend, that's all.'

'Well, if there's anything I can do to help, just let me know.'

Did she know? Chrissy glanced across at Natalie and smiled. She couldn't know. No one did. 'Thank you, but it's fine.'

'Good. Are you looking forward to the school Christmas Concert tomorrow?'

'Oh, yes.' Chrissy bit her bottom lip, how could she have forgotten about that? The girls had been so excited practising their lines and the songs all last week, but with everything that had happened over the weekend, she hadn't even thought about it.

'It's normally really good, the school as a whole put a lot of effort into it. They normally go to town with the decorations and, a major plus point, they give out mulled wine and mince pies to the audience!'

'Really? The girls' last school just used to throw something together last minute. I remember Evie having a meltdown last year because they'd only given her four days to learn her lines. She's quite the perfectionist, so it had completely thrown her and she'd rather not do something at all than be rushed or feel as though she's not prepared.'

'That's awful. You'll be in for a treat tomorrow then.'

'It sounds like it.' Although she'd have to spend time in the same room as both Andrew and Luke. Two men who had cheated on her. She focused on a pink teddy lying on the floor and took a deep breath. She'd get through it, for the girls, she'd be fine.

* * *

'Sophia, Evie. Did you both have a good day?' Smiling, Chrissy accepted their rucksacks, slipping them over her shoulder before leading the way across the playground and through the gates.

'It was great! We practised the Christmas Concert and then we baked mince pies to give out to the parents.'

'That sounds like a really good day, Evie. How about you, Sophia?'

'It was OK.' Sophia shrugged her shoulders.

'Hey, what's the matter?' Chrissy slowed her pace to walk alongside Sophia.

'She got told off for rushing her spellings.'

'Did you, Sophia?'

'Yes, but if Evie hadn't rushed me this morning I could have done them properly and made my handwriting better.' Sophia scowled at Evie.

'Hey, don't blame me. It was you who forgot to do your homework over the weekend.'

'No, it was my fault, Sophia, not your Evie's. I should have reminded you to do your homework. Never mind, let's forget about it now. Your teacher knows how neat your handwriting is normally and, besides, as long as you were learning your spellings I can't see what difference it makes if you were rushing to write them or not.'

'I suppose.'

'Right, well, I thought we could go home, practise

your lines and songs for the concert and then have a movie night with the Christmas lights on. What do you think?'

'Yes, OK.'

'Good.' She needed to make it up to the twins for being so rubbish lately. What with feeling drained and sick with the pregnancy and upset over what had happened with Luke, she'd taken her eyes off of what she should be doing. But now it was just the three, soon to be four of them, things would get better.

21

Standing in the queue tailing across the playground, Chrissy rubbed her hands together. She'd left her gloves at the cottage and by the time she'd realised she'd been halfway down the lane and hadn't had time to turn back. She had wanted to get to the school and into the hall before Andrew turned up. If she'd known there would be this many people coming to watch the school's Christmas Concert, she would have left earlier to get a better space in the queue.

Looking in front and behind her, there was still no sign of Andrew, but she spotted Luke with Natalie and Graham near the front of the queue. She quickly ducked back behind the person in front of her, the last thing she wanted was for Natalie to spot her and wave her to join them. She was here to focus on the girls, it was going to be hard enough having to share the same air as Andrew, she didn't want to be forced to sit next to Luke and have all of her hopes and dreams for the future rubbed in her face.

'It's cold, isn't it?' An elderly lady in front of her pushed a strand of loose grey hair behind her ear and turned to face Chrissy.

'Absolutely freezing.' Nodding in agreement, Chrissy stuck her hands in her pockets.

'Shouldn't be much longer now though, love. They normally open the doors at o'clock.'

'Oh, good. Let's hope it's a little warmer in there.' Smiling, Chrissy checked her watch, it was three minutes to.

'Is it your first time at the Christmas Concert? I don't remember seeing you around school?'

'Yes, we only moved out here a couple of months ago.'

'Ah, that'll be why I haven't seen you then. My grandchildren come here and I've never missed an assembly, concert or performance yet. I'm Elsie, by the way.'

'Nice to meet you, Elsie, I'm Chrissy. What years are your grandchildren in?'

'We have Gemma who's in Year Six now and little

Thomas who just started in Reception this last September.'

'Lovely ages.' Chrissy pulled her scarf up higher against the wind. 'My girls are in Year Five.'

'Not the twins, by any chance?'

'Yes, that's them. Evie and Sophia.'

'I think they're the only new ones in Year Five since last June, I think, when Harry started the school. I pop in a couple of times a week to help hear readers and change books.'

'Wow, that's great. Well, thank you, and I hope my girls have been good for you.'

'Yes, yes, very polite. Good little readers too.'

Glancing around, Chrissy spotted Andrew joining the end of the queue. He'd brought Susan. It was definitely her, the bleach blonde highlights and high heels were unmistakable. Taking a deep breath in, she quickly turned back to Elsie.

'Are you OK, love? You look as though you've seen a ghost.'

'Yes, yes, I'm fine. Sorry. I just spotted someone I don't particularly want to run into tonight.' What had they been talking about? Reading, that was it. She needed to keep her mind off of Andrew and Susan, she needed to focus. 'So what made you volunteer at the school?'

'I used to come here, and after that, my own children came here. I even worked here for a while.'

'Oh, lovely.'

'Yes, it is. It's a very good school. My children and my grandchildren have done well here.'

'It does seem a nice school.'

'Here we go, they're letting us in now.' Elsie shuffled a few steps forward until the line paused again.

* * *

As they made their way into the hall, the warmth hit Chrissy. The difference in temperature between outside and in the hall was huge. Unzipping her coat, she immediately unwound her scarf.

'You enjoy it, love.' Elsie patted Chrissy's arm and made her way to a seat which had been saved in the second row, waving at the couple who were already sat down.

'You too.' Chrissy watched Elsie settle into her seat, chatting away to the couple and shook her head. The hall was filling up quickly and she needed to find a seat before Andrew and Susan came in.

'Excuse me.' A woman carrying a baby with one hand and holding onto a toddler with the other squeezed past her.

Making her way down the fourth row of plastic chairs, the closest row to the stage still available, she sat down. Tugging her arms from her sleeves, she slid out of her coat and lay it across her lap. This was the first time she had ever been to a school function on her own. Andrew had always managed to get the time off work, or as she'd realise later, away from Susan to come or if he really couldn't then his parents would have.

She quietly laughed at herself, she supposed she wasn't alone really, was she? Andrew was here and he'd brought Susan too. She twisted around in her seat, trying to spot them in the crowds. She needed to know where they were sat. Two rows back, on the left. Hopefully, when the lights were dimmed they wouldn't be able to see her, she just needed to avoid eye contact with them until then. She tugged on a loose strand of hair, the messy bun she'd tied up to get her hair out of her face as she'd thrown up her lunch was getting messier by the minute. If she'd known he was bringing her she would have at least straightened her hair.

'Chrissy.'

Jerking her head up, she spotted Natalie as she squeezed down the row towards her. 'Hi, Natalie.'

'There's a spare seat next to us on the third row, if you want to join us?'

'No, it's OK, thanks though.' She couldn't sit next to Luke.

'OK. I'm going up to get some mulled wine, shall I bring you one back?'

'What? No, sorry, no thanks. I had a coffee before I came out. I don't think I could fit any more liquid in my bladder at the moment.' Laughing, Chrissy cringed, her answer had sounded over the top even to her. She bundled her coat up in her lap and fiddled with her scarf.

'OK, I'll catch you later then.' Smiling, Natalie turned and squeezed back down the row towards the drinks table that had been set up.

Dipping her head down, Chrissy tried not to let her eyes be pulled towards Luke who was sitting to her right in the row ahead. He hadn't taken his black beanie hat off yet, he must be too warm, surely? With all these people in the hall, it was quickly becoming uncomfortably hot. He hadn't brought Laura then. At least one of her exes had done the decent thing and not brought their mistresses along to remind Chrissy that she hadn't been good enough.

The lights dipped as 'Jingle Bells' played over the speakers. Stage lights were switched on, shining on groups of children at either side of the stage who must have entered the hall when the lights had been dimmed. Chrissy searched in the groups and found Sophia on the left towards the back, mumbling along to the song. Evie was on the other side, standing tall and proud, singing as loud as she could.

The children retold the Nativity, with numerous adaptations and jokes thrown in. Each year group had taken a section to re-enact beginning with Reception and leading up to the last scene played by the pupils in Year Six. Every child had a turn on the stage, the majority even had a small speaking part.

When it was the turn of the twins' class, Evie played her part of the Star showing the way perfectly, happily skipping around the stage and reciting a short poem instructing the shepherds to follow her.

Grinning, Chrissy gave Evie the thumbs up as she finished her poem and skipped back across the stage. Although she had always been the quieter of the twins, Evie had always come to life on the stage, exuding a confidence she struggled to find during her everyday life.

Sophia, on the other hand, although the more confident of the two, absolutely hated any form of acting or anything where she was put in the spotlight and came onto the stage, head down and mumbling her words under her breath, barely audible above the normal rustling and toddlers talking from the audience. Sitting up as tall as she could, Chrissy caught her eye, giving her the thumbs up and smiling at her, letting her know that she was proud of her. Sophia had been worrying about the Christmas Concert for weeks now, and had woken in the night telling Chrissy that she just couldn't bring herself to talk in front of everyone. So Chrissy knew how much effort it had taken Sophia to come up on stage in front of them all, act out her part of a Shepherdess and mutter her lines.

Instinctively turning to her side, Chrissy bit her tongue as she remembered she was on her own. There was no Andrew or his parents next to her to tell each other how well the twins had done or to say that Evie had outperformed last year's part or that they were so proud of Sophia for managing to do something she was so clearly uncomfortable with.

Twisting around in the dark, Chrissy watched as Andrew leant in towards Susan, whispering to her. No doubt telling her the same things he normally said to Chrissy. Tearing her eyes away from them, their silhouettes highlighted from a stage light behind them, she shook her head and reminded herself that she was far happier sat on her own than she had been last year at the twins Christmas Concert with Andrew. She didn't need his hand on her knee, a front to pretend to the world that they were a happy couple, providing a happy and secure upbringing for their girls, when in truth, and unbeknown to all, including Chrissy, Andrew had been planning to rush off to 'work' on a 'callout' as soon as the curtains had closed on the production. No, she didn't need the lying any more, the façade. She was just fine on her own.

* * *

The whole school squeezed onto the stage to sing 'Away in the Manger' before bowing and heading back to their classrooms in an orderly line.

Chrissy slipped on her coat as the hall lights were turned on, she needed to get outside and around to the Evie and Sophia's classroom door before she ran into Andrew. At least she knew he wouldn't be hanging around to see them, being as it was during the day he really would have to head back to work, Susan would too.

'Excuse me, please?' Chrissy weaved through the crowds of parents milling around chatting to each other. Pulling at her scarf, she wished she hadn't put it on until she'd made it outside, it really was hot and stuffy in the hall. Too stuffy, she could hardly breathe. Looking back, she could see Andrew helping Susan with her coat, they had barely even stood up. She had time.

'Sorry.' Why she was apologising when the pushchair had come out of nowhere, she had no idea, but she steadied herself and smiled before striding the last few steps to the door.

The cold wind whipped in her face and she braced herself against the chill. Pulling her scarf up higher over her chin, she made her way to where the twins would be let out once they'd got changed.

* * *

Slowly, parents, friends and grandparents joined Chrissy on the playground after filtering out from the hall. Checking her watch, she realised she'd only been waiting five minutes. They'd probably take at least ten or fifteen to get changed and get their things ready to come home. She wriggled her toes in her trainers, glad she had kept her thick slipper socks on.

'Chrissy.'

Jerking her head up, Chrissy slowly turned, holding her breath. She'd recognise that voice for the rest of her life. 'Andrew. Susan.'

'We just thought we'd pop over to tell the girls how proud we are of them after their performance.'

'Right.' Had he really used the term 'we', referring to both himself and Susan? Susan had no right to be proud of them. She was nothing to them. Apart from being the woman to break up their parents' marriage, of course. As for Andrew, well, it was debatable whether he had any right to be proud of them either. He hadn't helped them practise their lines or learn the songs or encouraged them in any way.

'I hope you don't mind me tagging along? Now that I'm a big part of the girls' lives, I feel we all need to be mature about the situation and show the girls that we are getting along for their benefit, don't you think?' Susan smiled, her coral pink lipstick cracking at the corners of her mouth.

A 'big part of their lives'? She saw them once every two weeks, and then from what the twins had said she was often out anyway. Who the hell did she think she was? What gave her the right to talk down to Chrissy? To make out that Chrissy wasn't 'being mature'? She hadn't even clapped eyes on the woman since Andrew's Christmas party three years ago. How could she even suggest that Chrissy wasn't being mature? Had Andrew said something? What though? She'd always been civil to him. In fact, it was Andrew who had the tendency to be immature, not her.

'I know this must be difficult for you, but we do really need to make the effort to get along, I'm sure you agree.' Susan pursed her lips, her cheeks concaving to reveal high angular cheekbones.

'Hey, Chrissy, I just need a quick word, please? You two don't mind if I steal her for a moment, do you?' Holding Chrissy by the elbow, Natalie guided her towards the edge of the playground, away from Andrew, Susan and their ongoing interrogation. 'Is that your ex? Are you OK? You look really pale. You're not going to faint or anything, are you?'

'No, I'm fine, thanks. Yes, that's Andrew and his mistress, Susan. Apparently, I need to make an effort with her now that she's "going to be a big part of the girls' lives".' Holding her fingers up, Chrissy used her index fingers to make quotation marks.

'She actually said that?'

'Oh, yes. And then she wonders why I'm rendered speechless!' Chrissy laughed, it was either that or burst into tears. 'Anyway, thanks for rescuing me.'

'That's fine. Just promise to do the same at the wedding if Graham's parents corner me and start talking about their bunions.'

'Your wedding? I didn't expect to be invited, not

now that...' Chrissy let her gaze be drawn to Luke, still with his beanie hat on, who was stood talking to Graham.

'Of course you're still invited, and the girls, obviously. If it wasn't for you, I'd be wearing a bin bag as my wedding dress!'

'Thank you.' Patting her cheeks, Chrissy let the cold seep from her gloves to her cheeks, hoping it would dull the crimson blush flooding her face. 'Are you all set for the big day now?'

'I think so. I mean, Gina has everything planned down to the last detail, but there are still things out of her control that seem to be going wrong.' Natalie rolled her eyes.

'Oh no, what like?'

'Well, for a start Graham's great grandma was rushed into hospital with a broken hip last night, so I can't see her being able to come. The 1970's red bus we thought we'd hired to take the guests up to the reception has apparently blown a gasket or something, and then, of course, there's Laura.' Natalie ticked each one off on her fingers.

'What about Laura?' So she knew then? Was she worried that Chrissy would have a go at her at the wedding or something? Maybe she should reassure her.

'Well, the fact that she's in Italy and, now, it seems she's not going to make it back in time for the wedding. So I'm afraid all those hours you put in working on her dress may actually have been for nothing.'

'Right, I didn't realise.' Chrissy stole a glance at Luke, maybe that's why he looked so down, standing next to Graham with his head bent as he kicked at something with his feet. He'd more than likely stay around for the wedding and then go and join her.

'Yes, Phil rang her the morning of the meal and asked her to meet him back in London, which was why she didn't come out that night. Apparently, he's confessed his undying love for her and had already booked a holiday for them both.'

'Wow.' She was with Phil? Laura had been with Phil the night of the meal? She hadn't gone. Luke hadn't been with Laura that night. He'd been telling the truth.

'Umm, I don't know if it's romantic or presumptuous. I mean, to book a holiday like that for the same day he had planned to apologise for being an idiot.' Natalie shook her head. 'He's a nice bloke, I guess. I just hope he doesn't break her heart again.'

'I'm sure he won't.' Chrissy walked towards the wobbly bridge and gripped hold of the metal railing.

Closing her eyes, she waited until the dizziness had passed.

'Are you OK?'

Feeling Natalie's hand on her arm, Chrissy opened her eyes and smiled. 'Yes, sorry. I just felt a bit weird then, I should have had something to eat before I came out.'

'Hold on, I might have something in the nappy bag.' Leaving Chrissy standing alone, Natalie went back to Graham, Luke and the pram and began rummaging through her bag.

Looking across towards Andrew and Susan, Chrissy wound a loose strand of hair around her index finger. They looked so happy. It looked as though they were actually talking, having a proper conversation rather than the stilted one-sided conversations of the last years of their marriage, when Chrissy would talk to Andrew and he would nod here and there half-heartedly pretending to listen. No, they both had their heads dipped towards each other and Andrew was actually talking to her. Chrissy shook her head, good for them if they were happy. It was completely her fault that she wasn't. Luke *had* been perfect. She'd just messed it all up because of her own insecurities. She had no one else to blame.

She shifted her gaze across at Luke who was now

holding Natalie's nappy bag as she delved into it, pulling out Babygros and wet ones to pile into Graham's waiting hands. Chrissy watched as Luke pointed inside the bag and pulled out a fruit bar before handing it to Natalie.

She dipped her head as he looked across at her and pulled her mobile from her pocket, tapping in her password she scrolled down reading old messages from him. He had ended every single one of them with a kiss. What had she done? Why had she jumped to the wrong conclusion so quickly? Just because Andrew had been unfaithful, it didn't mean every other man she met would be. And Luke hadn't.

'Here you go. It's a bit squashed but it might help. I must warn you though, they don't look very pleasant, although Kane devours them quickly enough so they can't be all that bad.' Natalie brandished the bent fruit bar.

'Thank you, that's great.' Unwrapping the bar, Chrissy swallowed trying not to gag on the strong taste of manufactured blueberries. She'd have to eat it and hope she could keep it down until she got home at least.

'Luke was worried about you, he said you look ill.' Tipping her head to one side, Natalie looked her up and down. 'Which you do.'

'I've probably got a cold coming on, that's all.' Waving Natalie's concerns away, she finished the bar and shoved her hands in her pockets, trying to pull her coat away from her middle.

'Well, make sure you're better for the wedding. I can't have anyone else drop out, everyone will think I don't have any friends.' Laughing, Natalie looked across at the classroom door again. 'Here they come.'

Stepping forward, they both joined the throng of parents and grandparents who had pushed forwards, trying to catch a glimpse of their child or grandchild. With each child who exited the class, the crowd dispersed a little.

'Evie, Sophia.' Waving, Chrissy called to the twins as they came to the door.

'Mum, did you see my dance? What did you think?' Running across to her, Evie slung her bag onto the floor by Chrissy's feet and jumped up and down.

'I did. It was fantastic and so was your singing. I'm so proud of you, you did so well.' Grinning, Chrissy pulled each one to her, kissing the tops of their heads. 'And Sophia, you were great too. I'm so proud of you too.'

'Umm, I was rubbish, just admit it.' Sophia slipped her bag off her shoulders, letting it drop to the ground next to Evie's.

'No, you were not. You were great.'

'No, I really wasn't, but that's OK, I hate acting.'

'Sophia, you did really well.' Too late, Sophia was already halfway across the playground on her way to the tyres to join a game of tag with her friends.

'Evie, darling. You were amazing. The star of the show.'

Grimacing, Chrissy turned around and watched as Susan sauntered over, her arms wide, ready to give Evie a hug.

'Thanks.' Evie glanced back at Chrissy as she was enveloped in Susan's arms.

'Yes, you really were very good.' Andrew patted Evie on the arm, waiting until Susan had let go and stepped back before he hugged her. 'Where's Sophia?'

'Over there playing.' Chrissy pointed to the other side of the playground.

'You, miss, are definitely the actress of the family.' Susan tapped Evie on the nose.

'Sophia was really good too.' Looking down, Evie scuffed her shoes against the tarmac, something Chrissy hadn't seen her do since she was four.

'Of course, she was, but you were wonderful.' Pulling her leather gloves off one finger at a time, Susan opened her clutch bag and pulled out two chocolate Santas. 'Here you go, one for you and one for Sophia when she has time to come over and say hello.'

Biting her tongue, Chrissy took a deep breath in. 'She's just playing with her friends, I'm sure she'll be over soon when she realises you've both come over to say hello.' She decided not to mention that she had seen Sophia pause in her game and watch as Susan hugged Evie before running off again in the opposite direction. 'And, both myself and Andrew decided before the twins were born that we'd try very hard not to compare the girls.'

Susan pursed her lips and put her gloves back on before turning to look at Andrew.

'Chrissy, Susan didn't mean anything by it. She was just complimenting Evie, which she deserved.'

'Anyway,' Susan linked her arm through Andrew's. 'We really must be going to avoid the rush hour on the way home.'

Home? Was she doing this on purpose? Was she trying to make Chrissy feel awful? Chrissy looked across at Luke who was giving Kane a piggyback ride while chasing Adam. Well, it wasn't working. Susan was welcome to Andrew. Let them go home to their perfectly decorated and furnished detached house. It wasn't Andrew who was making her feel awful.

'Good idea. Evie, love, will you run over and ask

Sophia to come over to say bye, please?' Slowly, Andrew extracted his arm from Susan's before plunging his hands in his pockets and staring at his shoes.

'Well, thank you for coming. It means a lot to the girls.'

'We wouldn't miss it for the world.' Susan straightened her floral scarf against her coat.

'No, of course you wouldn't.' Smiling, Chrissy glanced across at Evie and Sophia, willing them to hurry up. 'Here they come.'

'Sophia, darling, you were a very good shepherdess.' Placing her hands on Sophia's shoulders, Susan leant across and kissed her on the forehead.

'Thanks.' Looking across at Chrissy, Sophia stepped back, letting Susan's hands fall to her sides.

'You're very welcome. Maybe next time, just come over and say hello to your dad when he's travelled this far to watch one of your shows instead of going off and playing with your friends.'

'Excuse me...' Stepping forward, Chrissy put her arm around Sophia's shoulders, pulling her back towards her.

'Yes, you were a lovely shepherdess but we need to get going now, so I'll see you both on Boxing Day.' Andrew looked across at Chrissy. 'If that's still OK with you?'

Chrissy nodded. What was the point of saying anything else, he'd only cut her off again. He could always make her feel that small with a mere look or insinuation that what she had to say was worthless. In a way, it was probably a good thing that Susan was so very confident and egocentric, at least he wouldn't be able to make her feel as insignificant as he did Chrissy. Good luck to her. Stepping away, she let them say their goodbyes to the twins.

'Bye, bye, Chrissy.'

'Goodbye, Susan. Goodbye, Andrew.' Narrowing her eyes, she watched them walk out of the school grounds, Susan's arm once again linked through Andrew's.

'Right, I bet you two are hungry after your big performances. Let's go home, get the wood burner on and bake some Christmas cookies. One more day of school and it'll be the Christmas holidays!' Picking up the two abandoned rucksacks at her feet, Chrissy led the way home.

'At last! I feel like we've been at this school forever now.'

'Hold on, I just need to tell Rachel something.' Evie ran across the playground to a huddle of girls standing around a bench.

'Are you OK, Sophia?'

'Yep.'

'Just ignore Susan. Your dad understands that you were off playing and it was nice for him to see how well you've settled in and that you've made so many friends.'

'I know. I do ignore her. I don't care what she thinks.'

'Good.'

'She's out most of the time when we're at Dad's house anyway, so at least we don't have to put up with her for long.' Taking her rucksack from Chrissy's hand, Sophia flung it over her shoulder.

'Right.' Pulling her scarf up over her mouth, Chrissy silently laughed. If Susan was like that all of the time, no wonder Sophia had got into an argument with her that time. Did Andrew know exactly what he had got himself into? It was one thing having all the excitement of an extra-marital affair, but Chrissy would imagine living with someone twenty-four seven would be completely different. She shrugged, he'd got himself into this.

'Come on, Evie. It's freezing.' Sophia ran towards Evie and her friends.

22

Pulling her royal blue satin dress over her head, Chrissy breathed in. If this one didn't fit she'd end up going to Natalie's wedding reception wearing jeans and a shirt. Wriggling her hips, she reached around and pulled up the zip.

She looked in the mirror, the royal blue fabric clung to her curves, which was OK, that was the style of the dress but it still didn't improve her confidence. Turning to the side, she smoothed the dress over her stomach, a slight bump was obvious but maybe it was only because she was so conscious of it. To other people it would hopefully just look as though she'd put a bit of weight on. She put the palms of her hands against her cheeks. Would it though? Her face was looking gaunter by the day. The morning, or more fitting all day, sickness meant she'd hardly kept a thing down for weeks so she'd actually lost weight everywhere else apart from her waist area. It had been the same with the twins and she'd always joked that if she wanted to lose weight she just needed to get pregnant again.

Untying a floaty white scarf from the end of her bed, she wound it around her neck, letting it rest across her stomach. That was better, the contrast of the white against the royal blue took away the attention from her increasing waist.

Sitting on the edge of the bed, she pinched the bridge of her nose. She really didn't want to go. She didn't want to see Luke. She didn't want to be reminded of how stupid she had been and how little she had thought of him. Over the last few days, he'd been going out of his way to avoid her and she didn't blame him. Only yesterday when she'd taken the girls on a walk with Star, she'd spotted him duck into the pub when he'd seen them coming.

Maybe she was being paranoid, maybe it was her mind making things up. Still, it was definitely going to be awkward today, and if Natalie hadn't been insisting they went, she'd gladly just stay in and have a movie night with the twins.

Standing up again, she took a silver diamanté necklace out of her jewellery box and put it on. She had to make the effort, Evie had been crying only last night upset that this Christmas things were going to be so completely different to last year. They'd always gone round to Andrew's parents' house on Christmas Eve for a big family party. They'd then stay overnight along with Andrew's brother's family so the girls had always been busy playing with their cousins. On Christmas Day, they'd wake up to a stocking and some share-me presents to keep at their grandparents before they'd go home after a big roast to open the presents Santa had left under their own tree. At least the girls would enjoy the wedding. Their friends at school had been talking about it for weeks. She couldn't make them miss out.

Chrissy slipped her feet into her heels, this Christmas Day would be quiet and boring in comparison. They'd decided tomorrow they'd wake up to their presents, go for a long walk to the woods with Star and then have a Christmas movie marathon. It would be lovely in its own right, but much quieter than they were used to. On the plus side, they'd be no snide comments under Andrew's breath at his parents' house, no in-laws to try vainly to please and no arguments when they got home, and above all, no walking on eggshells until Andrew finally stormed out of the house.

Opening the wardrobe door, Chrissy ran her hand over the small wooden Christmas Eve Box she'd picked up at a craft fair at the beginning of December and smiled. Christmas would be good this year, she'd make sure of it. They would have a good time at the wedding reception and come home to the Christmas Eve Box, one of a few new traditions she had decided to implement.

She just needed to put Luke out of her mind and try to enjoy the night.

* * *

'Are you sure my hair doesn't look funny like this?' Evie pulled one of the curls between her fingers before letting it go, watching in the mirror as it pinged back.

'It looks lovely.' Chrissy smiled and turned the curlers off. 'Are you sure you don't want yours doing, Sophia?'

'No way. It's too girly for me.' Sophia pulled her hair up into a ponytail and wrapped a hairband around it. 'It suits you though, Evie.'

Peering into the mirror, Evie shook her head, the

mound of curls dancing around her. 'I like it. Thanks, Mum.'

'You're welcome. OK, let's get a photo of you both before we go.' Pulling her mobile from her silver clutch bag, Chrissy indicated to the twins to stand side by side in front of the Christmas tree. Although they were identical, due to the way they were dressed you could hardly tell. Evie wore a pale pink chiffon dress and held a black purse in her hand, while Sophia had refused wear a dress, instead opting for smart dark jeans and a glittery purple T-shirt. 'That's it. Smile.'

'Do you think there'll be a buffet?'

'I should think so, Evie. Right, you two go and wait in the car, I just need to make sure I turned my bedroom light off.'

'OK.' Sophia caught the car keys as Chrissy threw them to her.

Waiting until the girls were outside, Chrissy then ran upstairs and brought out the Christmas Eve Box.

Back downstairs, she lifted the bottom branches of the Christmas tree and slid the box underneath. Taking a tube of green glitter she had hidden behind a photo on the mantelpiece, she gently shook it over the floor. As she backed out into the hallway, she watched the tiny grains of green foil flutter down, landing in swoops leading from the front door to the tree.

'Mum...'

'Hold on, just coming.' Slipping the small tube into her clutch bag, she turned and went outside, pulling the front door shut behind her.

* * *

'Doesn't it look beautiful?' Following the thin red carpet, Chrissy led the way through the field towards the large marquee by the stream. The green of nature served as the perfect backdrop to the white marquee illuminated by hundreds of white twinkling lights wrapping around the outside. She had to admit when Gina had told her that the reception was going to be in a marquee in the middle of the local farmer's field, she hadn't pictured something so picturesque.

Two tall fir trees, again covered in white lights, flanked the entrance. In a sleigh stood to the right of the entrance, lit by an old-fashioned style lamppost, children sat gripping the reins to two wicker reindeer while their parents took pictures.

Chrissy, Evie and Sophia joined a small queue of guests arriving for the reception which wound out from the entrance along the red carpet.

'Why are we stopping here?' Sophia fidgeted with her scarf.

'The bride and groom are probably waiting just inside ready to greet their guests. Have you got the card and present still?'

'So we've got to wait to say hello? But they already know us?'

'I know, but it's so we can congratulate them on getting married. Remember, there's a lot of people here and it would take them forever to go around to everyone to speak to them, so it's traditional for the bride and groom to greet everyone as they come in.'

'Oh, OK.'

'Will they have a disco?'

'I expect so, Sophia.'

'Can we dance?'

'Why not? Look, we're almost at the entrance now.' Putting her arms around Sophia and Evie's shoulders, she led them forward a little into the stream of warm air escaping through the doorway.

Following the couple in front of them, they stepped into the marquee through an archway of gold sprayed bamboo covered in fairy lights. Waiting for their turn to greet the happy couple, Chrissy paused, letting her eyes adjust to the bright of the inside.

'Wow, it's warm in here, isn't it? We may as well take our coats off and hang them here.'

Slipping out of her coat, Chrissy hung it on one of the coat stands grouped beside the entrance before turning to hang Evie and Sophia's up too.

'Who are those other people?' Evie pulled on Chrissy's elbow and pointed ahead. 'We obviously know Adam, Kane and Luke, but who's that woman and man?'

Looking ahead, Chrissy froze. Why hadn't she realised that Luke would be in the line-up for greeting people? Glancing down at her stomach, she centred the fabric scarf. 'I should think they are Graham's parents.'

'Hey, Chrissy. Hi, girls. So glad you could come.' Leaning forward, Natalie held Chrissy's shoulders and pulled her in for a hug.

'Congratulations! You look beautiful.'

'All thanks to you.' With a champagne glass in one hand, Natalie twirled, the train swirling around her ankles.

'Not at all. You look stunning. And this place is gorgeous.'

'It is, isn't it? All of Gina's painstaking planning has paid off, hasn't it? Come here and give the bride a hug, girls.'

'Congratulations.' Evie smiled as she was pulled in for a hug.

'Thank you, sweetie. Loving your curls.'

'Thanks.' Touching her hair, Evie grinned.

'Congratulations on your wedding.' Sophia stood awkwardly in front of Natalie.

'Thank you, Sophia. Come here.' Natalie hugged Sophia to her.

Making their way down the line of the wedding party, Chrissy, Evie and Sophia congratulated Graham, said 'hello' to Adam and Kane before introducing themselves to Graham's parents.

Pushing the girls in front, they made their way towards Luke who was standing awkwardly at the end of the line.

'Hey, Sophia. Hey, Evie.'

'Hi. Do we have to say congratulations to you too?'

'You can do if you want, Sophia. But, no, you don't have to.'

Luke smiled at them and pointed to the far side of the marquee. 'There's a pic-n-mix stall over there, you best get in there before all the adults hit it.'

'Oh, can we, Mum?'

'Yes.' Watching Evie and Sophia make their way through the busy marquee, Chrissy fiddled with her scarf before looking up at Luke. Blinking her eyes, she forced herself to smile. 'Congratulations on your sister's wedding.'

'Thanks.' Leaning forward, Luke pecked her on the cheek.

Without thinking, she held onto his elbow, forcing both of them to freeze momentarily. She breathed in his distinctive aftershave, the woody fragrance making her think of security, love and home.

Placing his hand on her shoulder, they were locked in position, so close and yet emotionally still miles apart. The warmth and weight of his hand through the satin of her dress filled her with longing. What had she done? Why had she ruined something so perfect?

'I'm sorry.' Closing her eyes, she bit her bottom lip before turning her head and pulling away to find the twins.

* * *

With the buffet eaten, the dance floor began to fill. Sitting at a table against the edge of the marquee, Chrissy watched as Evie and Sophia wound their way through clusters of Natalie and Graham's friends and family to meet up with their classmates standing by the disco booth.

Taking a sip of her orange juice, she twisted the glass, tiny silver sequins in the shape of wedding bells stuck to the bottom. To her right, a couple sat with their heads bowed, deep in conversation. The other couple who had been seated with them had already said their goodbyes and left to collect their daughter, who had apparently just thrown up over the babysitter.

Gina had transformed the inside of the marquee into a winter wonderland with elements both for the adults and the children. A Santa's grotto set up towards the far corner of the marquee boasted a winding walkway filled with glittering silver wicker animals. Small children holding their parents' hands chattered to two elves as they waited their turn to meet Santa. The pic-n-mix stall stood next to a craft table laden with glitter glue, sequins and plain baubles to decorate. While for the adults, a photo booth complete with an array of hats, wigs and accessories stood waiting to capture drunken memories. The sparkly black dance floor was set up in the centre of the marquee, red and green disco lights illuminating guests enjoying classic Christmas hits.

Taking a deep breath in, Chrissy smiled, it was amazing what Gina had achieved. She had mentioned that she might start her own events business and, if this was anything to go by, she'd be very successful. Chrissy was glad they had come in the end, it would be a Christmas Eve to remember and the girls were definitely enjoying themselves. Leaning back in her chair, she watched as Evie, Sophia and about five other children from their school gathered in a circle at the edge of the dance floor, taking it in turns to step into the middle and perform a silly dance to make the others laugh.

Looking around, although she recognised quite a few of the guests as parents of pupils from the school, she only really knew Natalie and Gina to say more than a cursory hello to and they were both busy. The happy couple were making their way around the tables, sitting down and chatting with their guests, and Gina was nowhere to be seen, probably busy organising something or other.

Shifting in her seat, she picked up sequin bells, piling them around the bottom of her glass. Luke had sat down at a table on the opposite side of the dance floor, straight in her line of vision. He sat alone, his arm resting on the table, clutching a bottle of lager in his hand. Had he sat there on purpose just to remind her of what she had done? Her eyes stung as she thought about how she had ruined their future. Looking from her stomach to him and back again, she took a gulp of orange juice, the acidic flavour sticking in her throat. She had to tell him, didn't she? People would begin to notice soon and it wouldn't take long for him to realise the baby was his. As much as it terrified her, it was the right thing to do.

Twisting the ends of her scarf together, she watched as he ran his hand through his hair and nodded at someone dancing on the floor in front of him. Maybe she should just tell him everything, that she'd made a huge mistake, that she'd been stupid to finish with him, that she should have trusted him.

Standing up, she pulled her dress down over her thighs. If she didn't do it now, she'd lose her confidence.

Weaving her way through the tables and around the dance floor, she made her way towards him.

'Luke?'

'Chrissy?' Looking up at her, he tilted his bottle towards her.

'Can I have a quick word, please?'

'Of course, sit down.' Leaning towards the chair next to him, he pulled it out slightly.

'Not here, outside. If that's OK?'

'OK.' Standing up, he held the bottleneck between his thumb and index finger and followed her through the crowds and out of the marquee.

The cold air stung her cheeks as she glanced around, trying to find a quiet spot where they could talk. A few people sat on chairs watching their children play tag across the field. A small group of smokers huddled together towards the back end of the marquee.

'There's a bench up here.' Pointing his bottle towards a small copse of trees, Luke strode across the field.

Keeping her head bent, she looked down at the ground, stepping over the uneven tufts of grass and mounds of soil. There was no going back now. She had to explain why she'd acted the way she had. If she did, maybe there was a chance that he would forgive her and they could start over. Maybe.

Stopping a short distance away from the copse of trees, Luke led them to the side to a bench which faced back across the field towards where the festivities continued, everyone else completely oblivious to how important their conversation would be. Shrugging out of his suit jacket, he laid his across the damp wooden seat.

'Here, sit on this.' Lowering himself down onto the bare wood, he patted his jacket.

'Thanks.'

'So, what did you want to talk about?'

Taking a deep breath, Chrissy looked at him. 'There's something I need to tell you, but first, I wanted to explain why I pushed you away.'

'Why you finished with me, you mean?' Tipping his bottle up, he took another sip.

'Well, yes.' Clasping her hands together in her lap, Chrissy looked across the field as people began exiting the marquee, gathering in pockets opposite them.

'I think they're going to start the fireworks in a minute.'

'Fireworks? Did you want to go back? This can wait.' Standing up, she looked back at Luke. She was only kidding herself anyway. She'd done far too much damage for Luke to forgive her.

'No, I'm happy watching from here.'

'OK.' Sitting back down, Chrissy shifted and crossed her legs. 'I'm sorry for the way I treated you. I know it's nothing to do with you, but the girls' dad, my ex-husband, was having an affair before we split up.'

'You're right, that has nothing to do with us.'

Looking down at her shoes, the heels caked in mud, she whispered. 'Laura.'

'What about Laura?'

'When I met her and I altered her dress, she was talking about you. And then, when I didn't go out for

Natalie and Graham's dinner and you stayed out all night, I just...'

'You thought I'd cheated on you?'

'I... yes. I jumped to the wrong conclusion. She's just so beautiful and successful, and everything I'm not. I got the impression she regretted splitting up with you, and then you didn't come back, and...'

'She wasn't even at the dinner. And we were completely different people when we were together.' Leaning forward, he leant his elbows on his knees and stared ahead at the illuminated marquee.

'I know that now. I'm sorry.'

'When did you find out she didn't go?'

'The other day after the Christmas Concert. Natalie mentioned it.'

'Until then, you'd thought I'd cheated on you?'

Rubbing her hands together against the cold, Chrissy looked across at him. 'I'm sorry. I made a mistake.'

Closing his eyes, Luke leant back against the bench, lifting his head to the sky.

'Luke, say something. Please.' Tapping her foot against the ground, she stared at him. Forgive me, forgive me. Say you want to get back, say you want to give us another go, please.

Opening his eyes and leaning forward again, Luke

stared at a tuft of grass in front of him. 'What do you want me to say? You actually thought that little of me to think I would do that behind your back? And then lie about it? What sort of person do you think I am? You think I'm a liar and a cheat?'

'No, not at all. I made a mistake that's all. Andrew...'

'I'm not Andrew.' Without looking at her, he stood up and begun striding towards the marquee.

'Luke, please? I know you're not, you're nothing like him. I was feeling rubbish and I just let my imagination run away with me. I'm sorry, I really am.' Standing up, Chrissy picked up his suit jacket and followed him, running to catch up with him.

They were nearing the crowd gathered waiting for the fireworks.

'Luke. Please? Just listen to me.'

'Chrissy, I can't do this.' Turning around, he paused, holding up his hands towards her. 'I had really fallen for you and I told you that. I thought we had a future together. I thought we could build a life together and then you just went cold on me. You didn't even give me a reason.'

'I know. I'm sorry.'

'You didn't even confront me with the ludicrous idea you had that I had been with Laura behind your back. You didn't even give me a chance to fight for us.'

Standing in front of him, in the middle of the field, Chrissy hugged his jacket to her chest. He wasn't going to forgive her, was he? She had messed it up forever. The fireworks began to the side of them. A small white fountain, followed by a larger rocket, the lights cascading from it mid-air, taking the form of bright, shining falling leaves.

'I love you.' Shouting above the crackles and bangs, Chrissy bit her bottom lip. Had she really said that? She hadn't meant to. She had been thinking it, yes, but she hadn't meant to actually say it aloud.

Rubbing his hands across his face, Luke looked at the ground.

'Luke, I...' She'd made things worse, she could tell.

His eyes met hers as he slipped his hands in his pockets. The fireworks illuminated the bright white of his long-sleeved shirt. 'I can't do this now. Not now.'

'Look, I know I've messed up, I know that. The way I just shut you out can't have been nice, but I had my reasons.' Surely he must understand that?

'I cannot be judged by your ex's actions. Besides, it too late anyway.' Turning on his heels, he strode towards the marquee, his head down, oblivious to the light show above him.

Holding his jacket to her nose, Chrissy breathed in deeply, the fragrance of his aftershave plunged her straight back to the first time they had spent the evening in the pub, laughing, joking and drinking. They had really clicked and it hadn't been just lust. They had both had feelings for each other. What they had felt had been real. It couldn't be too late. She needed to fight for him, tell him again how she felt.

Besides, regardless of whether they did get back together or not, he still deserved to know about the baby. It would be up to him if he wanted to be a part of the baby's life, but it was his choice to make. She couldn't take that away from him.

With her heels sticking in the mud with every step she took, she avoided the worst mud patches and tufts of grass as she made her way after him. Running around the outskirts of the group of guests watching the fireworks, Chrissy followed Luke into the marquee.

Pausing in the entrance, she let the warm air envelope her. 'Luke, please?'

Grabbing a new bottle of lager from the edge of the bar, Luke turned back to her. 'I don't know what else to say. What's done is done.'

'It doesn't have to be. You're right, I did just think you'd done the same as Andrew and that wasn't fair on you, but it was a mistake. I'm sorry, I really am, but can't we just get past it and try again? What we had wasn't just some quick fling, it was real.'

'Regardless of how I feel about you, it's too late.'

'So you do still have feelings for me then?' He did. He had said 'feel' not 'felt'. He did still want a relationship with her. 'If you do, then it's not too late.'

Taking a swig from his bottle, he placed it on a table to his left and cleared his throat. 'I've brought a property up north. It's that old hotel that needs renovating. I managed to get hold of it. I have a lot riding on it and I'll need to be on site.'

'You're moving.' Gripping the back of a chair, Chrissy stared at him. He was leaving?

'If I'd even have thought there was any chance of us working things out, I wouldn't have even given it a second thought but you'd made it quite clear and, truth be told, I needed to get away.' Running his hand through his hair, he looked at Chrissy, his eyes glistening.

'Right, well, OK.' Squeezing her eyes shut, she rubbed her temples with her index finger and thumb. She'd well and truly messed things up. Opening her eyes, she looked down at her shoes. 'When are you leaving?'

'Boxing Day.'

'How long are you going for?'

'The hotel will take six months to a year to complete, all being well.'

'And then you'll come back?'

Taking a deep breath, Luke shrugged his shoulders. 'I wasn't planning to.'

This would be the last time she'd see him. She wouldn't see him again. She blinked the tears away, she needed to tell him then. She had to. 'I need to tell you something then.'

'Look, I know you're sorry. I get that. I'm sorry too. Like I said, if I'd known, if you had told me what you were thinking...' He held his hands out in front of him, his palms up.

'No, it's not that.' Glancing up at the ceiling, Chrissy hugged his jacket to her. 'I'm pregnant.'

'Pregnant?' Dropping his hands to his sides, Luke stared at her.

'Yes. I didn't know how to tell you.'

'Is it mine?'

Had he really asked that? Who did he think she was? Narrowing her eyes, she took a deep breath before throwing his jacket on the table to her side and turning on her heels and coming face to face with Natalie. How long had she been standing there? Had she heard? 'Natalie?'

'I just popped in to see if you were both OK.' Her face blushed ashen.

'Sorry, I need to go.' Looking at the floor, Chrissy mumbled as she ran out of the marquee. Natalie had heard. Luke thought she'd been sleeping around. Everything was wrong. Everything. She needed to get the twins and get home.

23

Watching Evie and Sophia pulling presents from underneath the tree, the room buzzing with excitement, Chrissy plastered a smile on her face and tried to keep her eyes open. She couldn't have had more than an hour's sleep after getting home from the wedding last night. She and Luke's conversation had been on constant replay in her mind.

'Mum, look! I've got the guitar I've been asking for!' Grinning, Sophia held up a green acoustic guitar.

'Wow. That looks great.' Chrissy smiled, a real one this time. Sophia would find a voucher for guitar lessons further under the Christmas tree.

'And I've got the roller skates I wanted!' Pushing

the robin adorned paper aside, Evie pulled a pair of bright pink skates from a box.

'Maybe we can go for a walk and test them out after Christmas dinner then.'

* * *

'Can I hold Star's lead?' Sophia held out her hand.

'Yes, here you are.' Handing the lead over to Sophia, Chrissy watched as she ran ahead to catch up with Evie, Star bounding along beside her. It had only taken Evie a few minutes and one stumble to get used to her new roller skates before she had zoomed off up the path.

'Girls, we'll go this way.' Catching up with the twins at the end of the lane, she pointed to the road out of the village. She didn't want to go past Natalie and Graham's house. Luke would likely be round there all day and, even if he wasn't, she didn't want to run into Natalie. Not now that she knew about the baby. She shook her head, she wasn't even going to think about having to face her on the school run in January.

'Can we go to the basketball court? They'll be no bumps there and I'll be able to go super-fast.' Evie spun around on her roller skates, making circles around Chrissy.

'Yes, we can do.' Pulling her scarf up over her nose, Chrissy nodded.

Following the girls as they sped ahead, Chrissy checked her mobile. Nothing. No missed call or text message. She shoved it back into her pocket. What had she expected? Luke had made himself perfectly clear last night. She'd just have to get used to the idea of this baby having no father. Wiping her eyes with the tip of her gloved fingers, she watched the girls as they laughed and joked together, each trying to tag the other with Star barking excitedly at the commotion. They were happy. She must be doing something right at least. She'd cope. She'd have to. The girls would probably be overjoyed anyway.

*** * ***

'Mum, are you OK?' Skating up on her roller skates, Evie came to a stop in front of Chrissy.

'Of course I am.' Smiling, Chrissy held out her arms, wrapping them around Evie as she skated into them.

'You just look a bit sad, that's all.' Looking up at Chrissy, Evie frowned.

'Honestly, I'm fine. Thank you for asking though.' Chrissy kissed her on top of her head. 'Are you enjoying your Christmas?'

'Yes, definitely! I like being at home for the whole of the day because we can play with our toys.'

'It's nice, isn't it? You go off and play with Sophia and Star. I'm fine.'

'OK. I love you, Mum.' Pulling away from her, Evie grinned before skating off.

Turning away, Chrissy walked towards the bin, pulling receipts from her pocket. She didn't want the girls to see the tears rolling down her cheeks. It wasn't Andrew she was missing, it was the thought of what she could have had with Luke and the knowledge that it was all her fault that she wasn't sharing today with him.

She tore the receipts into tiny pieces and watched as they fell like confetti into the bin. That was her life at the moment, broken, and she knew there was a long path ahead to get back on track. Closing her eyes, she took a deep breath. Today she just needed to focus on keeping a happy face on in front of the girls, tomorrow when they went to Andrew's, she'd allow herself to think about it all properly.

'Mum! Look, it's snowing! It's actually snowing on Christmas Day!'

Looking up at the sky, Chrissy allowed the small, cold snowflakes to land on her face. Sophia was right, it was actually snowing and the pure white sky was full of it. Turning around, she smiled. Sophia was spinning around, her arms wide and her mouth open, catching snowflakes on her tongue. Evie raced around the basketball court, every now and then cruising on her skates, letting the momentum propel her along. Star, whose lead had been dropped, jumped excitedly in the air trying to catch the flakes as they drifted down to settle on the tarmac.

'Right, we'd best head back now and start dinner. You two can go and play in the garden while I'm cooking, if you like?'

* * *

By the time they rounded the corner to their lane, the snow was falling thick and fast and had already covered the ground in a soft, white blanket at least an inch thick.

'Look, Mum, Luke's here.' Skating back and circling Chrissy, Evie's voice was softened by the snow surrounding them.

'Luke? Are you sure it's him?' He couldn't be here. Why would he be? Not unless he was here to tell her he was going up north now, earlier than he had planned. Or else, maybe he wanted to know why she hadn't told him about the baby when she had found out.

'Yep, definitely him.'

'Right, OK.' She didn't want to deal with this now. She didn't even want to see him.

'Come on, then. He'll be covered in snow and look like a snowman by the time we get there.' Evie laughed. 'Or shall I take the key and go and let him in?'

'Good idea.' Rummaging in her pockets, she located the front door key and passed it to Evie. At least with the girls here, he couldn't say much. He might be annoyed with her, but he wouldn't say anything in front of them.

'OK, see you in a minute.' Evie skated back to the cottage, the fallen snow slowing her down.

Slowly, Chrissy made her way down the lane, she'd just give them time to get inside. Once Luke realised that he wouldn't be able to have any time with her alone then hopefully he'd just go, he wasn't the sort of person to make a scene in front of the girls.

* * *

Gently pushing the gate open, Chrissy looked up towards the door.

'Luke.' Sat on the front step with his hands shoved in his pockets and his beanie hat covered in snow, Luke looked up.

'Chrissy.' Standing up, he brushed the snow from the back of his jeans.

'I thought Evie was letting you in?'

'She offered, but I was rather hoping to be able to talk to you by ourselves.'

'Right.' Glancing behind her, she stood aside as he made his way down the path. Maybe he'd just leave.

'Look, the way I reacted last night... I'm sorry.' Standing in front of her, he pulled his beanie hat off, running his hand through his hair.

Looking down at her feet, Chrissy stamped until the snow had flown from her trainers.

'Please, say something.'

Raising her head, she looked him in the eyes. He looked as though he hadn't slept at all, dark circles surrounded his bloodshot eyes and the usual stubble had grown that tiny bit too long to be fashionable. 'I can't believe you had to ask if it was yours.'

'It's no worse than what you accused me of, not if you think about it.'

'I guess so.' He had a point, he must have felt as

she did when she'd told him why she had finished with him.

'I shouldn't have said it though. I know you, and I didn't need to ask if I was the father. I guess it was just a shock reaction.'

Nodding, Chrissy clasped her hands in front of her. 'I'm sorry too. I really am. I completely jumped to the wrong conclusion about you and Laura and ended up spoiling what we had. I should have known you wouldn't treat me like that.' She cleared her throat. 'Are you leaving today? Is that why you've come round?'

Looking past Chrissy and out onto the lane, Luke blinked against the snow before looking back at her. 'I don't have to.'

'You're not leaving early?'

'No, I mean, I don't have to go.'

'Oh, I hope you're plans haven't fallen through? Did you lose the hotel?'

'No, the hotel still needs renovating, but I've spoken to a mate of mine who lives a few miles away from it. He's happy to oversee the project.'

Where was he going then? Had he decided to go travelling again? He had when he was younger, maybe he had caught the travelling bug again. Maybe Chrissy had driven him away. 'Where are you going then?'

Shaking his head, he dismissed her question, instead, he took her hands in his. 'Did you mean it when you told me you loved me?'

'What? Well, yes. I did.' He *had* heard her then.

'Good, because I feel the same way.' Hooking his finger under her chin, he gently tipped her head up. 'I love you, Chrissy, and if you still feel the same way, I'd like us to make a real go of it. I want to be a proper dad to our child. I want to be a family, you, me, the twins and our baby.'

'You don't just feel like you have to? Because you don't. I can cope on my own.' Looking into his clear blue eyes, Chrissy didn't even need to hear his answer to know how he felt, to know that he wasn't doing this out of obligation but because he did truly love her. Closing her eyes, she let him kiss her, his soft lips warm against hers.

'Is that the answer you were looking for?' Grinning, Luke wrapped his arms around her, leaning his head against hers.

'It is indeed.' Breathing in his aftershave, she let herself sink into his embrace. 'I love you, Luke.'

'I love you too, Chrissy.'

Pulling away, Chrissy looked back at the cottage and laughed. 'I think we've been rumbled.' Pointing to the living room window, she watched as Evie and Sophia waved at them, their lips pursed as they pretended to blow kisses out of the window, teasing them.

'Oh, whoops.' Turning to face the cottage, he waved at them.

Holding out her hand, she waited until she felt Luke's warm skin through her gloves and led him towards the cottage. 'Are you staying for Christmas dinner?'

'I was hoping you'd offer, Natalie's terrible at cooking.'

'Oi. Is that all you're here for?' Laughing, Chrissy patted him with her free hand.

'That and the fact that I'm excited to start our new life together.'

EPILOGUE

'Anyone for gravy?' Holding the gravy jug, Chrissy looked down the long table filling Natalie and Graham's family room.

'I do.' Sophia waved her hand and pushed her green paper hat away from her eyes.

'Here you go.' Leaning over the table, Chrissy poured the gravy. 'Evie, Adam, Kane, do you want any?'

'I'll have some please, love?' Shifting the small bundle in his lap, Luke grinned at Chrissy.

Making her way down the table towards Luke, Chrissy bent her head and pecked him on the cheek. 'Did you hear that, Harry? Daddy wants gravy.' Placing her hand on Harry's small blonde head, she smiled. 'Do you think he's enjoying his first Christmas?'

'A noisy, chaotic family Christmas, what's not to like?' Gripping Chrissy's hand with his free one, Luke pulled her down towards him, kissing her on the lips. 'Happy 'Getting Back Together Anniversary', Chrissy.'

'You too.'

ACKNOWLEDGMENTS

Thank you, readers, for taking the time to read to read *Christmas at Corner Cottage*. I hope you've enjoyed reading about Chrissy's new start and her romance with Luke as much as I enjoyed writing her story.

A huge thank you to my wonderful children, Ciara and Leon, who motivate me to keep writing and working towards 'changing our stars' each and every day. Also to my lovely family for always being there, through the good times and the trickier ones.

And a massive thank you to my amazing editor, Emily Yau, who reached out and believed in me – thank you.

Thank you also to Shirley for copyediting and proofreading Christmas at Corner Cottage. And, of course, Clare Stacey for creating the beautiful cover. Thank you to all at Team Boldwood!

ABOUT THE AUTHOR

Sarah Hope is the author of many successful romance novels, including the bestselling Cornish Bakery series. The first book in her new series with Boldwood, *The Wagging Tails Dogs Home*, is set in a fictional Cornish village and will be published in May 2023.

Sign up to Sarah Hope's mailing list for news, competitions and updates on future books.

Follow Sarah on social media here:

f facebook.com/HappinessHopeDreams
🐦 twitter.com/sarahhope35
📷 instagram.com/sarah_hope_writes
BB bookbub.com/authors/sarah-hope

ALSO BY SARAH HOPE

The Wagging Tails Dog's Home Series

The Wagging Tails Dog's Home

Escape to... Series

The Seaside Ice-Cream Parlour

The Little Beach Café

Christmas at Corner Cottage

Boldwood

Boldwood Books is an award-winning fiction
publishing company seeking out the best
stories from around the world.

Find out more at www.boldwoodbooks.com

Join our reader community for brilliant books,
competitions and offers!

Follow us
@BoldwoodBooks
@TheBoldBookClub

Sign up to our weekly
deals newsletter

https://bit.ly/BoldwoodBNewsletter

www.ingramcontent.com/pod-product-compliance
Lightning Source LLC
Chambersburg PA
CBHW010857130726
47900CB00017B/2754